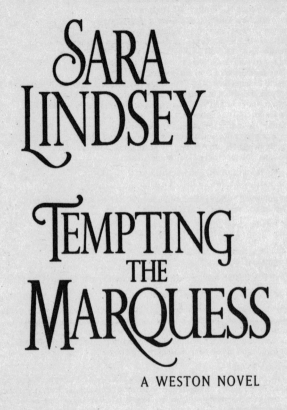

SARA LINDSEY

TEMPTING THE MARQUESS

A WESTON NOVEL

A SIGNET ECLIPSE BOOK

SIGNET ECLIPSE
Published by New American Library, a division of
Penguin Group (USA) Inc., 375 Hudson Street,
New York, New York 10014, USA
Penguin Group (Canada), 90 Eglinton Avenue East, Suite 700, Toronto,
Ontario M4P 2Y3, Canada (a division of Pearson Penguin Canada Inc.)
Penguin Books Ltd., 80 Strand, London WC2R 0RL, England
Penguin Ireland, 25 St. Stephen's Green, Dublin 2,
Ireland (a division of Penguin Books Ltd.)
Penguin Group (Australia), 250 Camberwell Road, Camberwell, Victoria 3124,
Australia (a division of Pearson Australia Group Pty. Ltd.)
Penguin Books India Pvt. Ltd., 11 Community Centre, Panchsheel Park,
New Delhi - 110 017, India
Penguin Group (NZ), 67 Apollo Drive, Rosedale, North Shore 0632,
New Zealand (a division of Pearson New Zealand Ltd.)
Penguin Books (South Africa) (Pty.) Ltd., 24 Sturdee Avenue,
Rosebank, Johannesburg 2196, South Africa

Penguin Books Ltd., Registered Offices:
80 Strand, London WC2R 0RL, England

First published by Signet Eclipse, an imprint of New American Library,
a division of Penguin Group (USA) Inc.

First Printing, June 2010
10   9   8   7   6   5   4   3   2   1

For my mother.
I love you even bigger than the sky.

Acknowledgments

Like the proverbial village needed to raise a child, there are a number of people who helped this book grow from a dream to reality. Thank you to: my editor, Kerry Donovan; my agent, Kimberly Witherspoon; Dana France and the NAL art department (for another beautiful cover); Kathryn Tumen (for her publicity savvy); the Vanettes (for being with me through all the ups and downs, responding day and night to my often frantic e-mails, and somehow knowing when I needed help staying grounded and when I needed the extra lift to fly); Lindsey Faber, Courtney Milan, and Janice Rholetter (for their thoughtful and detailed critiques); Jennifer Goodman and Elyssa Papa (for reading chapters at a moment's notice and cheering me on to the finish line); Stacey Agdern (for discussing this book over and over and over, and then coming back to do it again the next week); Kristin (for being remarkably understanding of a deadline-crazed bridesmaid); Alexandra, Jenny, Kara, and Lindsay (for being my Scripps sisters); Lizy (for always bringing sunshine into my life); and the biggest thank-you of all has to go to my family (for your endless love, your constant support, and yes, even for your nagging).

The Weston Family Tree

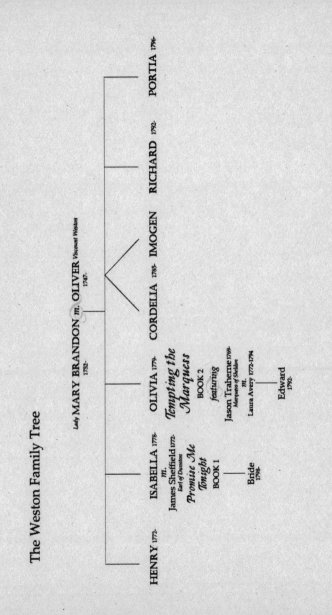

Lady MARY BRANDON *m.* OLIVER *Viscount Weston*
1752-   1747-

HENRY 1773-   ISABELLA 1776-   OLIVIA 1779-   CORDELIA 1785-   IMOGEN   RICHARD 1792-   PORTIA 1796-
                m.
                James Sheffield *m.*   *Tempting the*
                Earl of Dunston   *Marquess*
                Promise Me   BOOK 2
                Tonight
                BOOK 1   *featuring*

                                        Jason Traherne 1769-
                                        Marquess of Sheldon
                                        m.
                                        Laura Avery 1772-1794

                Bride   Edward
                1798-   1792-

Chapter 1

"If this were played upon a stage now,
I could condemn it as an improbable fiction."
Twelfth Night, Act III, Scene 4

Olivia stood before the castle's thick wooden portal, inwardly bracing herself against what lay in wait on the other side. Freezing rain had plastered her shabby traveling gown to her body, and the biting wind whipped at her sodden locks. She thought wistfully of her blue velvet pelisse with the ermine trim, but she had left the garment—and the elegant, easy life it represented—behind when she had chosen to run away rather than marry the lecherous Duke of Devonbridge. And now she was a lowly governess, dependent on the kindness and goodwill of her employer . . . and her new master was purported to have little of either.

A lone wolf howled somewhere out on the misty, moonlit moors that stretched for miles around the isolated edifice. She shivered with cold and fright, wondering if she might not be safer with the wolves than inside the castle's walls. A different sort of beast lay within that impenetrable stone fortress. A caged beast, confined not by chains but by his own despair.

The villagers called him the Mad Marquess, for he had been crazed with grief since the death of his wife some four years past. He eschewed all company . . . not that there were many eager to subject themselves to his foul *humor. In the past year alone no fewer than eleven maids had resigned their posts at Castle Arlyss. She'd heard rumors, too, of a centuries-old curse. . . .*

Olivia raised her face to the heavens, searching for a sign that this was indeed the path she was meant to travel—that she was meant to save this tormented soul and show his son a mother's love. Lightning flashed and crackled through the night sky, setting her hair on end. The angry rumble of thunder followed close behind.

Stiffening her spine, Olivia raised her fist to knock. Then, all of a sudden, a strong gust of wind snatched at her sleeve, as if trying to stop her. The air swirled around her, rustling through the dead leaves underfoot.

It seemed to whisper a name.

Her name.

Livvy, it murmured. Livvy . . .

December 1798
A Carriage Bound for Castle Arlyss
Pembrokeshire, Wales

"Livvy!"

Olivia opened her eyes and stared unseeing out the coach window. She blinked at the few rays of sunlight that dared penetrate the winter gloom lingering over the southwest of England. She shook her head. The wild, stormy night had vanished, and she was back in her aunt's well-sprung carriage.

A wistful sigh escaped her. The dream had been so real. . . . And now she was back to being ordinary Olivia Weston.

She turned her head to look at her young cousin, Charlotte, who was tugging rather insistently at her sleeve.

"Livvy!"

"What is it?" Livvy asked in as understanding a tone as she could muster. The journey from Scotland to Wales had already taken close to a fortnight, and though she loved Charlotte dearly, the boundless energy of a five-year-old was ill-suited to the close confines of a carriage. Not that Olivia was any stranger to small children. As the third of seven siblings, she knew all about them.

The little girl frowned, tugging at one of her glossy, dark ringlets, then shrugged. "I forget."

Livvy bit back a groan and stifled the urge to tear at her hair, which, to her everlasting disappointment, was neither curly nor dark. Neither was it blond and straight. Olivia's hair was a very ordinary, indeterminate shade of brown, and it had just enough of a wave to always escape its pins and make her look unkempt.

"Livvy?"

"What, Char?"

"I remembered. I had a secret to tell you." Charlotte crossed her arms over her chest and flopped back against the plush squabs with a satisfied smile.

"And?" Olivia prompted. She waited for further elucidation, but none was forthcoming. "Did you wish to tell me this secret you remembered?"

Charlotte thought a moment before shaking her head. "I'll tell Queenie instead."

Queen Anne, a doll in lavish court dress, was Charlotte's most prized possession, a distinction it had held since being unwrapped a few weeks past. Yes, Livvy thought, she had been replaced in her cousin's affections by an inanimate object. How distressing! She consoled herself with the knowledge that her conversational skills far surpassed those of Queenie. Then again, so did a squirrel's. As was her wont, she began composing a list in her head:

Ways in Which I Am Superior to Queenie

1. I can read.
2. I can write.
3. My head is not made of wood.
4. I can breathe.

Hmm, perhaps that last should have been first on her list; it seemed a fairly important distinction. Of course, squirrels also breathed. Maybe she ought to list the ways she was superior to squirrels instead. . . . She stopped herself, wondering if it was possible to go mad from boredom.

Aunt Kate looked up from her book to address her daughter. "Charlotte, I do believe Queenie looks a bit peaked. Perhaps you should both try to rest for a time and let your poor cousin alone."

Charlotte was disgusted by this suggestion. "Mama, Queenie is a *doll*. How can she rest when her eyes don't close?"

Aunt Kate sighed and peered out the window at the passing scenery. "At least we are getting close to the end. We should arrive tomorrow provided the weather doesn't change—" A choked laugh escaped her. "Dear heavens, that child will be the death of me!"

Livvy glanced at Charlotte, who had apparently decided to take her mother's advice. She was curled into the corner of the carriage, with her feet drawn up under her and her head pillowed against one hand. Her eyes were closed, a beatific smile on her face. Queenie lay in the crook of her free arm— Olivia smothered a laugh as she realized the reason for her aunt's proclamation.

As the doll's eyes did not, as Charlotte had pointed out, close, her enterprising mistress had contrived other means by which Queenie might rest. Raising Queenie's gown up over her head *did* shield her face from light, but this also exposed the doll's lower half. And while Queenie's ensemble boasted exquisitely detailed garters, stockings, and shoes, it did not apparently run to petticoats.

Ha! Petticoats! There was another way in which she was superior to Queenie *and* squirrels, too, for Livvy had never encountered a petticoat-wearing squirrel and very much doubted she ever would. The closest she was ever like to come was the stable cat her younger sisters had caught long enough to dress it in a bonnet and christening gown.

Aunt Kate leaned forward and spoke quietly so as not to disturb Charlotte. "I feel I ought to warn you about my stepson."

"Warn me?" Olivia's cheeks grew warm. "I hardly think—"

Her aunt waved a hand dismissively. "Heavens, child, I'm not suggesting anything of *that* nature. No, I only meant to caution you about the welcome we are like to receive."

"You mentioned Lord Sheldon keeps to himself a great deal of the time. I am not expecting to be met with a grand parade. I wish to inconvenience the marquess as little as possible."

That wasn't precisely true.

If all went to plan, she would put the man to a great deal of trouble. . . .

But that was her secret, one she didn't dare share with present company. Not with Aunt Kate, certainly not with Charlotte, and not even with Queenie, who was by nature most admirably closemouthed.

"Jason," Aunt Kate began, then sighed. "I know I should call him Sheldon, but I can't seem to get my mind round it, no matter that he's held the title for five years

now. I suppose his Christian name is rather too familiar
for polite conversation, but he has always been Jason
to me."

"Did he not have use of a courtesy title?"

"There is one," her aunt admitted, "but most of the
heirs would rather do without it." Her eyes sparkled with
laughter. "Most understandable, really. Would you like
to go through life being addressed as Bramblybum?"

"B-Bramblybum?" Olivia burst out laughing. She
caught her aunt's sharp glance at Charlotte and lowered
her voice. "Surely you are joking."

Aunt Kate shook her head. "The marquisate was created for the ninth Viscount Traherne, who was, I gather,
a great personal favorite with James I. The viscount's
son, who went on to become the second Marquess of
Sheldon, openly disapproved of his sire's, ah, special relationship with the king. The Traherne men have never
been ones to keep their opinions to themselves, which
perhaps accounts for the dearth of ambassadors and
politicians in the family. In any case, the young man's
outbursts angered the king, and he might have met a
very sorry end had not his father intervened. The viscount begged the king to disregard his son and joked
how the boy had been born with nettles stinging his
backside. The king's revenge was to bestow a marquisate *and* an earldom upon the viscount. While his father
was alive, the second marquess was known by his courtesy title."

"The Earl of Bramblybum," Livvy whispered, torn
between horror and hilarity.

"Earl Bramblybum, actually, but I wouldn't suggest
you let that pass your lips once we reach Castle Arlyss. Jason always gets fussed on hearing it. He certainly
doesn't use the title for Edward. I have told you about
Jason's son, Edward, haven't I? He's nearly seven now
and such a dear, sweet boy."

Olivia nodded. She wasn't sure if Aunt Kate had told her about Edward, but she knew about him all the same. But that was part of her secret.

Unconsciously, she bent forward and smoothed her hands over her skirts, her fingers searching out the almost imperceptible bump of the little fichu pin she wore affixed to her garter. The dainty brooch featured a tiny silhouette set in a gold frame surrounded by garnets. The portrait was no bigger than her thumbnail, but the artist had rendered the gentleman's profile in great detail, from the slight curl in the hair at his nape to the soft ruffles of his shirt frills. An elegant man, but Livvy reserved final judgment until she met him in the flesh, which, with any luck, would be on the morrow. *Finally,* she thought, a little sigh escaping her.

"I'll stop nattering on and let you rest." Aunt Kate's eyes twinkled. "You needn't go take the same drastic measures as poor Queenie and cast your skirts over your face."

"I wasn't— I mean, you weren't—" Livvy stammered out a protest.

"Calm yourself, my dear, I'm only teasing. I know I have a tendency to ramble, especially when I don't have to mind my tongue." She winked and nodded in Charlotte's direction.

A rush of pride swept over Olivia at her aunt's words. In the eyes of Society she was an adult and had been since her eighteenth birthday close to a year earlier. Girls her age, and even some younger, had already had their come-outs this past Season. She should have come out then as well, but her sojourn in Scotland with Aunt Kate, Charlotte, and Livvy's newly married (and freshly abandoned) older sister, Isabella, had lasted longer than expected.

Nine months longer, give or take a little.

Olivia hadn't minded putting off her come-out. She

wasn't overly anxious to put herself on the Marriage Mart, and besides, her sister had needed her. That last trumped everything else as far as Livvy was concerned.

Aunt Kate reached forward and patted Olivia's knee. "I've grown accustomed to having you and Izzie around. I was so pleased when you asked to come along with us to Wales. I would have invited you had I known you were so interested in this part of the country."

"I must confess, some of my interest stemmed from wanting to avoid traveling home with Mama, spending countless hours trapped in a carriage listening to her expound on some Shakespearean heroine or other."

For as long as Olivia could remember, her mother had been writing a critical work about Shakespeare's heroines. Life in the Weston household was all Shakespeare, all the time, at least when her mother was present. The rest of the family bore it with equanimity—mostly because they tended to ignore her—but over the years her mother's obsession increasingly grated on Livvy's nerves. She adored her mother, really she did, but she could easily do without hearing, at least once a week, as she had for her entire life: "Be not afraid of greatness: some are born great, some achieve greatness, and some have greatness thrust upon them."

Lady Weston particularly enjoyed tailoring her recitations so that each of her children would be familiar with the plays from whence had come their names. Though Olivia resented having Shakespeare's greatness constantly thrust upon her, not for the world would she have hurt her mother's feelings by telling her so. All in all, she felt lucky to have been named for a character in *Twelfth Night*, which, in her opinion, was one of Shakespeare's more tolerable works, and not only because it was relatively short.

Her younger sisters, identical twins Cordelia and Imogen, were stuck with *King Lear* and *Cymbeline*, two plays that were, in Olivia's opinion, entirely too puffed up with melodrama. The first words Richard, her precocious little brother, babbled had sounded suspiciously like: "Now is the winter of our discontent." Portia, the baby of the family, hadn't got much past cooing and gurgling when Livvy had left for Scotland. . . .

She realized with a slight pang that she had missed her youngest sister's first words, and a wave of homesickness swept over her. These past months marked the longest time she had ever been away from her younger siblings.

"What's caused that long face?" Aunt Kate asked. "Have I scared you off with this talk of my stepson? You mustn't let him upset you. He is very changed since Laura's death, and grief affects us all in different ways. Perhaps, given time . . ." She trailed off, her hopes for the future unspoken but entirely clear.

Olivia wanted to say she knew, or at least had an inkling, of what the marquess had been like before his wife's death—but she could not. Instead she smiled brightly and said, "Then we must do our best to bring some cheer to both him and his son this holiday season. If you don't mind, Aunt Kate, I think I'll read a bit while Char is quiet."

Her aunt laughed. "Yes, living with Charlotte one does learn to seize those rare moments of peace. They certainly don't last long."

Olivia nodded distractedly, already absorbed with her book. Or rather, with the piece of paper hidden inside. In bold, scrawling script were the words—the first clue—that had led her to the brooch, thus prompting her seemingly impromptu journey to Wales—words penned by none other than the Mad Marquess of her dreams.

*   *   *

Castle Arlyss, Pembrokeshire, Wales
December 22, 1798

Under his butler's disapproving gaze, Jason Traherne, Marquess of Sheldon, reached for the box of sand on his desk and sprinkled some over the letter he had just completed. He waited a moment for the fine grains to dry the ink before brushing the sand back into the box. He set the paper aside and stood, noting how Gower's shoulders relaxed.

The butler shuffled his feet, edging toward the door of the study while Jason made a great show of neatening up, taking his time to straighten the various piles of papers, books, and other odds and ends spread across the polished mahogany surface. Then, with a satisfied nod, he settled back down in his chair and reached for the ivory paper knife with one hand and a stack of unopened correspondence with the other. Lord, he had come to a pretty pass when twitting his butler was the brightest spot in his day.

"M-my lord," Gower spluttered. "Perhaps you misunderstood. Your guests have arrived. You cannot mean to—"

"I did not misunderstand, but my stepmother is hardly a guest. She should know her way around after all these years, but if she wants a tour, have the housekeeper—"

"Beg pardon, my lord, but Mrs. Maddoc is occupied just at present."

Jason took the top letter off the pile and slid the edge of his knife under the wax seal. "I, too, am occupied. I have put off responding to, ah—" He glanced down to ascertain the sender. It was from his stepmother. He cursed and set the paper aside, reaching for the next letter. A glance at the handwriting showed it was from the same source. He thumbed through the remainder of the stack before setting it back upon his desk.

Gower shook his head. "Her ladyship is the only person who still bothers to write you. Everyone else has either given up or addressed their concerns to your man of business."

Jason rubbed his temples. This was the problem with having retainers who had known him from the time he was in short coats. They had no compunction about making their displeasure known.

"Do I pay you to be impertinent, Gower?"

"If I may be so bold, my lord, you don't pay me at all. Your dearly departed father left me a generous pension in his will. I've the means to retire if I so choose."

"Are you tendering your resignation, then?" Jason asked flatly, as though the butler's answer meant nothing to him.

"You would be rightly served if I did, and Mrs. Maddoc, too, but neither of us is leaving while there's life in our bodies and Trahernes residing here at Castle Arlyss."

Jason released his breath. "I can't get rid of the servants I don't pay or keep the ones I do," he grumbled. "The maids don't last long enough to learn their way about the house. I swear not a month goes by without Mrs. Maddoc informing me that yet another maidservant has quit her post. That would mean, what, eleven maids have come and gone this year?"

"Twelve. Bess left this morning."

"Bess," Jason repeated, frowning. "Wasn't she the one who—?"

"She was the only one, my lord."

"The only one who what?"

"The only maid, my lord." Gower's expression was that of a long-suffering parent saddled with an unnecessarily stupid child.

"Don't be ridiculous, Gower. A place this size can't function without maids."

"Quite so, and we're in a fair bind being so short-staffed, but perhaps I should clarify: Bess was the only remaining chambermaid. The under-maids usually aren't scared off, as they never come in contact with, er—" The butler cleared his throat. "In any event, Mrs. Maddoc has placed several advertisements—"

"Scared off?" Jason pushed to his feet and began to pace the room. "Christ, has some ninnyhammer been spreading tales about that bloody ghost again? Or is it the curse on the Traherne brides this time? You know I won't stand for gossip among the servants."

"My lord, your guests are waiting for—"

Jason stopped, fixing his butler with an icy stare. "Answer the question."

"Very well," the butler replied stiffly, drawing himself up to his full height. With his back straight, the man's bushy white eyebrows were in line with Jason's collarbone. "There has been no mention of ghosts or curses, at least in my hearing, since you forbade such talk."

"Then what the devil is scaring these silly chits off?" Jason snapped.

Gower fixed his attention on the study's coffered ceiling. "I couldn't say, I'm sure," he murmured. "Mayhap they're frightened of those demon hounds always trotting along at your heels."

Jason looked over at the two massive Danes sleeping on their backs in front of the fireplace. With their front paws drawn up to their chests, they looked more comical than ferocious. "They wouldn't harm a flea—" He held up a hand as Gower opened his mouth to protest. "—without some provocation. Yes, I remember how they viciously atta—assaulted you. You certainly take every opportunity to remind me. Give over, Gower. You weren't harmed and neither of them has so much as barked in your direction in years."

Jason shot a sideways glance at the dogs he'd rescued years before from a bear-baiting in London. They had recovered from the experience in most respects, but there were certain commands so harshly beaten into them, an eternity wouldn't be long enough to forget.

A familiar anger welled up, its dark currents flowing through his veins, stirring his blood. Being deceived and abandoned by the one most implicitly trusted ... Such betrayal cut deep. The physical scars had healed and faded, but there were other scars no amount of patience or affection could erase.

"My lord, are you well?"

Jason heard the butler speak as from a great distance. He forced his eyes to focus on the older man's worried visage. "Quite well," he responded, unclenching his fists. "I got lost in the past for a moment."

"If there is anything I can ... ?" Gower trailed off as Jason shook his head sharply.

"There is nothing anyone can do, short of turning back time."

The butler fiddled with one of the buttons on his austere black coat. "May I suggest you allow yourself to be distracted for a while? Your guests are waiting in the Great Hall—"

"Damnation, didn't you hear me before? I have no wish to play at being the gracious host, and it isn't necessary in this case. My stepmother is not a guest, nor is my half sister."

"The marchioness and Lady Charlotte are family and thus more deserving of your attention. As it happens, however, you do have a guest. There is a young woman come with them."

Jason shrugged. "She's probably Charlotte's nurse."

"I hope your lordship is not suggesting I cannot tell a gentlewoman of good breeding from a maidservant." Gower's tone had more starch than his cravat.

"I wouldn't dare." Jason sighed. "You're not going to leave off until I greet them, are you?"

"No, my lord."

"Very well," Jason grumbled, stalking toward the door. "You're a nuisance, Gower. Remind me later to turn you out without references."

"Of course, my lord," the butler agreed. "The day would feel woefully incomplete were I not dismissed at least once."

Chapter 2

"My purpose is, indeed, a horse of that color."
Twelfth Night, Act II, Scene 3

As she stood in the medieval entry hall of Castle Arlyss, there were three things about which Olivia was absolutely certain. One, the Marquess of Sheldon was far too attractive for his own good . . . or for the good of any female in close proximity to him. And her proximity to him was escalating with every purposeful step he took in her direction.

Two, judging by his scowl—and Livvy felt certain that scowl was directed at *her*, not at her aunt or her cousin—the man did not want her in his home for another moment, let alone for the remainder of the holiday season.

Which brought Olivia to her third certainty, which was that she should never have come.

This had been a mistake.

She had absolutely no business being there.

None at all.

Then again, she had never been very good at minding her own business.

"Hello, Katherine. Charlotte." The marquess gave each a sharp nod before settling his gaze on Livvy. He briefly took in her appearance before turning to the harried-looking butler. "No, I don't suppose she is a maidservant. More's the pity, for we're in short supply."

Apparently Aunt Kate had not been jesting about her stepson's indifferent manners.

The marquess braced his hands on his hips and focused his attention once more on Olivia. "Who the devil are you and what are you doing here?" he demanded. The hostile words hung suspended in the air for a moment before being swallowed up by the heavy tapestries blanketing the impenetrable stone walls.

It was, for all intents and purposes, a simple, albeit rather rude question, and yet Olivia did not know quite how to respond. She couldn't imagine he'd be pleased if she answered truthfully, but starting their acquaintance with lies seemed impolitic.

Thankfully her aunt saved her from having to answer. "Jason! I do not know where you have forgot your manners, but you will promptly find them and greet us with at least a modicum of civility."

A sardonic smile twitched at one corner of Lord Sheldon's mouth as he sketched a bow. "Forgive me. You are most welcome to Castle Arlyss," he drawled as he came forward and took her aunt's hands, then pressed a kiss to the cheek she presented. "A pleasure as always, my lady."

Aunt Kate chuckled, a low, husky sound, which attracted men like moths to a flame. Livvy had once tried to make her laugh sound like her aunt's, but she had ended up with a sore, scratchy throat and difficulty speaking for a few days after her attempt.

"I know you don't mean a word of it, but we are glad to be here all the same. Now, permit me to introduce my—"

She broke off as Charlotte wriggled free of her mother's restraining hand and launched herself at her brother with a happy cry. The marquess stooped to embrace her, his expression momentarily softening. The rest of him stiffened in contrast, clearly ill at ease with this display of emotion. He patted her back clumsily before setting her apart from him.

"I'm not certain this is the same girl who visited last Christmas." He looked her up and down. "This girl is far too grown up to be Charlotte."

"It's me! It's me!" Charlotte bounced with excitement. "This is Queen Anne. You can call her Queenie." She thrust the doll in the marquess's face, or as near as she could reach, which was more in the realm of his midsection.

Lord Sheldon gingerly accepted the proffered offering and held the doll at arm's length, turning it first this way, then that. He appeared to be giving the doll a very thorough inspection, but it was Livvy, not Queenie, who was the recipient of that intense scrutiny. The heat of his gaze burned her as it swept over her body.

Her spine stiffened. Let him look. She might not be the Great Beauty her older sister was, but she had long since come to terms with that and had decided she was at least passing fair. And while the marquess stared so boldly at her, she would take the opportunity to study him.

At once her fingers itched to sketch him, first the strong, hard line of his jaw, then the broad sweep of his forehead and the inky slashes of his eyebrows above equally dark eyes. She wanted to capture the slightly flattened ridge near the base of his nose, the faint hollows beneath his high cheekbones, and the gentle wave in his black hair. The planes and angles of his face were an artist's dream—no single feature was perfect in and of itself, except perhaps his lips, which could have been sculpted by the great Michelangelo—but everything worked in absolute harmony.

Livvy was no stranger to handsome men. Her older brother, Henry, was quite good-looking, though she would never tell him so, and her brother-in-law, the Earl of Dunston, was another splendid specimen of masculinity. The marquess put them both to shame. There was a swirling, smoldering undercurrent in the air around him that spoke of tightly leashed emotions—a mighty tempest held in check by a will forged of iron.

He was nothing like what she had expected. Her mind had conjured the image of a man so worn down by years of embittered grief that all that remained was a fragile, brittle shell. She could see nothing weak about Lord Sheldon. The marquess radiated strength from the proud set of his broad shoulders to the muscular thighs bulging beneath his tight-fitting riding breeches. Not that she, a young lady of good breeding, would do anything as improper as express an interest in the marquess's inexpressibles. She quickly looked up lest she be caught but, from the hint of a smile lurking about his mouth, she feared she was too late.

"Delightful," he drawled, catching Olivia's gaze as he handed the doll back to Charlotte.

His dark eyes smoldered in blatant masculine appreciation. Livvy's cheeks flamed despite the icy draughts that always seemed to plague old castles.

Aunt Kate reached out a hand to her daughter. "Come, Charlotte, leave your brother be a moment so I may introduce him to—"

"Mama-promised-I-could-have-a-great-Danish-dog-like-you-have." Charlotte spoke the words in a rush, determined to get them out before she was reprimanded for interrupting.

Sure enough, she had just eked out the last word when Aunt Kate began to scold. "Promise or no, you will not be getting a dog, great Danish or otherwise, unless you display the requisite maturity to care for the creature."

As if their words had manifested it, the largest dog Olivia had ever seen lumbered into the room.

"Blue!" Charlotte squealed.

The dog—or perhaps it was really a small horse—gave an answering bark, which exposed far too many sharp teeth for Livvy's comfort, and then began to gallop toward the little girl. The beast could eat her in a single bite and still be hungry for more.

Olivia lunged forward and grabbed her cousin's arm, pulling her to safety.

"Let go of me, Livvy! I want to see Blue." Charlotte shook off Olivia's grasp and bounded toward the horse-dog.

Livvy cast anxious glances at her aunt and the marquess. "Aren't you afraid it will attack her?" Her voice rose sharply on the last words as the beast reared up on its hind legs.

At her words, Lord Sheldon's head jerked up. He quickly scanned the room before his gaze focused on her, or rather on something beyond her. His eyes widened in alarm. "No, Red, no!" he commanded sharply.

"Red? I thought its name was Blue—oomph!"

Something plowed into Olivia from behind, knocking the breath from her as she went sprawling to the ground. The carpet was but a thin barrier against the hard, cold stone that lay beneath. She heard a snarled growl and heavy panting and came to three new certainties.

One, she was about to die.

Two, Blue—*and really, what sort of name was Blue?*—had a friend.

Three, the other horse-dog-beast was called Red, an equally ridiculous name.

Red and Blue.

Together they made purple, which was the color her body was going to be tomorrow if the pain coursing through her was any indication. Supposing, of course, she didn't die of mortification first. She shut her eyes tightly, hoping this might turn out to be some dream gone horribly wrong.

"Oh, Livvy, dearest, are you all right?"

Olivia drew some air into her lungs, answering her aunt with a pitiful sound that fell somewhere between a grunt and a groan.

"I think she's dying," Charlotte proclaimed, not seeming overly concerned by the prospect. "Bad, Red Dog, bad!"

"No, Charlotte, do not scold Red. He hasn't been around strangers in a long time and he heard a word that made him so angry he forgot his manners for a moment."

The marquess's voice grew increasingly loud and clear as he said this, and suddenly Livvy found herself lifted by a pair of strong arms. Her eyes flew open in surprise. She had never been held by a man other than her father, and that had been when she was a child.

This felt quite different.

She was close enough to see the stubble shadowing his jaw, though it was clear he had been clean-shaven that morning. Close enough to discover his hair wasn't black, but rather a deep, dark brown, like rich, freshly turned soil. Close enough to breathe in the faint scent of the stables that hinted at an early-morning ride. Close enough to feel the whisper of his breath against her temple when he exhaled.

"This is some welcome you have provided," Aunt Kate huffed. "It's a bit late for formal introductions, but I suppose we must observe those proprieties still left to us. Jason, allow me to present my niece, Miss Olivia Weston. Livvy, as you may have surmised, you are being held by my stepson, the Marquess of Sheldon."

Her aunt's mention of propriety caused Olivia's face to heat. She was in the arms of a man to whom she had never been introduced. Livvy pushed at Lord Sheldon's chest. It was like granite, hard and unyielding, but she could feel the heat of his body through the layers of his clothing. The thought of his skin, of his bare torso, sent a shiver of excitement through her. His eyes narrowed on her flushed face, then dropped to her mouth. She shivered again and a predatory, knowing look came into his eyes.

Oh, my! She had guessed the marquess had a powerful effect on women, but given the weakness stealing over her body and turning her bones to jelly, she had clearly underestimated his potency.

"Miss Weston, I trust you are not seriously injured?"

She felt more than heard the deep rumble of his voice. She nodded automatically, slightly breathless, held captive by the wicked promise in his deep brown eyes. She hoped she hadn't just agreed to anything untoward, or rather, anything unpleasant. She suspected untoward behavior with the marquess would be very pleasurable indeed. . . . She needed to get away from him before her brains were permanently scrambled. She squirmed and shoved harder at the muscled wall of his chest.

His arms tightened about her as he strode to the far end of the hall, carrying her as though she weighed no more than Charlotte. He deposited her on a low settle placed before the massive hearth, then straightened, crossing his arms over his chest.

"I must apologize, Miss Weston. I rescued both dogs from a particularly vicious bear-baiting, and while they generally act like overgrown lapdogs, Red in particular still responds badly to hearing the word A-T-T-A-C-K."

"Oh," Olivia gasped. "I'm so sorry. I had no idea."

"Obviously, or you would not have said it. Of course, you shouldn't be here in the first place, and if you hadn't been here, the incident never would have occurred, but I apologize all the same. Now, you look like the missish sort who will insist a doctor be sent for, but I give you leave to prove me wrong."

She stared, astounded not only by his sheer audacity

but by his ability to insult not only her but her entire gender in one breath.

"What are you saying, Jason?" Aunt Kate asked suspiciously as she came near.

"I was merely inquiring whether Miss Weston wished me to send for a doctor."

"That won't be necessary," Livvy snapped.

"Olivia!" her aunt scolded. "Jason has expressed concern for your well-being. If you have no need of a doctor, you will thank him and politely decline his offer."

Livvy drew in a deep breath and pasted a smile on her face. "Thank you, my lord, but I hardly think we need send for the doctor just because I was A-T-T-A-C-K-E-D by a dog the size of a pony."

Lord Sheldon began to laugh. It was a bit rusty sounding, as though he had not used it in a long time. Of course, from what she knew of him, he probably hadn't. Despite her annoyance, the thought wrenched at Olivia's heart.

She had come to Wales hoping to satisfy her curiosity about the marquess. Her aunt had spoken despairingly of the changes grief had wrought in her stepson, painting a portrait entirely at odds with the man Livvy had come to know through the terribly written but very cleverly hidden clues that had led her to the brooch. He might not want her there, and perhaps she ought not to have come, but there she was, for better or for worse, and though it was doubtless a fool's errand, she had to see if she could help him.

Perhaps she was the one who needed help! A man who looked like that must have had scores of women offering to help him move past his grief. Of course, if he was as surly and rude as he had been to her, there were probably some who had run away. But Olivia was willing to bet there were plenty of others who saw him as a challenge. And no mistake about it, from a purely aesthetic standpoint, Lord Sheldon was a prize worth winning.

Not that Livvy planned on winning him. She wasn't even entering the competition. She wanted to help him, and that was all. Though Lord Sheldon was good-looking enough to make her heart skip a beat, and though he had at some point been possessed of rather romantic sensibilities, he was not for her. Nor, she reminded herself, did she want him to be. Perhaps she ought to be seen by a doctor after all. That knock to the ground had clearly addled her wits.

"Perhaps I might lie down for a while?" she ventured.

"Certainly, dear," Aunt Kate said. "Ah, Mrs. Maddoc, what excellent timing."

An older woman, all round and soft about the middle, bustled into the hall. "Mr. Gower just told me what happened." She paused to catch her breath. "Are you all right, miss? Shall I send for—?"

"No!" Olivia and Lord Sheldon spoke simultaneously.

"Thank you," Livvy told the housekeeper, "but all I need is a short rest and I shall be as good as new."

"Ladies, if you will excuse me, I've recalled a matter of business I must attend to without delay. I leave you in Mrs. Maddoc's capable hands. If you need anything further, please don't hesitate to ring for Gower." With that, he bowed and walked off.

Aunt Kate shook her head. "Amazing the way gentlemen always seem to recall pressing matters of business just when they wish to avoid company, but I suppose for every man claiming urgent business there are probably two women claiming headaches to avoid, er, unwanted company of another sort."

"While I have no objection to the present company, my head *is* starting to pound," Livvy admitted.

"Mine too." Aunt Kate winked. "And no wonder, with such a welcome as this. My stepson swears this place is quiet as a tomb the rest of the year, and it only turns to Bedlam the moment Charlotte and I arrive." She turned to face the housekeeper. "Mrs. Maddoc, I trust you are well?"

"As well as can be expected at my age. Now, this must be your niece."

Aunt Kate nodded. "You received my letter?"

"I did. Miss Weston, I hope the rest of your stay with us will prove more pleasant. Your aunt mentioned you've a liking for old houses and such, so you should find a great deal here to interest you. His lordship is just the same, or at least he used to be. He doesn't take much interest in anything these days."

The housekeeper spoke in a lovely lilting cadence, the sounds rolling gently like the hills and valleys of the surrounding countryside.

"Olivia, dear, Mrs. Maddoc will show you to your room. I shall check in on you once I have Charlotte settled in the nursery."

"I'm to have the room in the Old Tower, yes? The one that's said to be haunted by the White Lady?" Livvy asked excitedly, for she and her aunt had spent a great deal of time during the long coach ride discussing the castle. She would rather have spoken of the castle's owner, but there were only so many questions she could ask without arousing her aunt's suspicion. A genuinely haunted castle was quite thrilling, but Livvy's preoccupation was with the clue-writing, letter-writing, and most assuredly living marquess.

Mrs. Maddoc fretfully shifted her not inconsiderable weight. "The maid going over the rooms this morning found one of the windows shattered in the tower room. It will be fixed as soon as can be arranged, but right now it's not fit for the dogs, much less a guest."

Livvy's breath caught. "It was the ghost, wasn't it?"

It seemed the castle's ghost was as unwelcoming as its owner.

The housekeeper shook her head, sighing. "Young folk are so full of whimsy-whamsy nowadays. Bess, the chitty-faced maid what discovered the window, thought much the same. If anyone is to blame, it's Mother Nature. There was a fierce storm a couple days past—hailing, it was. I expect the window was hit hard by hailstone or some such."

"The force responsible for the broken window isn't important," Aunt Kate broke in. "The chamber is uninhabitable, and that's that. What room shall we give Olivia in the meantime?"

"That's just the problem, my lady." Mrs. Maddoc wrung her hands. "All the other chambers are put away in Holland cloth and closed up. None of the other rooms have been aired, and I haven't had the time or the help to start airing another. Bess left this morning. Said it was the final straw and she wasn't going to stay another minute in such an accursed place. We've had trouble keeping maidservants these past years, what with the master's moods. Now Bess is gone, there's no one left. I'm at my wit's end, my lady, and I don't mind telling you."

"I could share a bed with Charlotte," Livvy suggested.

Her aunt thought a moment, and then a mischievous glint came into her eyes. "No, I don't think that will be necessary. There is a bedchamber here that I am sure is kept in good order. And, as it happens, this room also contains a ghost. Perhaps your presence will be the needed exorcism."

Mrs. Maddoc sighed. "I reckon I know what you're about, milady. The master isn't going to like this," she muttered, shaking her head.

"Yes." Lady Sheldon smiled broadly. "I know."

Chapter 3

"I hate ingratitude more in a man
Than lying, vainness, babbling, drunkenness,
Or any taint of vice whose strong corruption
Inhabits our frail blood."
                    Twelfth Night, Act III, Scene 4

As he dressed for dinner, Jason Traherne could not help thinking about his unexpected, unwanted, and undeniably female houseguest, probably because he never bothered dressing for dinner when he was alone. He might not have bothered, even with guests, had Gower not come to his study and announced that it was past time for Jason to be getting ready.

The butler's tone had been firm and stern and, in truth, Jason's earlier behavior was weighing on his mind as well. He should not have told Miss Weston that she was not welcome. It was the truth, but he was a gentleman and he should have acted like one.

His only excuse, and he knew it to be a poor one, was that her presence had thrown him.

He was not a man who enjoyed surprises.

He craved order.

He relished peace and quiet.

And yet, every December he invited—perhaps *allowed* was the better word—chaos into his home.

Chaos in the form of his well-intentioned-if-somewhat-prone-to-meddle stepmother.

Chaos in the guise of his rambunctious little sister.

And this year, he had a grim suspicion chaos had wormed its way into Castle Arlyss under a new name ... Miss Olivia Weston.

Wasn't there some saying about bad luck coming in threes?

He couldn't say why, exactly, Miss Weston's presence seemed to bode ill for his peace of mind, but he had the pricking sensation across his nape that always heralded some sort of disaster. It had been there the day his father had shown up at Harrow with the news that Jason's mother had died in a carriage accident. And it had been there the morning he had learned of his wife's death. . . . He tensed against the familiar rush of pain and anger the memories still brought.

Damnation, he hated this time of year. His stepmother didn't seem to understand that these annual gatherings also brought out the ghosts of the past. All he wanted was to be left alone, but arguing with Katherine was a futile endeavor. She insisted the family come together for the holidays, and that was that.

Miss Weston was not a family member, though, or at least not *his* family member, and that meant she had no business being in his home. As he barely tolerated his family, Katherine could not have imagined he would be pleased at her bringing a guest. But he also knew she fretted over his isolation.

Had she brought the chit along for company or. . . ?

Damnation. He should have realized the moment Gower informed him that Katherine had a young woman with her. His stepmother had brought the girl to tempt him. Since he refused to go out in Society, she had brought it to him, done up in a neat little package.

Pretty misses were excellent temptations, especially for a man who had been celibate as long as he. He had to resist, though, since unwrapping this particular package was as good as having the banns read.

He smiled grimly at his reflection in the looking glass, straightening his cravat. He knew Katherine's motives were pure, however misguided, but she had gone too far this time. He would never marry again, and woe betide the scheming stepmother or ingenious ingénue who tried to convince him otherwise.

His guard up, Jason made his way to the drawing room, only to realize he had underestimated his opponent. The sight of Miss Weston—every luscious inch of her—hit him like a broadside. He had noticed earlier that she was pretty, but he had done her an injustice. There was not one specific feature of hers whose perfection caught his eye—excepting, perhaps, the creamy expanse of flesh swelling above her bodice—but the complete picture, from her upswept golden brown hair to the toes encased in dainty satin slippers, was a masterpiece.

He forced his eyes up to hers, which gleamed like twin sapphires, set off to perfection by skin the color of fine ivory. She was little and delicate, but rounded in all the right places, and he was very much aware— too much aware—of her as a woman. A pronounced cough from Katherine told Jason he had been caught in his admiration. He glanced at her, expecting her to be pleased, and received instead a look that would curdle milk.

Jason eyed his stepmother as they sat down to dinner, trying to decide if he could possibly be mistaken about her motives in bringing her niece along with her. He had been certain Katherine was hoping he'd fall in love with the chit—or at least compromise her—and marry her. Or, at the very least, that he would begin to remember what life had been like and be lured back into the glittering lights of Society, but her disapproving reaction was proving confusing.

Katherine could hardly blame him. He might live like a monk, but he didn't think like one, and his body didn't bloody well respond like one. Jason shifted uncomfortably in his seat.

Lord, anyone would think he'd never seen breasts before. Hers were rather large for her frame and then it was only a small step from there to wondering how they might feel in his hands and—

"Jason!" Katherine's voice was sharp.

"Eh?" Jason looked up, feeling as though he'd been rapped soundly on the knuckles.

"You are unusually distracted tonight. I just told you Olivia did wonders with the library at Haile Castle."

Jason frowned. "I was not aware there was anything wrong with the library to necessitate work being done upon it."

"Aunt Kate, I am sure Lord Sheldon doesn't wish to be bored with the trifling little changes—"

"Trifling little changes? My dear, you are far too modest. Olivia took everything off the shelves, did all the dusting and cleaning herself, wouldn't even let the maids help her."

"Well, some of the older books were in very fragile condition. I didn't want to risk them getting ruined by careless hands," Miss Weston explained.

"And then," Katherine went on, "she organized the books according to some system she has thought out—"

"By subject, and then by author within each subject, though naturally the size of the volumes had to be taken into consideration."

"—and she set aside books to go into special boxes, making lists about what went where. I don't know how she was able to finish it all before we left to come here."

"It was a close thing," Miss Weston agreed. "I should never have managed if I had gone home with Mama as originally planned."

The pulse in Jason's temple throbbed. Good Lord, when one of them paused for breath, the other picked right up. The upcoming weeks stretched out before him in an unending spate of feminine chatter. "Why was I not consulted before such a project was undertaken?" he ground out.

Katherine's brow furrowed. "Consulted about rearranging the books in the library? The thought never occurred to me. And how should I have gone about asking, pray tell? I doubt you bother to open my correspondence; you certainly never deign to send a reply."

"I open them," he muttered sulkily. He *had* opened one of her letters. That he hadn't read it was beside the point.

"You're lying." Katherine sat back in her chair, a smug smile on her lips. "Don't bother to deny it. Your ears turn red when you lie. Charlotte is the same way, and so was your father."

Jason fought the urge to clap his hands over his ears. "You could have written to my man of business," he grumbled.

"I could have," she agreed, "but as I did not require any funds, I daresay he would have told me to do as I liked. The books are certainly the better for Olivia's care. I would never have brought it up if I hadn't thought you would be pleased."

Miss Weston got to her feet and braced her palms on the table. Her eyes blazed and a splash of color spread across the ridge of her nose and onto her cheeks. "I don't see why you should be consulted," she huffed. "As far as I understand, you haven't left here in years and I doubt you are planning on leaving anytime in the foreseeable future. As you apparently have no interest in your other properties, you will forgive me if I have trouble believing you know or care overmuch about the state of the library at Haile Castle. And if someone else should take a notion to care—someone like me, for instance—I cannot see why you should be so put out."

Jason stared at her. He had a feeling it was less his imperious lord of the manor stare than a bewildered, bowled-over sort of stare. He told himself he didn't give a damn what she thought about him, but he resented being made to feel as though he had been in the wrong.

It was true he trusted the running of his other properties to estate managers, but they were all men he trusted. Besides, Katherine visited Haile Castle nearly every year, and she stayed at the town house in London frequently. She would let him know if there was a problem that wasn't being addressed. He was not going to feel guilty over some moldering books that had likely been moldering since before his grandfather was born.

Miss Weston had some nerve to accuse him of neglecting his responsibilities, riding the high horse with her talk about caring. His time was spent caring for his son, and Edward was a damned sight more important than her books. Dusting off books wasn't *caring*; it was cleaning. Caring was staying awake all night, watching over your child, praying for his breathing to ease. Caring was remaining strong and calm in those moments you most wanted to collapse. Caring was pleading with a God you had long since stopped believing in. . . .

What right did she have to criticize him? She was a guest in his home. Actually, if he thought about it, she had been a guest in his home for many months. And just look how she repaid him. She ransacked his library, she insulted him at his own table, and she made him *lust*, damn it.

So much that although he *wanted* to rise, doing
so would only give her another reason to berate him,
supposing she knew what a bulge in a man's breeches
meant. Of course, even if she didn't, Katherine certainly
did, and he wasn't about to embarrass himself that way.
And if she was trying to pair him off with this shrewish
creature, he had no intention of giving her the advantage of knowing the chit affected him.

"Since your opinion of me is so low, Miss Weston, perhaps you would like to leave. I'm certain I can arrange a
carriage and suitable escort to take you home."

She gaped at him. He found he quite enjoyed ren-
dering her speechless. He couldn't imagine there were
many able to best Miss Weston in a verbal battle.

"Or have you been pawned off on your aunt, and by
association on me, because your family can no longer
stomach your foul temper?"

She looked fit to burst. He bit his cheek so as not to
let his amusement show. Damned if part of him hoped
she *wouldn't* take him up on his offer. Ribbing Miss
Weston was the most fun he'd had in years.

"First, my family adores me. Second, *I* am not the one
suffering from perpetual ill temper. Third, in the event
I did want to leave, you would be hard-pressed to find
an escort for me. Perhaps you are unaware, but you happen to be more than a little short-staffed. Not that I can
imagine why anyone should wish to be quit of *you*—"

"Enough!" Katherine ordered. "If I wanted to listen
to childish bickering at the table I would take my meals
in the nursery. Jason, I would never have allowed Olivia
to accompany me had I realized you would be unable
to show a guest the most basic courtesy. And as for you,
Livvy, the marquess is your host and deserving of your
respect, no matter how provoking he may be."

Nothing killed a man's desire as fast as being scolded
by a parental figure. Now that he could do so without

embarrassing himself, Jason rose to his feet. He found his height was a greater advantage than he had foreseen. Looking down at Miss Weston gave him an unexcelled view of her plump breasts. His fingers twitched. . . .

Christ. He was a grown man. He was above this. And speaking of above, he really needed to stop staring at her breasts. He raised his eyes to meet her gaze.

"Miss Weston, I beg your pardon if I reacted too strongly. I am certain you meant no harm rearranging the library. Perhaps you even meant to be helpful."

Her lips pursed with displeasure.

Damn, that wasn't what he'd meant to say. At least, not in those precise terms. "I am not used to having things in my life upset," he tried to explain. "I dislike change."

"Sometimes change can be a good thing," Miss Weston said softly. "There are times in every life when events occur that make change inevitable. If a person learns to embrace change rather than rail against it, perhaps it is less troubling when control is wrested away and one is forced to accept some change."

They weren't talking about books anymore, that much was certain.

The room was silent, so silent he could hear his heart beating in his ears. Jason gazed at her, wondering if she was a sorceress of some kind. Her eyes, deep and clear as the azure water in nearby Carmarthen Bay, seemed to see right inside him, straight into the darkness of his soul.

It was unnerving.

It was hogwash.

He was delirious, Jason told himself. He hadn't been sleeping well of late and that, combined with this sudden surge of lust, had clearly addled his wits.

"Just so we are clear, Miss Weston, the books here at Arlyss have no need of your wonder-working. Is that understood?"

"Perfectly." Her chin rose in the air. "If you will excuse me, Aunt Kate, I'm afraid I have lost my appetite. I think it would be best if I went to bed."

"Of course, my darling. I admit, I am exhausted, too. Such a lot of traveling we've been doing, and on top of that you've been entertaining Charlotte a good deal of the time. It's a wonder you haven't collapsed. I'm certain you'll feel more yourself after a good night's sleep. You can ring if you need me, or I suppose the ingrate here will be close at hand."

Jason coughed. "I beg your pardon?"

"Well, you must concede that you reacted most ungraciously to all the work Olivia has done—"

Jason waved a hand to stop her, a terrible suspicion taking root in his mind.

"Right, I understand. Your niece is the patron saint of libraries and I'm the big, bad dragon."

Miss Weston laughed. It was a warm, rich sound, clear and true, and it made him think of happier times, of racing through snowy fields in a sleigh pulled by horses with jingling bells on their harnesses, of drinking brandy before a crackling fire, of wicked, whispered promises, of heated glances, of making love—

He stopped himself.

He would not go there.

It was too painful.

"What did you mean, I would be close at hand should Miss Weston need someone in the night?"

Katherine smiled at him, a gleam of wicked amusement in her eyes. "There was a slight problem with the room that was prepared for Olivia. It should all be taken care of in a matter of days, but as you never entertain, all of the rooms are kept closed up. Olivia offered to share a chamber with Charlotte, but I thought that unfair as Charlotte kicks dreadfully in her sleep. Wouldn't you agree?"

"Er, quite, but I'm afraid I don't follow. How could a room have been prepared for Miss Weston when she's only just arrived?"

"My dear boy, you can't think I expected Mrs. Maddoc to accommodate an extra guest with no forewarning. No, I wrote to her as soon as it was decided Olivia would be traveling with us. I knew you would not object to Olivia's presence once you met her and realized what a pleasant companion she is."

Jason found her presence entirely objectionable, but he held his tongue.

"If you can believe it," Katherine went on, "there is only one room in this great behemoth of a place that is aired out and suitable for someone to stay the night in. Can you guess?"

Jason knew what was coming. He knew, and yet he hoped his stepmother was going to mention some part of the castle hitherto unknown to him. Perhaps some lovely little one-room cottage on the perimeter of the estate.

It was not to be.

"Very well, I shall tell you: the Marchioness's Chambers."

Jason considered bashing his head into the table. "Are you certain that is proper?" he ventured. "The chambers adjoin."

His stepmother shrugged. "I grant you the situation is not ideal, but needs must suffice. I very much doubt that my innocent niece is going to take advantage of you."

Funny, that was exactly what he feared was going to happen. At least, the rational part of him feared it. From the neck down, he was only too eager to be compromised.

"In any case," she continued, "this arrangement will only be until Mrs. Maddoc can arrange for a glazier to repair the window in the tower bedroom. If you fear for your virtue, you can lock your door. Does that set your mind at ease, sir?"

It did not set Jason's mind, or any other part of his body, at ease, but he saw there was little to be done. "Madam, if you are not troubled by the impropriety of the situation, I certainly shan't lose sleep over it."

That was a lie. He wouldn't sleep a wink. Knowing the delectable Miss Weston was in the chamber next to his was going to be pure torture. To have a willing woman so close at hand . . .

And she *would* be willing. Even if she were a complete innocent, which he doubted, Jason hadn't missed her earlier reaction to him. Not the reaction earlier that evening when she had all but accused him of being a selfish monster, but earlier that day, first when he had caught her looking at a part of him no innocent miss would know about, and again when he had held her in his arms.

He had heard the slight hitch to her breathing . . . felt her heart pounding . . . watched as a rosy flush stained her cheeks. He'd been affected then, and that had been before he'd had a taste of her saucy little mouth. What wouldn't he give to taste her in truth. . . .

He dug his nails into his palms.

His stepmother had somehow arranged for her niece to be placed in the bedchamber adjoining his and, innocent or no, that young lady was a tender pullet ripe for the plucking. And no mistake, he was a man in need of a good pluck. The events of the day had borne in on him just how desperate was his need.

Christ. If a locked door was the only obstacle in his path, Miss Weston would be lucky to last the night.

"I certainly don't have to worry *you* will misbehave," Katherine added. "You haven't so much as looked at a woman since . . ."

Since Laura, Jason silently finished for her.

The mention of his wife was like a bucket of icy water thrown upon the flames of his desire. Good God, what had he been thinking? How had he let himself forget, even for a moment—

He needed to do more than lock his door that night. He needed to lock up, batten down, strengthen, fortify, and otherwise secure every portion of himself that was vulnerable to Miss Weston. He wasn't entirely surprised by his body's enthusiastic response—in truth, he was relieved such bountiful stimulus still elicited the proper reaction—but he couldn't go about with a cock-stand for the duration of the gel's stay.

Nor could he allow himself the fun of teasing her and drawing her into a battle of wits. That bespoke a closer relationship than he planned on having with Miss Weston or any other female. No, it was essential he remain detached. His heart was a stronghold with sentries at every entrance. If he relaxed his guard, if he allowed her to affect him, she might have a chance at breaking in.

A chance at breaking *him*.

A man could only bear so much hurt in a lifetime before the pain became crippling. He couldn't risk that, for his son's sake. Edward needed him to be strong. To protect his son, Jason would be invulnerable. Invincible. Infallible. And, if such behavior kept the castle's inhabitants at a safe distance, he would be utterly inhospitable, inimical, and otherwise insufferable.

If Miss Weston thought to ride roughshod over him as she so clearly did her aunt, she was going to be sorely disappointed. Arlyss was his domain, and he would not tolerate any interference. In the event his unwanted guest made advances toward either himself or his home, she would not get far. He was going to lock his door at night, to be sure, but just in case Miss Weston thought to go traipsing about the castle in search of some new project, Jason decided to lock the door to the library as well.

Olivia could not get to sleep. She tried lying on her right side, then on her left, on her back and on her stomach. She pulled the coverlet up to her chin before throwing it off entirely. She pushed the bed hangings open, then shut them tightly again. Nothing worked.

She couldn't banish the sight of the marquess's angry face from her mind's eye. He had truly been furious with her. Had he guessed what she had discovered in the library? Of course, even if he remembered hiding the clues and the brooch, she very much doubted he knew that his wife's diary had ended up there—if he had known she kept a diary at all.

Livvy guessed that after the marchioness's death, the London servants had packed her belongings and sent them to the family seat at Haile Castle. When the trunks were unpacked and the contents sorted through, the diary must have been mistaken for a novel and placed in the library. That was where Livvy had found it.

Taking the diary, which was carefully hidden at the bottom of her trunk, was an even worse transgression than taking the brooch.

She had stolen from a dead woman.

Twice.

But, she consoled herself, Laura had never actually found the brooch, so perhaps it wasn't really hers. Besides, the poor woman had no need for it now, or for her journal. Livvy needed them. She needed every fragment she could glean from these glimpses into his past to piece together the puzzle Lord Sheldon presented.

There was another matter nagging at her as well. She did not much care whether or not she adhered to her mother's steadfast notions of propriety, but she did mind—or tried to mind—her parents' insistence on civility. She had been less than civil—hostile, even—to her host, and while she had been provoked, the marquess had apologized for his behavior and she had not.

She was fairly certain the marquess had not yet gone to bed, so she decided to wait in the hall until he came upstairs. All that was needed was the word "sorry," and though it might choke her, she wouldn't die from it. She got out of bed and donned slippers and the quilted flannel wrapper that Alice, her aunt's maid, had laid out in case she got chilled at night.

It was cold in the hall, and dark, and there was no place to sit other than the floor. The carpet was probably priceless, but it did little to soften the hard wood beneath. Her physical discomfort made it difficult for Livvy to focus on anything worthwhile, and she soon stopped trying. She wondered how long Lord Sheldon would take before coming to bed. Minutes? Hours? Oh, perish the thought!

She counted to one hundred. She counted backward down to zero. She counted all her fingers and toes, wiggling them to make sure they had not succumbed to frostbite. All were cold but accounted for. She thought about making a list—Appendages I Would Be Loath to Lose to Extreme Cold, Beginning with Those Least Important to Survival—but she got stuck on the first point, trying to decide if each toe should be numbered independently, or whether all ten toes comprised an item. . . .

"Miss Weston?"

The marquess's deep voice startled her awake. She scrambled to her feet and rubbed her eyes.

"I know there must be a reason you are sleeping in the hall, Miss Weston, but I don't particularly care to hear. I'll ring for Mrs. Maddoc." He reached for the door handle.

"No, wait," Olivia said quickly. "That is, I need only you."

One dark eyebrow shot up and Olivia blushed furiously as she realized how her words must have come across.

"That did not come out right at all." She shook her head. "What I meant to say is that you were the person with whom I wished to speak."

"Pity," he murmured.

Livvy stared at him, wondering what exactly he thought a pity.

"There was something you wished to speak to me about, was there not?"

"Oh, yes, of course. I want to apologize. My behavior at dinner was shameful."

"Mine was no better," he admitted.

"Yes, but you apologized. What's more, I have been invited into your home against your wishes—"

He held up a hand. "Miss Weston, this is as much your aunt and Charlotte's home as it is mine. If they wish to bring a guest with them when they visit, such is their prerogative."

"But—"

"No, wait. I have made you feel most unwelcome and it is not well done of me. I pray you will forgive me, Miss Weston, for I have been a very ill-mannered host. May we begin again?"

His smile was just a bit crooked, and it made him look boyish and vulnerable. Something warm unfurled in the region of Olivia's chest. She dropped a quick curtsy and smiled up at him.

"Olivia Jane Weston."

He bowed, a faint twinkle in his eyes. "Jason Traherne. I won't bore you with the litany of names betwixt the first and last."

They stood in silence for a moment.

"Now what happens?" he asked.

"You should express your delight or at least your

very great pleasure at making my acquaintance," Livvy told him.

Lord Sheldon stroked his chin as if in deep thought. "Delight?" he repeated aloud. "No, I don't believe that is quite the word I want."

Olivia pursed her lips. Really, the man was insufferable.

"A very great pleasure, eh? No, that's not right, either."

"Oh, for goodness' sake, lie if you must," she bit out.

"Do you know," he mused, "I don't think that will be necessary. Miss Weston, I say this with the greatest sincerity. Heaven knows why, but I find myself charmed."

Livvy could have dealt without the "heaven knows why," but beggars could not be choosers. This teasing man with the twinkle in his eyes was the man she had hoped to find. The man who wrote atrocious poetry and hid presents for his wife's amusement. The man she had come here to save, but had feared was lost.

Her fall to the ground wasn't the only knock she had suffered since entering Castle Arlyss. No matter that Aunt Kate had warned her, the marquess's acrid, disdainful manner had shaken Olivia's confidence. His behavior at dinner only cast her down further. Now her spirits shot back into the air.

"I do believe there's hope for you yet, my lord."

It was the wrong thing to say. She knew it as soon as the words left her lips. He stiffened and drew away, physically and emotionally.

"No." He shook his head. "I am past hope. Or perhaps hope is past me. Either way, we would both do well to remember it."

"You are too young to have such a dismal view of the future," Olivia protested.

"Experience has made me old."

"In spirit, perhaps, but it will not make the years fly by any faster. You have a long life ahead of you."

"If there is one thing I have learned, Miss Weston, it is that none of us knows how much time we have been given on this earth."

Livvy knew he was thinking of his wife.

"All the more reason to spend every day full of hope and wonder for life's possibilities," she countered.

"You are young. I am afraid you will come to find that expectation leads to disappointment."

"I am not so young as I look. I am very nearly nineteen. I should have come out this past spring, but my sister needed me. I shouldn't mind putting it off another year, but one doesn't want to run the risk of being thought an old maid."

"An old maid at twenty." He shook his head. "And I have nearly ten years on you. By your calculations I must be ancient."

"Men are not held to the same standards. You are in the very prime of life. But you are a marquess and so would be thought a good catch even if you had one foot in the grave."

"Pursued for my title." He heaved a sigh. "And all these years I thought it was my sunny disposition."

Olivia choked on a laugh. "If ever I were to pursue you, my lord, it would certainly be for that."

"And if I were to pursue you, Miss Weston?"

Livvy's heart jumped. "I beg your pardon?"

"If I were to pursue you, what would be your great attraction?"

"My dowry, likely."

"I have no need of funds."

"My connections, then. My father is a viscount, and my grandfather on my mother's side was a duke. My brother-in-law is the Earl of Dunston."

He shrugged. "Good breeding is important, but as

you pointed out, I am a marquess. I don't particularly need to cultivate aristocratic connections."

"I tell very good bedtime stories."

The corner of his mouth twitched in amusement. "I am not a child."

"No, but you have one."

"You speak of your maternal abilities. A good try, Miss Weston, but a nursemaid serves the same purpose."

Olivia folded her arms across her chest. "Then apparently I hold no attraction for you, my lord, and you will not be pursuing me. I must hold I am greatly relieved."

He shook a finger at her. "I didn't take you for a liar, Miss Weston."

"You plan to pursue me, my lord?" Olivia smiled sweetly.

"No. On that count you were correct. You are not, however, greatly relieved to hear it. That was your lie. All women wish to be pursued."

She braced her hands on her hips. "Why should I, or any female for that matter, wish to be pursued by someone for whom I hold not the slightest attraction?"

"Ah, but I never said you held no attraction for me. You came to that conclusion on your own."

"You made it quite clear—"

"As it happens, you failed to mention your greatest attraction."

"Oh?" She regarded him suspiciously. "And what might that be?"

"Why, your equally sunny disposition to be sure, though I've not discounted your apparent gift for, er, organization. Tell me, does this talent extend to all rooms, or is it particular to the library?"

Livvy took a deep breath and counted to ten. Then to fifty. It didn't calm her in the slightest. First the man had tried to kill her by ordering his dog to attack her, and then he'd had the temerity to be ungrateful about

all her hard work on his library. And now *he* had the gall
to criticize *her* personality, which was charming most of
the time . . . just not around him.

This was not to be borne!

"You can forget that apology, my lord," she hissed.

The low, gravelly sound of his amused chuckle rang
in her ears. He leaned forward to chuck her under the
chin. *"Charmed,"* he whispered, his breath hot against
her cheek.

Before she did something she would regret, Olivia
turned and hurried into her chamber. She resisted slamming the door, but only because she was certain the action would further amuse the wretch next door. When
Aunt Kate had spoken of the changes in her stepson,
Livvy had imagined a quiet, sorrowful recluse. She
would coax him into the holiday spirit, gently remind
him of the pleasure to be had in good company, and perhaps permit a kiss beneath the mistletoe. . . . This was not
the sort of adventure she had reckoned on!

But then, that was the problem with adventures. You
could organize and plan and make lists all you liked,
but you were never prepared for the actual setbacks, all
of the unforeseen problems and pitfalls. By then it was
usually too late and, for better or for worse, there was
no turning back. Not that she was thinking of turning
back.

She reached down absentmindedly for the familiar
lump of the brooch, and then realized she had hidden
it away for the night. The marquess was unlike what
she had expected, to be sure, but he was still—or he
had been—the tender, passionate father and husband
depicted in his wife's diary. She had not come this far
to give up at the first sign of adversity. She fetched the
book she was reading—or purporting to read—off the
writing table where she had abandoned it earlier. She
flipped through the pages . . . There!

She removed the loose paper and moved to the window. Standing in the silvery moonlight, she whispered the words, weaving them into a healing prayer.

Livvy had to concede his rhyming of "cleric" and "esoteric" was clever, and it had taken her no little amount of time to puzzle out that her next clue was hidden in the castle's priest hole, but as far as poetry was concerned, Lord Sheldon was past saving. But, she assured herself as she hid the paper back inside the book, the rest of him was not. A man who had written poetry for his wife—however grating and unmelodic his verse—was not past redemption. He could be saved. No, he *would* be saved, and she, the ordinary (and ordinarily charming) Olivia Jane Weston, would be the one to do it.

Chapter 4

"Is there no respect of place, persons, nor time in you?"

Twelfth Night, Act II, Scene 3

As his housekeeper was scrambling to do the work normally delegated to the chambermaids, and as his stepmother planned to spend her morning attending to the matter of procuring new ones, Jason was informed over breakfast that the task of escorting Miss Weston on a tour of the castle fell to him. The situation was undesirable, to be sure, but he resolved to make the best of it. With any luck an hour or so in Miss Weston's company would dissolve any warmer feelings that might have arisen the previous evening.

God knew something else had arisen and he'd had a devil of a time getting to sleep. What little slumber he had managed was restless, spent drowning in a sea of lustful dreams wherein he and Miss Weston had engaged in libidinous acts amidst towering stacks of books. He would never again think of libraries in quite the same light. Fortunately he seemed to have recovered his control this morning, and if he chose to ignore the fact that his control seemed proportionate to the amount of flesh exposed by Miss Weston's gowns, that was his business. And if he decided the library need not be part of this morning's excursion, then that was his business as well. The damned room ought to be locked anyway, but

Gower's hearing was increasingly selective with regard to Jason's orders as of late.

"Miss Weston, if you have had your fill of chocolate . . ." He rose, beckoning her to follow him. "We'll start in the Great Hall, as that's the oldest part of the castle, though it has been improved upon over the past five hundred years or so."

The dining room had three doors; one led to the New Tower, which, on this level, housed the library. They were most definitely *not* going through that door. The door on the southern wall of the room led to apartments, and he had no intention of giving Miss Weston a tour of the castle's bedchambers. He was not going there. Not physically. Not mentally. Not nohow.

The door he guided Miss Weston through led into the solar, where, he supposed, some ancient relation dressed in a tunic and hose had sought solitude from the clatter and chaos of the Great Hall. Some other, not quite as ancient relation in a slashed doublet and codpiece had covered the walls with oak paneling and added an oriel window, which flooded the small chamber with light. The quiet nature of the room had not changed with the passage of time, but its purpose was less obvious now all of Arlyss was cloaked in a mantle of silence, rather like the castle in the story of the sleeping princess.

"Oh, what a lovely room!" Miss Weston exclaimed, flitting about to examine the carved paneling. She traced her fingers over the carved wood panels before gazing up at the plaster frieze, which continued all the way around the room. She circled the room twice, pondering the figures, before conceding defeat. "I'm afraid I can't make out the subject," she admitted. "It's not a battle scene, which I would never attempt to identify, but neither does it seem to be biblical or mythological. Is it peculiar to your family?"

Jason gave a curt nod. "Peculiar is a very apt description. One of my more fanciful ancestors, the third marquess, believed he was visited by the ghost of one of the castle's earliest residents, the ill-fated Rhoslynn Rhys. He commissioned this depiction of her star-crossed romance to commemorate his brush with the spirit world."

Miss Weston's eyes were alive with excitement. "I had hoped to see the White Lady during my stay, but with the window broken in the Old Tower—"

"There is no ghost, Miss Weston." He spoke forcefully, and in the small room his words were almost a shout. "The White Lady is naught but a legend passed down, embellished and elaborated upon by each successive generation. Whatever tale Katherine told you—"

"Aunt Kate only remembered bits and pieces," Miss Weston broke in. "Won't you tell me about her?"

He shook his head. "If everyone remembers only bits and pieces, the story will eventually be forgotten, and then maybe the maids will stop leaving."

She gave him an appraising look. "Do you really believe the maids leave because of an old ghost story?"

Jason shrugged. "Gower did suggest the dogs might scare them."

"They are somewhat intimidating, I grant you, but I doubt a dog would frighten a maid into giving up a post in a good household with decent wages."

He sensed she was trying to lead him to some answer, but he wasn't following. "There is no need to beat about the bush, Miss Weston. Tell me, why are the maids leaving if the fault lies with neither the ghost nor the dogs?"

She hesitated, plucking at the folds of her skirts. "You truly wish to know?"

He frowned. "Of course."

"Very well." She swallowed and turned her gaze back

to the frieze. "If I tell you why the maids are leaving, will you tell me about the White—about Rhoslynn?"

Jason was torn. He hated talking about his ancestress, not because her legend scared off the maids, but because people—usually women—always sighed and sniffed into their handkerchiefs and murmured how the tale was so romantic when it was nothing of the sort. On the other hand, he hadn't particularly enjoyed waking up to cold ashes in the grate and the lingering stench of the piss-pot.

"I will tell you the story as I was told it," he agreed, "since I imagine you'll pester everyone in the castle until you hear it."

"Probably." She grinned, revealing a dimple in her left cheek. "Tenacity is one of my strengths."

"Then I should hate to learn your weaknesses," he muttered.

"I heard that, my lord, but I shall let it pass. *My* weaknesses are not the issue at hand."

His brows rose. "And mine are?"

"Presuming one counts a choleric temperament as a weakness. I have only been under your roof for a day, but if you are always snapping and bellowing in this manner, I would guess *you* are to blame for terrifying the maids."

He laughed because the notion was so utterly ridiculous. Perhaps he *had* been a bit short with a few of the maids, and he *had* lost his temper with the maid who'd brought his son icy bathwater, claiming it would strengthen his constitution, but he could hardly be faulted for that. Or for dismissing the occasional maid who decided to offer more, ah, personal services. And the silly girls he'd berated for idle gossip clearly had flighty dispositions; they wouldn't have lasted long in any case. . . .

Christ, was it possible he was the reason the maids had left?

Miss Weston came forward and patted his arm. "I don't think they *all* left because of you. The castle is somewhat isolated and likely quieter than one might expect in a nobleman's household. I daresay some of the maids wanted a bit more excitement, and I've no doubt a number of them grew weary of pining for their master—" She clapped her free hand over her mouth, then brought it up to cover her eyes. "Oh, dear, I can't believe I said that aloud."

Jason chuckled, watching in wonder while her skin changed from creamy white to the color of strawberries.

"Pray, do not be embarrassed. That was the nicest compliment I have received in quite some time. You wouldn't think it, but Gower is unbelievably stingy with his praise."

He wasn't sure why, but he felt compelled to relieve her distress. And when she lowered her hand from her face and he saw that dimple again, he felt like he'd been given the moon and the stars.

A fragment of conversation surfaced in his mind, a shard from a vessel once shaped like a heart. Like his heart.

"Marry me, Laura. I'll give you everything. Jewels, gowns—the moon and stars if you want them."

"I don't want any of that, my love. I only want your heart."

His heart.

She'd wanted his heart, and he had given it to her.

And then she'd had to go and break it.

"What are you thinking of?"

Miss Weston's gently voiced question drew Jason out of his reverie.

"Broken hearts," he answered truthfully.

"Rhoslynn's? Or were you trying to count the number of maids you've left brokenhearted over the years?" she teased.

His wife's shadow had chased away the lightness that had briefly surfaced within him. "Neither," he responded coldly. "The broken heart in question is my own. Now, may we proceed on our tour?"

Olivia trailed Lord Sheldon out of the solar, silently cursing her stupid, wayward mouth. How could she have been so unfeeling, so thoughtless as to jest about broken hearts with this particular man? She berated herself all the way downstairs, and then she forgot everything as he led her into the castle's chapel.

The room was long and narrow, but light flooded in through the large stained-glass windows that ran along one of the walls. Colored patches, like scattered pieces of a rainbow, danced over the stone floor, carved oak pews, and whitewashed walls. The timbered ceiling was painted with a scene of God in heaven, so that one felt there was nothing overhead but a blue sky with a choir of angels. The space was simple, but divine; old-fashioned, but entirely fresh. Livvy knew she had never been in the chapel before, and yet it was somehow familiar. It took her a few minutes to realize why.

"This is just how I pictured the chapel in *The Shades of Hartsbane Hall*," she told Lord Sheldon.

"I beg your pardon?"

"It's a wonderful novel. There's a governess—Emmaline—who discovers a priest hole in a chapel just like this one. The master of the house, Lord Maxwell, is the dark, brooding sort"—Olivia gave the dark, brooding marquess a sideways look—"but he falls in love with Emmaline and rescues her after the evil housekeeper traps her in the priest hole."

"I'm sorry to say I must have missed that one," he

said, sounding not at all sorry. "An evil housekeeper, you say? Perhaps I should order it for Mrs. Maddoc."

"Oh, no." Livvy shook her head. "I am certain she would much prefer *The Bride of Moongate Manor*. That's the one where Emmiliana, an impoverished Italian *contessa*, disguises herself and becomes the housekeeper of Prince Maximilliano—"

He leaned back against the side of one of the pews and crossed his arms over his chest. "Let me guess, he's the dark, brooding sort as well?"

She nodded.

"And they fall in love, this prince and his housekeeper?"

"But she's really a countess—"

"Yes, well, as Mrs. Maddoc's family has been in service to the Trahernes for some years, I am quite sure she is not an aristocrat in disguise. Nor do I see myself falling in love with anything other than her tea cakes. I think it would be unkind to give her false hope."

"Go ahead and poke fun, my lord," Livvy sniffed. "You are obviously unaware of the great pleasure to be had from such novels."

He made a sound of disgust. "Nonsensical stories written for nonsensical women."

"I believe many men enjoy reading them as well," she replied stiffly.

"I take leave to doubt that."

She raised her brows in silent question.

"Men are logical beings," he explained. "These novels, though I doubt they deserve so lofty a title, clearly defy rational thought."

"I see," she said through clenched teeth. "And if men are logical beings, then women are. . . ?"

He didn't hesitate for a second. "Women are illogical, irrational, flighty creatures prone to ridiculous notions of love and romance."

Olivia wasn't sure whether she was more startled by his words or the utter conviction with which he spoke them. She gave an uneasy laugh. "Anyone would think you hate women, my lord."

He straightened. "Hate women? No, I am as fond of women as the next man."

"For a man fond of women, you certainly have a mean opinion of us," she retorted.

He shrugged. "I am simply aware of the weaknesses of your gender. It doesn't follow that I hold those flaws against you."

She gaped at him, unable to think of any suitable rejoinder.

"And speaking of women's weaknesses," he continued, "let us go into the Great Hall, where we can sit and I'll tell you of Rhoslynn."

He gestured her through a tiny wooden door that connected the chapel to the Great Hall. They made their way to the cluster of chairs set before the enormous stone fireplace where he had carried her only the day before. It seemed a lifetime had passed since she set foot in Castle Arlyss.

Lord Sheldon settled back and began his tale. "Long, long ago—"

"And not at all far away," Livvy added.

"Are you going to tell the story, or am I?"

She settled back in her chair and folded her hands primly in her lap.

"Very well then, as I was saying, long, long ago, there lived in this castle a beautiful maiden called Rhoslynn. Her mother had died giving birth to her, so she was the great pet of her father and her five older brothers. Such attention did not make her spoiled, though, and Rhoslynn grew up to be as lovely and kind as a woman can be.

"As her mother and her grandmother before her,

Rhoslynn had a gift for physicking; there were many who believed the Rhys women had fairy blood in them and with it the ability to heal. People would come from great distances for one of her salves or for the touch of whatever magic she might possess."

The marquess chuckled, shaking his head. "Great believers are the Welsh. In any case, one day, whilst gathering herbs in the countryside, Rhoslynn came upon a man lying on the ground. She saw a horse some yards off and figured he must have been thrown. Not knowing if he was unconscious or dead, she immediately dropped to her knees beside him and felt at his neck for a pulse.

"His skin was cold beneath her fingers, and she feared she was too late. She bowed her head and tears rolled down her cheeks, falling on the man's head like a gentle rain. Suddenly, the flutterings of a pulse tingled beneath Rhoslynn's fingertips, and when she placed her face on the man's chest to listen for a heartbeat, there it was, sure and steady."

"The magic," Livvy whispered, unable to contain herself. Then, before the marquess could roll his eyes or launch into a lengthy diatribe on the impossibility of magic, ghosts, or any other such metaphysical phenomena, she quickly went on. "So Rhoslynn brought the stranger back to life. What happened then?"

"The stranger opened his eyes and beheld the fairest maiden he had ever seen and, in an instant, he knew however far he might roam, whatever distant lands he might visit, his heart would always stay there with her."

"Typical male," Olivia muttered. "She's beautiful, so he loves her." She glanced at the marquess and saw he was watching her with bemusement. "I beg your pardon. I won't interrupt again."

"Doubtful," Lord Sheldon said, but he continued on. "When Rhoslynn gazed into the stranger's eyes, she too felt her heart swell and knew however long she lived, there would never be another she would love so well as this mysterious man."

There was a long moment of silence. Livvy was torn by the desire to stay quiet, as she had said she would, a need to know what happened next, and a growing itch to remark on Rhoslynn's ability to fall in love with a man without even knowing his name.

"That can't be it," she finally blurted out.

"No," he agreed.

Her brow creased. "Then why did you stop?"

"I felt certain you wished to make a comment."

She shook her head and motioned him to go on, unwilling to give him the satisfaction of knowing he was right.

"The man asked the name of his fair savior but, upon learning it, he knew himself to be cursed, for Rhoslynn's father was none other than the infamous rebel leader he had been sent by the Crown to destroy. The newly appointed Deputy Squire of Haverfordwest, Sir Philip Kentchurch, had been chosen by King Henry IV himself after Sir Philip's predecessor was killed defending the castle at Haverfordwest against a siege laid by Rhoslynn's father and his followers. Duty urged Sir Philip to take Rhoslynn captive and hold her as a hostage—"

"He wouldn't!" she exclaimed.

"*But,*" he spoke over her outburst, "he knew in his heart he could not. He asked Rhoslynn if she, too, felt the strength of the connection between them. She said she did and asked for the name of the man who had engaged her heart so quickly. Sir Philip warned her that her family would disapprove, but even after she learned his identity, Rhoslynn remained constant in her affections, though she could not imagine how they could ever be together.

"Sir Philip vowed to find a way and gave Rhoslynn his signet ring as a sign of his fidelity, though he cau-

tioned her to keep it hidden. They arranged to meet in
the same spot one week from that day, by which time
Sir Philip hoped to have worked out a solution to their
seemingly impossible situation. When the time came
for them to part, Sir Philip told Rhoslynn, 'I will think
of thee every second of every minute of every hour of
every day that shall pass ere we meet again.' And Rhoslynn replied, 'And I will see thy beloved face in every
seed of every fruit of every flower of every tree I pass
'til you come for me.'"

Olivia snorted. She couldn't help herself. "That's doing it a bit too brown, my lord."

"I didn't make up that tripe," he protested. "I am telling you the story as it was told to me." He frowned at
her. "It was my understanding women enjoy that sort of
overblown romantic sentiment."

"I am sure a great many do, but I do not count myself among their number. There is more to romance than
pretty, meaningless words. I would have been happier to
hear he swept her off her feet with a passionate kiss."

"Would you indeed?" he murmured, staring intently
at her lips.

Unused to such blatant perusal, or the hunger it
stirred within her, Livvy rose to her feet. "Perhaps you
could continue as we walk about the room," she suggested. "I would like to observe the tapestries in closer
detail."

The marquess stood and offered his arm to her. She
didn't wish to take it—she was too discomfited by the
way he made her feel—but she had no choice. She rested
her arm as lightly as possible upon his sleeve and tried
to ignore the heat from the skin beneath.

"Now, where were we? Oh, yes, your desire for a kiss.
You will be pleased to learn Sir Philip did steal a kiss
from Rhoslynn, but only one, lest he be tempted beyond bearing. Then he strode to his horse, vaulted into

the saddle, and rode off. Rhoslynn watched until he was out of sight, then gathered up her herbs and headed for home, nearly skipping in her happiness. Her father and brothers could tell she had met with some excitement while she was out, but mindful of Sir Philip's warning, Rhoslynn told them only that she had come upon a wounded hare and had been able to heal it. The Rhys men were also in high spirits, for they had spent the day planning their next assault against the English, but Rhoslynn knew nothing of this.

"Though she longed to tell someone, Rhoslynn dutifully kept the secret close to her heart, along with the ring. She placed it in a little pouch, which she filled with yarrow and rosemary and other lovers' plants, then hung it round her neck. Her father and brothers went out hunting two days before she was to meet with Sir Philip, and they came back in wild spirits. They took turns telling Rhoslynn how they had successfully taken the castle at Haverfordwest; how the new English lord had ordered his men to stand down; how he had sent a messenger bearing a white flag of truce."

"How wonderful!" Livvy exclaimed with delight. "Now *that* is a truly romantic gesture."

Lord Sheldon eyed her askance. "Perhaps you should hear the end of the tale first. Rebel forces, as you may know, rarely hold to the rules of civilized warfare. *Civilized warfare*," he sneered. "Now there's a contradiction in terms if ever I heard one. And in this instance, warfare is the wrong word. Slaughter is more appropriate."

Olivia gasped.

He nodded grimly. "When the messenger went forth, Sir Philip's men laid down their arms in a show of goodwill. Rhoslynn's father and his men struck while they had the advantage. The English lord refused to defend himself and was quickly dealt a mortal blow. After that, the soldiers surrendered the castle. When Rhoslynn heard this, she ran and locked herself in what is now the Old Tower, which has always been the tallest in the castle. The chapel used to be there, at the top, so no one would walk above God. The chapel you saw was built after Rhoslynn. . . . For all she was a healer, she couldn't mend her broken heart."

The hair on Livvy's neck stood on end. "She threw herself from the tower?" She knew the answer even as she asked.

"Her body was never found, but no one ever saw her alive again. The pragmatists insist the body must have been dragged off by wild animals. The fanciful claim she was spirited away by the goddess Branwen, who also died of a broken heart. In either case, the moral of the story remains the same."

"Don't fall in love with the enemy?" she guessed.

"Always a good rule to follow, but I believe the true lesson imparted by Rhoslynn's folly is that love is every bit as destructive as war."

Livvy pulled away from him. "You're wrong. War is destructive, but love is its antidote. Nothing could be worse than losing a loved one, but even then love triumphs over death, for the memory of those loves lives on in the hearts still beating. Love is the stuff of hopes and dreams, which are in turn the stuff of life."

"You, Miss Weston, are possessed of a romantic nature. I fear your life will be fraught with disappointments."

"As opposed to you, who have not suffered disappointment?" she shot back.

The corner of his mouth twitched in a smile, but his eyes were sad. "I too was once possessed of a romantic nature. I have found life is much simpler if one ceases to have expectations. If you will excuse me, I have important matters to attend to." He bowed and walked away.

She let him go. He had given her quite enough to

think about for one morning. The marquess was a puzzle to be sure, but she would figure him out. She wasn't one to back down from a challenge— No, that wasn't true. She had backed down from any number of her older siblings' dares, but really, their admiration was hardly worth her mother's wrath. She didn't give up, though. Not on puzzles, not on people, and certainly not on puzzling people.

Chapter 5

"Leave thy vain bibble-babble."
Twelfth Night, Act IV, Scene 2

Olivia awoke suddenly in the night. Heart racing, she scrambled out of bed, clutching her quilt to her chest. A fine sheen of perspiration coated her skin, causing her thin lawn nightgown to cling to her body, but the chill in her chamber soon turned it to gooseflesh. She squinted into the darkness, trying to discover what had awoken her, and then the hair on her nape rose. Slowly she turned around and what she saw left her stupefied.

On the opposite side of her narrow pallet she beheld a beautiful young woman, pale and diaphanous, clothed as in the Middle Ages. The apparition wore a flowing gown with wide, hanging sleeves, girded about the hips with a richly embroidered belt. For a moment, Olivia stared in incomprehension, frozen with terror.

The specter, seeing it had her attention, held out an arm. Olivia sucked air into her lungs and opened her mouth, but her scream died in her throat as the ghost gave a slight shake of her head and raised one pearly finger to its lips.

"Nay, be not affrighted. I mean thee no harm."

Though the ghost's lips never moved, somehow Olivia heard the antiquated words.

"I must be dreaming," she whispered shakily. She slowly sank down to the floor, unmindful of the rough wooden boards beneath her knees.

"Thou art not asleep. I am as real as thee, albeit somewhat less corporeal. Hast thou not yet heard of the White Lady of Castle Arlyss?"

Olivia wet her lips. "I have heard. . . . No, this is impossible."

"I pray thee, listen. I come on behalf of another, less tied to this world. She lingers, restless, unable to find peace until those she loves are also at peace."

A faraway look came over her pearly visage.

"She says you must remain strong. He will resist, but he needs you. They all do."

"I don't understand." Olivia shook her head in confusion. "Who is—? No, don't go. Not yet. Please, come back!"

The apparition faded into shimmering moonlight.

"He needs you."

The words reverberated through the tiny room, and suddenly Olivia sensed she was once more alone in her room. She rose unsteadily to her feet and moved to the door. He needed her. . . .

Olivia woke with a start. She scrambled to push aside the heavy curtains of the lofty tester bed, searching for some evidence of an otherworldly visitor. Nothing. *Of course there's nothing,* she berated herself. *You were dreaming.*

It hadn't felt like a dream, though. Everything had been so real. . . .

"He needs you."

The words echoed in her mind. Was she simply recalling her dream, or . . . ? In a flash, she was out of bed, reaching for her wrapper. Before she gave herself time to think about what she was doing, she crossed the room and rapped lightly on the door connecting her chamber to the marquess's. If he was asleep he likely wouldn't hear, and if he wasn't, if he needed her—

The door opened to reveal a harried-looking Lord Sheldon. His face was drawn and his hair was disheveled—but she couldn't deny he also looked quite splendid in his red silk banyan. Then she heard it. The sound of a child crying.

"Miss Weston? Is something amiss?"

"I— I heard something and grew worried. Perhaps the door between our rooms was ajar," she invented. Now was not the time to discuss the possibility that she had been visited by the castle's ghost.

"I am sorry to have woken you, Miss Weston."

Olivia peered past him and made out a little huddled mound in the middle of an enormous tester bed.

"Your son." The words hovered between a question and a statement.

The marquess nodded. "Yes, my son, Edward. Now, if you will return to your bed . . ." He took a step toward her, clearly expecting that she would retreat to her chamber.

Livvy held her ground. "Does he have night terrors?"

Lord Sheldon let out an impatient sigh. "If you must know, Edward suffers from a chronic chest complaint. He is prone to asthmatic fits."

"Has the doctor been sent for?"

"That old fool? His bleedings and blistering plasters nearly killed Edward."

"Have you no other physician treating him? There must be something that can be done."

He raked a hand through his hair, standing it on end. "I've sent for special doctors from London. I've bought special breathing contraptions and restorative elixirs. None of it does any good, and some of these so-called cures have left him a great deal worse. There is nothing for it but to wait it out." He cast a worried look back at the bed.

The sight of such concern over his son stirred Livvy's

heart and left her feeling decidedly unsettled. Of course, it was an excellent thing for Lord Sheldon to care for his son, because such tender feelings boded well for his ability to fall in love again. What she didn't like was her immediate, unfounded surge of jealousy toward the unknown woman who would one day claim his heart.

You are being ridiculous, she scolded herself. Feeling anything other than casual attraction to the marquess would be the very height of foolishness. *He* might have stepped out of one of her novels, at least when he kept his mouth shut. *She*, on the other hand . . . Well, no one would ever mistake Miss Olivia Jane Weston for a heroine.

No, she would never be a heroine, but she might be able to help Lord Sheldon's son if she could stop mooning over his father long enough to concentrate on the problem at hand.

"Do you know the cause of his ailment?" she asked.

"Anxiety. Excitement. A change in the weather." He waved his hands in an encompassing gesture. "Any number of seemingly benign events and emotions can trigger it. He can go to bed in fine health and, with no warning, wake an hour or two later struggling to draw breath."

"How awful," Olivia said feelingly.

"Quite." The marquess's tone was clipped. "If you will return to your chamber, I must attend to my son."

Olivia brushed past him and headed over to the bed. Perhaps it was having so many younger siblings, or maybe she had been born with more than her fair share of maternal instincts, but a child in distress was not something she could sit back and ignore.

Lord Sheldon snagged her arm, halting her progress.

"No. He is shy with strangers and crowding may exacerbate his symptoms."

"He is a frightened child who is feeling ill." She shook off the marquess's hand and strode to the bed. "Hello,

Edward. My name is Olivia, but you may call me Livvy if you like. That's what Charlotte calls me. I am her cousin, you know."

He was a beautiful child. With his dark hair and eyes, he was a tiny replica of his father, though his features still had the softness of youth. He was too pale, though, and the labored rasp of his breathing sent icy tendrils of fear spiraling through her. A fit of coughing wracked his slight frame, and Livvy took an involuntary step backward. She had no experience with sickness of this magnitude.

The realization left her feeling helpless and adrift. *What was she doing there?* Not just in the marquess's bedchamber, but here at Castle Arlyss. What madness had possessed her to believe *she*, Olivia Weston, could help the marquess or his son? She was about to run back to her chamber when a sense of calmness settled over her, and she suddenly knew what to do. She didn't know if the knowledge came from some deep-rooted instinct, or whether it came from outside her. Maybe it was a gift from the spirits residing outside space and time—a healer and a mother—who watched over the castle's inhabitants. Wherever the knowledge came from, she was grateful.

Olivia imagined that the boy's panic over the attack was contributing to it, feeding it in a vicious cycle. She needed to distract him. She saw that the boy was looking at her curiously. If he was focused on her, he would think less about being scared. She also imagined he would not be so frightened if he was not alone.

Livvy was also a firm believer in the healing power of touch. Whenever she fell ill, her mother's touch seemed to alleviate some of her misery. She wasn't Edward's mother, but perhaps any nurturing presence would do.

"Shall I climb in beside you and tell you a story, Edward? Would you like that?"

"I really don't think—" the marquess began, but he

stopped when Edward nodded and scooted over in the bed. The rasp of the boy's labored breathing filled the room.

Olivia hoisted herself into the enormous bed and drew Edward to her side. He nestled trustingly into her body as she pulled the quilts up over them. The marquess stalked over to a chair by the fireplace, seated himself, and crossed his arms over his chest, his expression inscrutable. She ignored him and focused on Edward.

"Once upon a time," she began, stroking the boy's silky hair, "there was a young prince—Prince Edward was his name—with a very special talent. He could talk to dragons. . . ."

Jason didn't know what to think as he listened to Miss Weston's nonsensical tale. He couldn't approve of the way she had barged in and taken charge of the situation. She had ignored his concerns, which were well-founded, and in doing so might have made Edward a great deal worse.

On the other hand, the chit clearly had a way with children. Her silly story was just the thing to distract Edward, and already his breathing sounded a bit better. The tension in Jason's shoulders lifted a little. Unexpected tears of relief sprang into his eyes, and he braced his elbows on his knees and buried his face in his hands.

Sometimes he wondered if having to stand by helplessly and watch his son suffer was a sort of penance for his wife's death. Laura's accident could have been prevented.

If only he had been more strict . . .

If only he hadn't let his pride get in the way . . .

If only he had insisted . . .

If, if, if, if, if . . .

"If ifs and ands were pots and pans, there would be no need for tinkers' hands," he muttered to himself, quoting one of his father's favorite sayings.

He didn't want to think of the dead any more tonight. He focused, instead, on Miss Weston's voice. By degrees he felt himself relax. His last thought, before he drifted off to sleep, was that perhaps he had been too hasty in dismissing her storytelling skills.

"My lord?"

Jason ignored the voice. Surely whomever it belonged to could see he was resting.

"My lord."

The voice came again, a bit louder and firmer this time. Damnation, couldn't a man even dream undisturbed?

The slight pressure of a hand on his shoulder catapulted Jason awake. He shot to his feet and glanced around in confusion.

"I beg your pardon. I didn't mean to startle you."

Disoriented, Jason blinked several times, finally focusing on the source of the words. At first he was certain he was still dreaming, and that the vision before him was a figment of his imagination, conjured up out of too many lonely, sleepless nights. Then he decided she must be real, for if he was going to fantasize about a woman in his bedchamber, her hair would be loose, not in a long plait, and she would not be dressed in an ugly wrapper that covered every inch of her.

She would be dressed in nothing at all. Or perhaps just in her stockings. There was something about a woman dressed only in stockings and garters that was more titillating than having her fully nude. Somehow it just seemed a little more . . . wicked.

He wondered if the woman before him—the woman who was likely real and not a dream—was wearing stockings under that bulky flannel monstrosity.

The woman folded her arms over her chest. "There is nothing wrong with my wrapper," she growled through clenched teeth. "It keeps me very warm. As for the other, it is absolutely none of your business!"

Jason wasn't sure if he had spoken aloud or if the woman had somehow divined his thoughts. There was something about her, something about the annoyance radiating from her, that was familiar. In a rush the day's events came back to him and he shook off his tired daze.

"Miss Weston!" he blurted out.

She put a finger to her lips and jerked her head in the direction of the bed. Before he could respond, she headed for her room, crooking a finger at him to follow.

"He is asleep?" Jason asked, once they were inside her chamber.

She nodded. "As were you. I only meant to wake you so that you might move into the bed. That chair could not have made a very comfortable place to sleep."

"My thanks, Miss Weston, and my apologies as well, to you and your wrapper. I fear I spoke before I was fully awake."

"That is all right, my lord. I should probably think this"—she waved a hand down her front—"a hideous monstrosity, too, if I had such a lovely dressing gown as yours."

He couldn't help himself. He was a man. And the slight longing in her voice made him imagine her in his banyan, the crimson silk sliding over her pale skin like a lover's caress. . . . A slight groan escaped him and, despite the distress it was currently causing him, Jason was grateful for the loose-fitting garment.

"Are you all right? Would you like to go to bed now?"

Jason clenched his fist and reminded himself that the girl had no idea what she was innocently offering. He wanted very much to go to bed, but not to sleep. No, his body was wide awake now.

Christ, this was just what he needed—another sleepless night. Soon he would be fit for Bedlam. Then again, given the direction of his thoughts over the course of the evening, perhaps he already belonged there.

"My lord?"

Jason shook his head. "I am perfectly well, just somewhat dismayed to find that the desire for sleep has fled. I'll leave you to your rest, then."

"That is probably for the best."

Was that disappointment he detected in her tone? No, surely not. Whatever her feelings when she entered his home, Jason suspected that by now Miss Weston rued the day she had decided to travel to Arlyss. His feelings had undergone a bit of a reversal as well. She was still a guest, and thereby a nuisance, but he could not regret that she had come.

For Edward's sake.

Not because the thought of her in his red silk banyan made his pulse race.

He headed for his chamber. "Good night, Miss Weston."

"Sleep well, my lord."

Jason closed the door between their rooms and resisted the urge to bang his head against the wood panel.

Sleep well, she'd said.

Right, as if there was any chance in hell of *that* happening. However good she might be for his son, Jason had a growing suspicion that Miss Weston was going to be very bad for him. He just wished he didn't find the prospect so bloody exciting.

Chapter 6

"I warrant thou art a merry fellow and carest for nothing."

Twelfth Night, Act III, Scene 1

Christmas Eve

Jason stumbled into the breakfast parlor the following morning. He acknowledged his stepmother and a bleary-eyed Miss Weston with a nod before dropping himself into the chair at the head of the table.

Katherine looked him over and immediately began to fuss. "You must start taking better care of yourself, Jason. You won't be any good to Edward if you fall ill. And you *will* fall ill if you don't get some rest."

"Thank you for that astute observation, Katherine. Your ability to state the obvious by means of circuitous logic never ceases to amaze."

She smiled warmly at him, undeterred by his rudeness. "After all these years, do you really think I will be put off by your foul temper? I only hope you can be persuaded to take a nap this afternoon along with Edward and Charlotte."

"Grown men do not nap."

"You will never stay awake tonight if you don't get some sleep."

"As I have no intention of staying up tonight, that should not pose a problem."

"But we must show Olivia a proper Welsh Christmas."

Jason glared at his stepmother.

"What makes a Welsh Christmas different from any other Christmas?" Miss Weston wanted to know.

"Everything," Katherine answered, just as Jason said, "Nothing."

"Don't listen to him. There is nothing like Christmas in Wales. Once you have attended Plygain services, you will never be happy celebrating Christmas anywhere else."

"Plug eye in?" Miss Weston repeated doubtfully. "It sounds most uncomfortable."

"It is," Jason quickly agreed.

"Oh, stop. He's bamming you, my dear. Plygain is the Welsh word for daybreak, which is when the Christmas services are held."

Her niece frowned. "You wish to go to church that early in the morning?"

Jason bit back a grin, schooling his face into a solemn expression. "As you said, most uncomfortable."

"It doesn't feel like early morning because you don't go to bed," Katherine explained. "Everyone stays up late on Christmas Eve. We decorate the house, and Mrs. Maddoc makes the most delicious toffee."

"That does sound fun," Miss Weston conceded.

"And the service isn't at all like what you are imagining. The sermon is very short and the rest of the time is taken up with carols."

"They are all in Welsh, though, so I doubt you would enjoy it." He tried to infuse the proper amount of regret into his voice. Not so much as to make her suspicious, but enough to persuade her that it would be a dreadful bore.

"Stuff and nonsense," his stepmother insisted. "I don't speak the language, and it has never hindered my enjoyment in the least. It is simply enchanting," she assured her niece. She turned and regarded Jason thoughtfully. "I know I have allowed you to mope and sulk and hide yourself away these past years, but there is to be no more of that. Edward and Charlotte are old enough to attend this year, so you cannot use them as an excuse."

"The cold isn't good for Edward," Jason protested.

"Then we shall take great care to ensure he is dressed warmly. There will be hot bricks and fur throws in the carriage, and we can bring them inside with us if need be."

"I don't like it," he muttered.

"I didn't think you would, but you have the whole day to reconcile yourself to it. By this evening I expect you to put on a good face."

"Charles should be arriving today. He could escort you instead," he suggested.

"No, it must be you. Edward will not enjoy himself if you don't come, and neither will Charlotte."

Katherine got to her feet. Jason made a move to rise, but she waved him down. She went to the sideboard and heaped food upon a plate, which she then set down, none too gently, in front of him.

"Eat," she ordered. "Perhaps, if we are lucky, a full stomach will improve your disposition. Clear your plate, too, Olivia. We've a long day ahead of us." She headed for the door.

"Leaving so soon?" Jason strove to look disappointed.

"Don't worry. I'll be back once I've seen to the *other* children."

After she left the room, Jason was left alone with Miss Weston. They ate in silence for several minutes before he said, "It occurs to me that I never properly thanked you for your help last night."

She looked up from her plate, her cheeks pink. "It was nothing," she mumbled.

"On the contrary. You seem to have a gift with children."

"I have four younger siblings," she said, as if that explained everything.

"Whom you love very much."

"Of course!"

"My dear Miss Weston, there is no 'of course' about it. From what I understand, younger siblings are a great trial. If I had been forced to deal with all that fussing and crying, I don't think I would ever want to see another child in my life."

"I cannot believe that," she protested.

"Like I said, you've a way with children. There's an understanding there and a level of compassion rare these days."

She squirmed in her seat.

"Does my praise make you so uncomfortable then? I should think you must be accustomed to receiving compliments."

"Yes. No. I don't know."

"I see."

"It is difficult to take pleasure in your compliments, my lord, when I know the other bit is still to come."

"The other bit?"

"The part where you insult me."

Jason roared with laughter.

"It was not my intention to amuse you," she sniffed.

"And yet you did. I find you unintentionally amusing. Could that be construed as an insult?" The thought set him off all over again.

"Edward slept through the night?"

Obviously Miss Weston had decided to change

the subject. Fine. Jason was feeling magnanimous. He couldn't remember the last time he had laughed so hard.

"Very nearly. He woke up thirsty at one point. You should thank me, Miss Weston. He wanted to wake you to hear the rest of your story, but I suggested he would do better to ask for a whole new story in the morning than half a story in the middle of the night. He agreed."

"Clever," she said approvingly.

"Yes, well, one does learn how to reason with children."

"I was referring to Edward," came the arch reply.

"Brava! And here I thought I was the only purveyor of the compliment-turned-insult."

She flashed a quick grin. "I am a fast study." Then her face turned serious. "Edward must have been quite young when you lost your wife."

"Yes." Jason turned his attention to his food.

"That must have been difficult for you."

He made a noncommittal sound, partly because his mouth was full, but mostly because he had no wish to discuss Laura with her.

Miss Weston took the hint. "I have been thinking about Edward's symptoms. He almost sounds as if he has a bad chest cold."

"Edward does not suffer from a chest cold," Jason bit out.

"I didn't mean to suggest that he did. Clearly his condition is far more serious. But I wonder if some of the treatments for the lesser ailment might not benefit him? Did the doctor who saw Edward try any natural remedies?"

The quacksalver had not, but his housekeeper had thought up any number of cures over the years. Mrs. Maddoc was a good soul and quite devoted to Edward, but her notions of doctoring were unusual, to say the least. She hadn't harmed anyone—yet—though he had once dumped one of her headache potions out his window, much to the detriment of the rosebush below.

When it came to his housekeeper, killed with kindness took on a whole new meaning. Jason found he was disappointed to learn that Miss Weston, who had seemed sensible—or at least as sensible as one could expect from a female—believed in such nonsense.

"I am not having my son walk thrice round a pig under the full moon, no matter how much it helped someone's grandmother's second cousin."

Miss Weston regarded him quizzically. " 'Thrice round a pig'?"

"That's what Mrs. Maddoc says."

"I regret to say I have not yet had the pleasure of conversing with your housekeeper about the restorative powers of farm animals during the full moon." She gave him a conspiratorial wink. "Personally, I wouldn't set much store in it."

"I don't."

"Then we are in agreement on that score. Now, when I was in Scotland, I remember seeing some herbals and other works on domestic medicines. Might I look for some similar volumes in the library here?"

He nodded. "I don't imagine you will find anything, but I will tell Gower it is safe to unlock the room."

She gave him a sideways glance. "Er, is it your usual practice to lock the library?"

"No," he admitted.

Her lips pursed in an expression of annoyance. It was a sight he was becoming familiar with. "I see."

"Miss Weston—"

She shook her head. "I cannot believe it. You actually locked your library against me." Then suddenly, she began to laugh.

Jason was puzzled. "You're not angry?"

"I was for a moment, but then I stopped to consider the sheer lunacy of such an action. Locking a room so that one of your guests doesn't go about the rather menial task of organizing its contents. Why, it's utter madness!"

"Since meeting you, madness is a condition with which I have become increasingly familiar. One has to wonder which of us is worse—you for taking on such a task or me for trying to stop you from doing it again. Ah, well, as Petrarch said: *Libri quosdam ad scientiam, quosdam ad insaniam deduxere.*"

She scowled. "An insult in a foreign language is still an insult."

"Permit me to translate: Books lead some to knowledge, some to madness. Did you gain any particular knowledge while organizing the library, Miss Weston?"

"Well, no, but—"

"Then madness it must be. You've been driven mad by books, and I have been driven mad by you."

"Another hit, my lord. You are in fine form this morning. I shall have to tell Aunt Kate her concerns were unfounded." She rose.

"I didn't mean—" he began.

"It doesn't matter. May I look in the library or not?"

"Yes, of course. Come, we'll go see Gower right now."

He'd had a lucky escape. He had been about to tell her his words weren't meant as an insult. She *was* driving him to madness, but not because she angered him.

Just the opposite.

And therein lay his problem.

As she browsed through the library, Olivia was thinking less of Edward and more of his uncle, Laura's brother. She had been stunned to hear he was expected. From what she had read in Laura's diary, Jason and Charles

did not get on at all. That was hardly surprising. Laura
hadn't been blind to her younger brother's faults, but
neither had she been able to say no to him. Perhaps he
had not meant to, but Chas, as Laura called her brother,
had used this advantage repeatedly and seemed to de-
pend on his older sister to rescue him from whatever
scrapes he landed himself in. And in the end she had
paid with her life.

No, that wasn't fair. Olivia shook her head, trying to
clear it of the unwanted thought. Laura's death was an
accident. In any case, she must at least be polite to Sir
Charles. It wouldn't do to let on that she knew more
than she should; that would raise questions she had no
wish to answer.

When he arrived late that afternoon, Livvy found, to
her very great surprise, that Sir Charles Avery seemed
a most respectable young man. He was probably in his
mid-twenties, which would put him around her older
brother's age, but he had a far more mature manner
than Henry possessed or would likely ever possess. Sir
Charles was an attractive man, as well. He was by no
means as good-looking as his brother-in-law, but his
boyish face was quite appealing. She had no doubt he
had a good many lady friends in London.

The smattering of Sir Charles's exploits that had
made their way into Laura's diary painted the picture
of a charming wastrel. The type of man who was really
still a boy, thinking only of his own pleasure, with no
thought to future consequences. And Livvy had read
enough novels to know that when one dealt with charming wastrels, there were always future consequences.

She had imagined he'd grown into a hardened gam-
bler in the intervening years, drawn further into London's seedy underworld, his sister no longer there to
rescue him. Instead she was met with chestnut curls and
a round, almost cherubic face. He was so very differ-

ent from her expectations, she found herself staring. He gave her a friendly smile and she saw in his sparkling green eyes a measure of masculine appreciation.

Livvy blushed.

"Jace," Sir Charles called out. "Who is this delightful creature? Surely she's been imprisoned here, for no maiden would consent to share your company."

Olivia laughed.

The marquess frowned.

"Charles, this is Miss Weston. She's Katherine's niece." His voice held a hint of warning. "Miss Weston, this is my brother-in-law, Sir Charles Avery."

"Uncle Chas!"

Edward appeared at the top of the stairs.

"Edward!" Sir Charles's genuine delight in seeing his nephew further improved Olivia's opinion of him. Edward raced down the stairs and his uncle caught him up in a big hug, spinning him about.

"Careful, Charles," the marquess cautioned.

Sir Charles set Edward down and ruffled the boy's hair. "No harm done. Now, where are the ladies of the family? This welcome feels quite incomplete without them!"

"Here we are." Her aunt glided down the stairs, almost seeming to float. Her aunt had an abundance of these feminine graces, though unfortunately they did not seem to be the sort of thing that manifested itself in families, like cleft chins or dimples.

As if to prove her point, Charlotte tripped on the bottom stair and would have gone sprawling on the floor—which Olivia knew from experience was rather hard and unforgiving—had Sir Charles not quickly stepped forward and caught her. He tossed her up over his head, making Charlotte squeal with delight.

"Hello, poppet!"

He set her down gently, then turned to Olivia's aunt.

"My lady." He turned a leg and made a courtly bow. "Still as beautiful as ever."

"Charles, you are a shameless flirt," Lady Sheldon declared, "but I wouldn't have you any other way. Someone must pander to the vanity of old women. Come here, dear boy, and give me a proper hug."

Olivia could tell that her aunt was truly fond of Sir Charles. Had Charles repented and been forgiven? The marquess didn't seem the forgiving sort, and though Charles wasn't responsible for Laura's death, her final diary entry mentioned an early-morning meeting, on Charles's behalf, in the park with a "Lord V" on Charles's behalf. Her riding accident must have happened on the way either to or from this assignation. This was all most curious. A mystery, one might even say. A mysterious man in a haunted castle—perhaps she'd have an adventure after all.

Aunt Kate held out a hand toward Livvy. "You met my niece?"

"I did indeed. I know it's shocking my brother-in-law remembered his manners long enough to make the introductions."

Lord Sheldon scowled.

"I am delighted to make your acquaintance, Miss Weston. Now we shall finally be able to make up a game of whist. We've tried to induce Dimpsey to play, but he refuses. I assume his massive self is lurking around here somewhere?"

"Right you are, Sir Charles." Aunt Kate's butler walked into the room.

Dimpsey was another mystery, though she doubted any of them would ever understand him. He had the look of a prizefighter, the manners of a gentleman, the stealth of a jungle cat, and the uncanny ability to appear at just the right time.

"Good to see you again," Sir Charles said as Dimpsey came closer.

"You too, sir." Dimpsey grinned. "And before you go asking me again, you still can't afford me."

Sir Charles gave a mournful sigh. "I suppose Jason already offered you a king's ransom?"

Aunt Kate gave her stepson a playful swat on the arm. "Will you stop trying to hire my butler out from under my nose? He's devoted to me, aren't you, Dimpsey?"

"Aye, my lady. You and Lady Charlotte." He winked. "I don't know how the two of you would manage without me."

"I'd scold you for impertinence if it weren't so true."

Dimpsey held out his hands. "Now, Master Edward, Lady Charlotte, I promised I'd take you out to look for holly and ivy and mistletoe to decorate with tonight, didn't I? Very well, then, let's go up to the nursery and get you both bundled up. I don't fancy having a pair of sick bairns on my hands come Christmas morning."

He hustled the children up the stairs, each of them perfectly obedient and charmed to do whatever he asked.

The marquess watched them go, his face a mixture of awe and skepticism. "There's something not quite human about that man."

"Yes," Lady Sheldon said fondly. "He truly is much more than a butler."

"That's just it," the marquess continued. "He's not just a good butler. He's also an excellent valet, and when he decides to set foot in the kitchen, his food is so good you think you've died and gone to heaven. Now I find he's on nursery duty as well. . . ." He shook his head and turned back to the company at hand. "Charles, you've been given your usual room."

"Dare I hope it is close to Miss Weston's?" He waggled his eyebrows suggestively.

Olivia blushed.

Her aunt laughed. "Charles, you devil, mind your tongue."

Lord Sheldon looked cross. "As it happens, Miss Weston is in the Marchioness's Chambers, so don't even think of trying anything improper."

"Yes, Lord Proper." Sir Charles saluted. "Well, I shall head upstairs to dust off the dirt of the roads and make myself presentable. When is dinner?"

"Seven," Lord Sheldon replied.

"Then I shall see you all in the drawing room at half past six," he said decidedly.

Men, Livvy had observed, had a distinct aversion to missing any sort of edible offering. Her older brother, Henry, could only be counted on to be on time for meals.

"I think I'll go to my chamber as well," Olivia said. She wanted to look over Laura's diary and see if there was anything she had missed about Sir Charles. He was so amiable; he hardly seemed capable of racking up vast amounts of debt, but appearances could be deceiving. Her preferred reading material might not be educational in the conventional sense, but the novels were vastly informative about sinister characters and nefarious deeds.

Had Sir Charles mended his ways after his sister's death? Was he the amiable young man he looked to be? Or was his easy conduct a mask for his true nature?

Perhaps Charles had known exactly what he was doing when he begged his sister for help. He might even have lured her into committing a crime. She didn't know the identity of "Lord V" or what might have transpired at their meeting. . . .

But she was getting ahead of herself. In this setting, it was sometimes difficult to remember that she was not the gothic heroine of her dreams, but ordinary Miss Olivia Weston. Just because she was ordinary, that did not mean she could not engage in a bit of discreet detective work. And if the suspect proved innocent, that was all to the good.

She had never been able to resist a good mystery. Her love of puzzles had started her on her current path and her journey would not be complete until she had unraveled every last knot, including her Gordian marquess. She had solved his riddles, clue by clue, and now she had to solve the riddle of him. He was infinitely more complicated than his poorly penned verses, but there was more than a brooch at stake. She was only just beginning to realize how much more and what price she might be forced to pay.

Jason saw the suggestive looks his brother-in-law was throwing in Miss Weston's direction. He didn't like them. At the moment there were a lot of things in his life that weren't to his liking . . . and nearly all of them involved Miss Weston.

Funny, that.

Still, he had a responsibility as head of the house, even if he only recalled that responsibility when it was to his advantage.

"Charles," he called out. "A word with you."

His brother-in-law trudged back down the stairs. "What?"

"Let's adjourn to my study, shall we?"

Once the two men were closeted inside the masculine domain, Charles turned to Jason. "What have I done this time?" he demanded.

"I am sure you've done a great many questionable things since last I saw you, but that's not why I asked to speak to you."

"Ordered, more like," Charles grumbled. "Go on, then. What's this matter of great urgency?"

"I wanted to speak to you about Miss Weston."

"And this couldn't have waited? Oh, very well, what about her?"

"She isn't one of your Town flirts. She's young and impressionable. She has probably never been exposed to attention from a man like yourself."

"A man like myself." Charles busied himself with brushing an imaginary speck of dirt off his pristine coat. "You certainly don't have a very high opinion of me."

"Damn it, Charles, you know what I mean. Your name's always being paired with some new woman or other—"

"Idle speculation. Every other bachelor in London with more than two shillings in his pocket suffers the same fate. One dance and a glass of orgeat and a man is practically engaged. You won't mind if I help myself to your excellent brandy, will you?"

Jason indicated that Charles was free to take what he wanted, at least as far as the cellar was concerned.

Charles continued to chatter as he poured himself a drink. "I had no idea you followed the gossip rags all the way out here. Are you only keeping tabs on me, or do the latest ladies' fashions interest you as well?"

"Don't be absurd." Jason moved to tend the fire. "Of course I don't read that trash, nor am I trying to keep tabs on you. That would imply a certain level of concern for your well-being. If you must know, my man of business in London takes great delight in regaling me with your exploits in his monthly letters." He poked at the kindling with unnecessary force. The logs crackled and hissed, shooting sparks every which way, as if to protest their mistreatment.

Charles seated himself in a leather wing chair near the marble fireplace. He took a sip of brandy and gave an appreciative sigh. "Such an overflowing of love warms my heart. I assure you the rumors are greatly exaggerated."

"Be that as it may, it would be very uncomfortable for everyone if you broke Miss Weston's heart."

"Set your mind at ease. I have no intention of toying with her emotions."

Jason looked up from the dancing flames. "Then you'll let her alone?"

Charles looked at him speculatively over the rim of his glass. "You know, I don't think I will."

"You can't mean you plan to seriously pursue the girl!" Jason swung around to face Charles, the red-hot iron in his hand.

"For God's sake, put that down before someone—namely me—gets hurt. I can't think why you're so shocked. I have to settle down eventually. Why shouldn't I see if Miss Weston and I suit?"

"Because . . ." Jason put the fire poker back as he weighed his words. "I just don't think it's a good idea."

Charles nodded sagely. "So the wind blows in that direction, does it?"

"What the devil are you talking about?"

"You've taken an interest in Miss Weston yourself."

"I have not."

"No need to be embarrassed. It's about time you remembered there's a fair sex," Charles said, clearly enjoying himself. "Being a widower doesn't have to mean a life sentence of loneliness. Laura wouldn't—"

Jason shook his head. "Don't."

"I miss her as much as you do, but you need to live your life. Edward is still at an age where he could benefit from a stepmother."

"What could a stepmother give him that I don't?"

"Lessons in how not to be so defensive?"

Jason massaged the tendons in the back of his neck. "My apologies. Edward hasn't been well and I haven't had enough sleep as a result."

"Damn. I keep hoping he'll outgrow it."

"Maybe he will. He went months without an episode before this last one. As you just pointed out, he's still young. Christ, I just feel so helpless every time it happens. He tries to be so brave. . . ." His throat swelled, making it impossible to continue talking.

Charles got to his feet and moved to stand next to Jason. "Wouldn't it help to have someone to share that burden with? I don't mean to say Edward is a burden, of course, but there's comfort in being able to let down your guard and confide in someone."

"Someone like a wife, you mean. What do you know about it? I don't recall you being married."

"It doesn't have to be a wife," Charles argued. "Laura was my confidante from the time we were children, ever since our mother died."

"I know. I always envied you that."

Charles was silent for a long moment. "I didn't realize. Is that why you disliked me so much in the beginning?"

Jason laughed. "I disliked you because you were ill-mannered and bent on ruining yourself, neither of which made your sister happy. You've grown up, though, and I'm glad to see you finally taking an interest in your estate."

"I . . . er . . ." Charles stammered, caught off-guard by the unexpected praise.

Jason grinned at him. "Don't mistake me, you're still an annoyance. Thank the Lord I only have to put up with you for a few weeks every year."

"Oh, good. For a moment there I was beginning to wonder who you were and what you'd done with my stuffy, sneering brother-in-law."

Jason sketched a bow. "At your service."

"Now, about Miss Weston . . . ," Charles started.

Jason sighed. "I thought we were finished with that topic."

"Hardly. We have barely begun to skim the surface.

A very pretty surface, too, though I haven't yet had a chance to closely examine it."

"Nor will you ever," Jason growled.

"So possessive already? How touching."

"Charles," he warned.

"Why is it so hard for you to admit that you're attracted to her?"

"Very well, I'm attracted to her. She's a pretty young woman and I've seen few of those in past years."

"And whose fault is that?"

"If I could think of a way for it to be yours, I would."

Charles's face broke into a huge grin. "No such luck, old man. It was all you. Fortunately for you, women seem to like the dark, brooding type. The harder to catch, the better to have or some such rot."

"Am I a fish to be hooked?" He meant the question to come out lightly, as a joke, but he couldn't conceal the underlying bitterness of such a situation.

"Do you mind if the bait is as enticing as Miss Weston?"

Jason crossed his arms over his chest. "I've no wish to be trapped."

"Does marriage have to be a trap?"

"Getting leg-shackled is always a trap. They don't call it the parson's mousetrap for nothing."

Charles shrugged. "That may be. But from what I've seen, and from what I remember of you and my sister, sometimes it is worth it."

Jason could see the discussion was going nowhere or, if it was, it wasn't someplace he wanted to go. "All right, you've had your say."

"And you yours."

"Right, then. Just so we're clear . . ."

Charles set down his drink on Jason's desk and folded his arms behind his back in the manner of a child reciting lessons. "I am not to seduce Miss Weston, no matter how prettily she begs me. I am to ignore her so that, in her despair, she turns to you."

Jason fought a smile. "So long as you let her alone, you may tell yourself whatever lies you wish."

"I realize it's been a while since you've interacted with the fair sex. If you need me to give you some pointers or—"

"Charles, don't you have somewhere else to be?"

His brother-in-law gazed around the study, as if searching for clues to jog his memory. "No. At least, I don't think so."

"Then think harder," Jason ground out. "I do not need your help, as I am planning on having as little involvement with Miss Weston as possible. I fear Katherine would be upset with me if I strangled the chit, and I have an alarming urge to do so nearly every time we converse."

"I would suggest that's frustrated desire, but I'm sure you would tell me I'm wrong."

"You are correct."

Charles eyed him warily. "I'm correct that your urge to strangle Miss Weston is frustrated desire?"

"No, you were correct that I would tell you that you were wrong. In any case, if I did happen to pursue a female, I would not need your help."

He pushed a laughing Charles out the door and locked it. He sat down at his desk, savoring the quiet. Lord, he hoped what he had told Charles was true. He had no real experience with rejection.

The women of his youth had put themselves in his path. Actresses, bored widows, and the like. He never knew if they wanted him for his title or for his looks. They hadn't wanted him for himself, that much was certain. Those women had had as little interest in knowing him as he had in knowing them. There was only one way they knew each other, and that was in the biblical sense.

And then, during his last year at university, Jason had met Laura. On the death of their father, Laura and Charles had moved to Cambridge to live with their uncle, the Master of Trinity College. From the first time he saw her, Jason was besotted. He had foolishly expected her to fall in line with the rest of the women of his acquaintance, but Lord, had he ever been wrong. Her serene, smiling exterior had masked a backbone of tempered steel. The first time Jason had tried to steal a kiss she'd given him a black eye.

The devil knew why, but he had gone back for more. Not for another shiner—he only had to be taught that lesson once—but for more of her. She hadn't believed he was serious in his addresses, but she'd let him court her, hoping to attract a more suitable suitor. After a few months, however, he had managed to persuade Laura of his intent.

Her uncle had given them his blessing at once, but then Hinchliffe was no fool. His brother-in-law had been awarded a baronetcy, the title of which had passed to his nephew, but having his niece land the heir to a marquisate was beyond his wildest imaginings. Jason's father had come from London, where he was relentlessly pursuing a young, beautiful widow, and had been delighted by his son's choice of bride.

Jason hadn't cared a whit for either Hinchliffe's or the marquess's approval—if necessary, he would have eloped to Gretna Green. To the moon, even. So long as he and Laura were together, nothing else mattered. They had been so happy, so in love. . . .

He should have known then it was too perfect to last.

Chapter 7

"Not to be a-bed after midnight is to be up betimes."

Twelfth Night, Act II, Scene 3

With Cook busy getting ready for the Christmas feast on the morrow, dinner that evening was a quiet, simple affair. Actually, most of Jason's meals were quiet, simple affairs, since he thought the preparation of elaborate dishes quite unnecessary for one person. For a long time he had found sitting alone in the dining room so dismal a prospect that he had taken his meals in his study or in the library, but eventually he had grown accustomed to his solitary repasts.

They were eating at a later hour than usual so as to sustain them through the long hours ahead, and a primitive hunger seemed to have won out over the civilized trappings of conversation. So focused on their food were the four adults, the only sound in the room came from the clinking of cutlery against china. As he listened to the oddly pleasant cacophony produced by a good meal, Jason heard a little whisper of a sigh from the vicinity of Miss Weston.

She was pushing her food about her plate, rather than tucking into it as the rest of them were. A lonely air—stiff and melancholy—hung about her, one he knew all too well. The emotion did not sit right on her . . . and it bothered him.

"You look pensive, Miss Weston. Is something amiss?"

"No, not really. A touch of homesickness brought on by the quiet."

"And how else should it be?" His words were more defensive than he meant them to be, but he somehow felt responsible for her unhappiness . . . and that bothered him, too.

"I don't mean to say it's a bad thing exactly, but it's very different from what I am used to."

Jason looked at Katherine and Charles to see if they were making any sense of this.

"You're forgetting that Lord Sheldon is an only child, Livvy, or he was for most of his life."

"What's that to do with anything?" Jason wanted to know.

"I've six brothers and sisters," Miss Weston explained, "and two are older than I am. So whether I was taking meals in the nursery or old enough to eat with the adults, I've always had at least one sibling, usually more, at the table with me."

"Which equates to noise?"

"Naturally. Or perhaps it is not at all natural. I suspect my family is unnaturally vocal."

"But ever so much fun to be around," Katherine insisted. "Why do you think your brother always had so many school friends wanting to come home with him for the holidays?"

Her niece looked at her in surprise. "I always supposed it was for Izzie, once she started showing signs of being a Great Beauty."

"Goose. It's because everyone in your family is so welcoming. You've big hearts, all of you, and you want to share the blessings you've been fortunate enough to have been given."

"Aunt Kate . . ." Miss Weston protested, looking quite pink in the face.

"You're right," Katherine said, a determined look on her face. "This place is too quiet."

"Hear, hear!" Charles raised his glass to her.

Jason had a feeling—one he was growing quite used to—he wasn't going to like whatever was brewing in his stepmother's mind. "Now see here—" he began, but he stopped when Katherine turned to him, her eyes bright with excitement.

"It's the season for giving, isn't it?"

No was the answer Jason wanted to give her, but she was looking at him so expectantly, he forced himself to say instead, "Where exactly are you headed with this?"

"I know it is short notice but I thought perhaps we could host an entertainment. Not a ball, for I doubt we've the numbers for that, but a dinner party with dancing and games. The neighbors will come, if only out of curiosity. This household has been kept in mourning too long. I know you still grieve, Jason, but—"

"What date did you have in mind for these festivities?" he asked quickly, hoping to distract her from talking about the past.

"It must be Twelfth Night. Olivia can be our guest of honor, for her birthday is nearly upon us, and she is named after the character in the play, you know."

"I did not. Shall I have a willow cabin made at the gate for the occasion?"

Miss Weston looked pained. Charles and Katherine just looked confused.

Jason gave a disgusted sigh. "Don't you know your Shakespeare?"

"Not particularly," Charles answered cheerily. "I'm afraid my mind is on other things when I attend the theater."

"I'm sorry, dearest," Katherine said to her niece. "I

should have warned you. My stepson is very fond of
Shakespeare."

"What have you got against him?" Jason demanded
of Miss Weston.

"How long do you have?" she retorted.

"I'm afraid my sister is a bit Shakespeare-mad,"
Katherine said. "It started when she was a girl and only
grew worse over the years. She's been working on a
book about all the great heroines for, oh, heaven only
knows how many years now."

"It's practically impossible to have a conversation
with her without some bit of Bardic brilliance worming
its way in," added Miss Weston. "And she named me and
all my siblings after characters in the plays, though my
father made certain she kept within the bounds of nor-
malcy. The truly outlandish names were reserved for the
horses and hounds."

"Poor beasts." Charles shook his head in sympathy.

Livvy laughed. "I doubt they know the difference
and, in any case, I must point out such literary names
are a bit more dignified than the, um, colorful names so
popular here."

"I am just thankful Edward was in the midst of learning his colors when I brought them home," Jason put in.
"Only imagine if he had still been learning to count. We
would be stuck with One Dog and Two Dog instead of
Red Dog and Blue Dog."

"Once Aunt Kate promised Charlotte a great Danish
dog, my mother began campaigning most vociferously
for the name to be either Hamlet or Ophelia, depending
on the gender, of course."

Jason laughed. "I think your mother sounds delightful."

"Oh, I love her dearly, but it is quite frustrating to ask
for a bedtime story and have your mother fetch a vol-

ume of the Complete Works. Not," she said thoughtfully, "that it didn't put us to sleep quickly."

"'Though this be madness, yet there is method in't,'" Jason quoted.

Miss Weston groaned. "Now you're just being cruel."

"Not to mention dull," Charles put in. "I fear you are going to need my pointers after all."

Katherine looked interested. "Pointers for what?"

"How to be sociable. So he won't scare off the . . . guests," Charles improvised, transferring his gaze from Katherine to Miss Weston as he spoke.

Jason wondered, not for the first time, if his brother-in-law wasn't a great deal more intelligent than he let on. Fortunately, Katherine misunderstood Charles's subtle jab.

"Then we may have our Twelfth Night revels?"

Jason thought of the torture such an undertaking would likely inflict. Not only would the entire place have to be thoroughly cleaned and aired out, but he would have to endure the actual party. The whispers and stares of his former friends and acquaintances . . .

"No" hovered on the tip of his tongue.

Then he thought about Miss Weston's concern for his son, and Charles and Katherine coming every Christmas to see that he and Edward were not alone. If this would make them happy, then he could suffer a bit of discomfort in return.

"Oh, very well. But keep it small, mind you. Charles, make yourself useful to the ladies. Laura always used to say I—" He stopped himself and rose. "Forgive me, I have some work I must see about. I cannot waste my time in idle chatter."

"Be off with you then." Katherine made a shooing motion. "We have important matters to discuss, Charles, Olivia, and I, and we will not have you meddling in our affairs. I shall send someone to fetch you when the children come down for the toffee making."

Jason stalked off to his study.

He feared he knew exactly what important matter they had to discuss.

Him.

Olivia could not, in all honesty, say she didn't remember the last time she had waited up long into the night. It had only been a few months since she had kept vigil for endless hours while her sister Isabella struggled to give birth. Then, nine months or so before that, there had been the equally long night when Izzie had set off to get herself compromised to save the life of the man she loved.

Livvy had pieced together that plan—and quick work she'd had to make of it, too—and there had been at least a thousand and one things that could have gone wrong. She'd bitten her nails to the quick imagining them all, though she hadn't given in to her fears until her sister was already out of the house and on her way to the seduction. It was nice to be awake at a late hour without worrying that something dreadful had happened, was in the process of happening, or was about to happen.

After dinner, she, her aunt, and Sir Charles had settled in the drawing room to discuss their plans for the Twelfth Night fete. Sir Charles and her aunt had discussed it, at any rate. Livvy could not help with the guest list as she had no knowledge of the neighboring families, nor could she say whether the dancing ought to be held in the Great Hall, which Aunt Kate thought would be festive, or in the ballroom, which Sir Charles believed would be more comfortable, as she hadn't known the castle *had* a ballroom. She voiced this last thought aloud.

"The ballroom lies above the gatehouse," Sir Charles

explained. "It may not have the same flair as the Great Hall, but it is far less draughty."

They decided Olivia must see the ballroom and have another look at the Great Hall, since her vote would decide the matter, but they only made it to the Great Hall, as the kitchen was on the way to the ballroom and Sir Charles, who was always hungry, insisted on a quick detour. They found Mrs. Maddoc there alone; Cook and the rest of the servants were off having their own celebration to while away the hours before going to church.

The kitchen was a spacious room with whitewashed walls and stone flagged floor, very much like the one she had grown up with at Weston Manor. Dark oak shelves and dressers displaying shiny copper cookware lined the wall opposite the hearth, where the housekeeper sat stirring the contents of a pot set upon the range.

"A good thing you've come by. I was just trying to figure out how to send for you." Mrs. Maddoc fanned herself with her free hand. "You'll want to be gathering everyone, now I've set the *taffi* to boil."

"Livvy, come with me and help me get the children up. Charles, you fetch Jason," Aunt Kate directed, "and do at least *try* not to provoke him."

The children had been given an early supper and then put to bed to rest before the festivities, so Olivia and her aunt had to wake them and get them dressed. By the time they made their way back to the kitchen, Sir Charles had successfully retrieved his quarry. They all gathered on stools and benches around the large pine worktable while they waited for Mrs. Maddoc to pronounce the toffee ready for pulling.

"How will we know when it's time?" Edward asked, yawning and rubbing his eyes.

"I think it's time now, lovey, but we'll check to be sure," the housekeeper responded.

"How?" inquired Charlotte.

"I'll tell you, Lady Inquisitive. See this cup of water I have here? I'm going to pour a spoonful of the hot *taffi* into the cup. If it hardens right away, then it's reached the right temperature," Mrs. Maddoc explained. "'Tis best if done by an unmarried girl." She beckoned Olivia over. "Go ahead, miss."

Livvy had heard that the Welsh were superstitious, and though she could not think how her gender or marital status possibly affected the outcome, she took the proffered spoon and dumped the boiling sugary mixture into the cup of cool water. As Mrs. Maddoc had hoped, it hardened at once.

"Good," the housekeeper exclaimed. "It's ready." She took the pot off the fire and carefully carried it over to a large marble-topped trestle table. She slowly began to pour the mixture onto the cool stone slab she had greased with butter.

Sir Charles ambled over and fished the piece of hardened toffee out of the cup. He was about to pop it into his mouth, when Charlotte spotted him. She tugged on her mother's sleeve. "Why does *he* get to have the first piece? The rules are girls first."

"Ladies first," her mother corrected, "though I doubt you'll be mistaken for a lady anytime soon."

"The only person who's touching that bit of toffee is Miss Weston," Mrs. Maddoc broke in. "No one is to eat it until we've had a chance to look at it."

Sir Charles examined the toffee. "It looks edible," he pronounced. "What more do we need to see?"

"We need to see what letter it looks like. The *taffi* forms the initial of a girl's true love," the housekeeper explained.

"Does it now?" Sir Charles mused. "Well, just look at that! I do believe this is a J. What do you think of that, Jace?"

At that, Lord Sheldon got up and came over. He took

the hardened toffee from his brother-in-law. "You're looking at it the wrong way. It is quite clearly a C, *Charles*."

"Don't everyone fight for me at once," Livvy muttered as she snatched the piece out of the marquess's hands. "You're both wrong. It is most definitely a U."

"A U?" Sir Charles shook his head. "What man's name begins with U?"

Olivia thought hard and came up blank. "I don't know," she huffed. "There must be someone."

"Maybe it's his title," her aunt suggested, coming over to see. "Lord Underwood must be out of mourning by now."

"I doubt he was ever in mourning," Sir Charles said. "Rumors are he killed his wife."

"Oh dear." Her aunt shook her head. "Not Underwood, then. Ulster, perhaps?"

Lord Sheldon shot her a disgusted look. "Ulster is eighty, if he's a day."

"In any case," Sir Charles added, "he just married a dairymaid."

"That would be awkward," Aunt Kate agreed. "And speaking of awkward . . ." She followed Mrs. Maddoc's example and covered her hands in butter, then reached for the hot, gooey mess on the slab.

Mrs. Maddoc was twisting and pulling a long rope of the stuff, which had turned a lovely golden brown and smelled simply heavenly.

"She makes it look easy," her aunt told her, nodding her head in the housekeeper's direction, "when really it's anything but. I always bungle it, but it's fun to try."

Rather than the rhythmic stretching that Mrs. Maddoc employed, her aunt's method seemed to consist more of juggling the hot toffee from hand to hand.

"Here, you work on this, miss." Mrs. Maddoc handed

Livvy some toffee she had been working on. "Just keep pulling at it until the color turns a light golden brown."

Olivia soon got the knack of pulling the toffee and thought it quite fun. Once all the toffee had been pulled, Mrs. Maddoc cut the long strands into smaller pieces and made up a plate for them to take back to the drawing room. Actually she made up two plates—one for Charlotte and another for everyone else—then sent them out of the way so she could clean up.

Eating the toffee, Livvy found, was even more enjoyable than making it. The candy was soft and chewy, and it seemed to have the very taste of Christmas. As they ate, they prepared to make garlands out of the evergreens Dimpsey and the children had collected that afternoon. Mrs. Maddoc had found a mess of red and green ribbons that had been used to tie up the greenery some Christmas past, which Livvy, her aunt, Charlotte, and Edward set about untangling.

Charlotte and Edward soon lost interest and quietly slipped from the room. They returned with armfuls of her aunt's bonnets, which they proceeded to try on the unprotesting dogs stretched lazily before the fire.

Sir Charles declared he had never seen more beautiful ladies, present company excluded, of course. When Blue rose to stretch, Sir Charles walked over to him and held out his hands. At once Blue leaned back on his haunches and lifted his front legs in the air. Sir Charles guided his paws onto his shoulders.

"Dance!" Charlotte clapped her hands in delight.

The expression on the dog's face was a combination of puzzlement and eagerness, which made for such a comical effect, even Lord Sheldon was moved to smile. He had to laugh, though, when Blue leaned forward and licked his companion's cheek.

"Ugh!" Sir Charles laughingly pushed Blue away. He

wiped his face against his coat sleeve. "I never smelled anything so foul in my life."

"Oh, goodness!" Her aunt wiped tears of mirth from her eyes. "Olivia, you must get your sketchbook and capture these poor beasts in all their finery. On second thought, I doubt my poor bonnets will survive that long. Charlotte, that dog is about to chew those feathers right off!"

Sir Charles and Lord Sheldon assisted the children in removing the dogs' headdresses, which was no easy task, as the dogs had decided this was some sort of game and refused to let themselves be caught. Livvy and her aunt laughed themselves silly watching the two grown men chase after the enormous, bonnet-wearing canines. Edward and Charlotte were very little help, as they mostly stood to one side, looking terribly proud of having so amused the adults.

Even with the dogs returned to their natural state and the bonnets put away—minus a few feathers—the fun did not end. The marquess and Sir Charles taught Edward and Charlotte how to play whist while Livvy and her aunt tied up bunches of holly, ivy, rosemary, mistletoe, and bay leaves. The scene was so cozy, with the warmth from the fire, the fragrant scents of the evergreens, and the happy chatter of the children, that the hours slipped past. With her fingers occupied, her mind began to wander. . . .

The marquess snagged Olivia's arm. "You have made the mistake of walking beneath the mistletoe, Miss Weston. Now you will pay the price." He caught her up against him and leaned her back over his arm.

"Is this why all the maids keep leaving, my lord? You believe you can force your attentions on the women in your employ?"

A wicked gleam came into his dark eyes. "Only you, my dear Miss Weston, and I've yet to find a woman who flees from my attentions."

"Such arrogance is most unappeal—"

He silenced her with a kiss. And, oh, what a kiss it was!

Olivia's knees turned to jelly, and she had to cling to the marquess to prevent herself from collapsing. Her heart was thundering so loudly she felt certain he must hear it. Oh, why had she no defenses against this man?

He laughed against her mouth, sensing her capitulation, and deepened the kiss.

She gave herself over to the magic, forgetting she was the lowly governess. She had come here for him—for this. She knew it was true. Whatever lies she told herself, in this moment, in his arms, she knew in her heart of hearts what had really brought her here. She had come for—

"Wake up, Livvy." Aunt Kate squeezed her arm. "It's after midnight, and we must get about putting on our winter wear. The service likely won't start until three, or perhaps later," she explained as they made their way upstairs, "but in this weather, we won't make it to town in less than an hour. And what with the time needed to get the children dressed and put our own things on and have the carriage readied, we'll be lucky to leave by half past one."

Her aunt had been right, Olivia realized, glimpsing the carriage clock as they drove off, with Dimpsey acting as coachman. The time was nearly two! Of course, as her aunt had pointed out on more than one occasion, she was nearly always right. It was, she thought, the one trait all the women in her family shared.

December 25, 1798
Christmas/Y Nadolig

St. Mary's Church was located in the village of Haverfordwest, which lay about ten miles west of Arlyss. The medieval town actually boasted three parish churches but, as Jason's stepmother informed the other occupants of the carriage, "The Trahernes have had ties to St. Mary's for three centuries. To go anywhere else would be unthinkable."

Jason needed no such reminding. He had been baptized in the font at St. Mary's, as had Edward, and it was under the oak-paneled roof, with its carved Tudor roses, that he had spoken his marriage vows. Damn Katherine for making him return to this place.

Miss Weston pushed the curtains aside and peered out the window of the carriage. Jason was just able to make out the church in the distance. The building seemed to glow in the near blackness, a welcoming beacon for all those cold, weary pilgrims who sought shelter within.

But there would be no comfort for him there that night. Only memories. And with the memories came anger and regret. The two emotions were so entwined for him, he no longer knew how to separate them.

He was careful to let none of this show on his face. Katherine would almost certainly notice, and he had no wish to have another of *those* conversations, but more important, he didn't want to do anything that might spoil the night for Edward.

The joy and magic of the holiday might be dead for him now, but Jason remembered a time when he had believed anything was possible on Christmas. That had been before he had learned that some prayers were too impossible to be answered and some sins were too grievous to be forgiven.

He knew there were those who would say he had lost his way, and perhaps they were right. Those were the same people who had tried to console him with the rationale that everything in life happened for a reason. He remained unconvinced.

For all his disbelief, Jason found himself hesitating on the steps to the church, waiting for a bolt of lightning to strike him down, but none was forthcoming. A punishment of another sort struck on the brief walk from the carriage to the church; icy gusts of wind pricked at his face like a swarm of tiny needles, making his eyes sting and water. He drew Edward close to his side, trying to shield him from the harsh elements.

Edward shrugged off his arm and nimbly dashed up the stairs behind Charlotte. Charles was helping the ladies mount the slippery steps, and Jason moved to help him. He offered his arm to the lady nearest him, which happened to be Miss Weston. That was how Jason came to see her face the moment they entered the church.

In the countryside, people from even the most remote farmsteads came to attend the Plygain at the parish church, which meant that St. Mary's was filled nigh to bursting. As was the custom, every person had brought a candle to help to illuminate the church. In addition to the candles held by individuals, the chandeliers held brightly burning colored tapers, and yet more flames danced from the hundreds of votives set upon every possible flat surface. There could be no doubt that the day marked the coming of the Light of the World.

Miss Weston gasped and clutched at his arm. He smiled down at her. "It is certainly a sight, is it not?"

"Oh!" she exclaimed, her face suffused with joy and her eyes shining.

Watching her, Jason forgot to remember. He forgot to be angry. Her happiness overflowed, spilling into him, and he found himself smiling back at her.

"How magical!" she whispered. "I don't think I've ever seen anything so lovely in my life."

An unfamiliar feeling settled in Jason's chest and took root somewhere in the vicinity of his heart. For once, he could not agree with her more.

Chapter 8

"Dost thou think, because thou art virtuous,
there shall be no more cakes and ale?"
                                    Twelfth Night, Act II, Scene 3

W hen they returned from services, Olivia was quite
     ready to seek her bed and sleep for the rest of the
day, but it was not to be. The Welsh, she kept finding,
were a people of a great many traditions. Along with
these traditions came an equally great number of proph-
ecies about what might befall should the customs not be
properly adhered to.

Upon their arrival back at the castle, Lord Sheldon's
tenants arrived with a plow, which they proceeded to
bring inside. This, her aunt explained, was to symbolize
that work was stopped for the holidays. Ale was sprinkled quite liberally over the plow to reward it for its hard
work throughout the year and to suggest that though it
was not being used, it had not been forgotten.

If she had not been so tired, Olivia was sure she would
have found this ritual touching. As it was, she thought it
perfectly idiotic. The plow didn't have feelings, but she
did, and she was feeling like she wanted to seek her bed.
But she could not, as it was then time for the feasting to
begin.

Goose was on the menu, along with many other
dishes, and by the time the plates were removed Livvy
felt certain she would not be able to eat another bite for

at least a week. After the feasting, Olivia was coaxed
into helping to finish the decorating started the previous
evening. She wanted to suggest that she could decorate
her room (and by decorate, she meant sleep, and by her
room, she meant her bed), but the excitement surrounding the day was contagious and gave her energy.

Lord Sheldon, Olivia noted, vanished after the meal.
She supposed he had hidden himself away in his study,
but she was surprised when he failed to appear for dinner. She was even more surprised that Aunt Kate seemed
unperturbed by his absence.

"Are you not worried?" she fretted.

"Not a bit," her aunt replied. "I have it on good au-
thority from Gower that my stepson is quite well."

"In that case, are you not going to insist he join us?"

Aunt Kate looked bemused. "I suppose I could try,
but Gower said it was nearly impossible to keep him
awake long enough to walk to his chamber. No, I think I
will be generous and let the poor boy sleep."

With the marquess absent from the table, Sir Charles
and her aunt began to discuss the upcoming party once
more. Olivia had little to add to the conversation, and
eventually she stopped trying to participate. Neither of
her companions seemed to notice her withdrawal.

Her thoughts turned unerringly, like the needle on
a compass, in the direction of the castle's enigmatic
owner. The day would have been trying for him. How
difficult it must be to witness so much cheer when one's
own life still seemed so bleak and empty. His coming to
the morning services had been a good step forward. She
couldn't expect him to heal all in a day, though patience
was not a virtue she possessed.

She would have to learn, though, for she sensed that
if pushed, the marquess would only retreat further into
himself . . . perhaps beyond reach. This slow coaxing was
the right attitude. She felt certain he had smiled more in

the days since their arrival than he probably had in the past several years.

It was not all her doing, of course, and she wasn't so vain as to think so. Livvy imagined the marquess had been gradually creeping out of his shell, a little bit every year, but perhaps more so this year since Aunt Kate was determined that she have a true Welsh Christmas. And this was just the beginning. After today, she still had eleven more days of merrymaking to look forward to. And the more noise and fun they made, the emptier the house would seem when they had gone.

Then Lord Sheldon would slowly begin to seek out the company of his neighbors and begin participating in Society. Perhaps one day he would even come to London, though he had said the city air was not good for Edward. And maybe he would meet a woman who would fill his heart, someone who would adore Edward and his too-serious yet passionate father, and make a family with them.

Livvy felt a sharp pang thinking of this mystery woman, which was silly. Of course she wanted what was best for him and Edward. She just had to remind herself that this woman would not be her . . . and, what took even more reminding, that she did not *want* it to be.

The marquess had no place in her future, especially because the more time she spent with him, the more she worried she could truly come to care for him. Perhaps, provided he refrained from quoting Shakespeare and locking his library, she might even fall in love with him. And that would be disastrous.

Love was her daily sustenance, her bread and butter, as it were, but she was practical enough to know that no living, breathing man could ever match the perfection of a carefully crafted hero from the pages of her books. It would be a futile endeavor for her to look for one. Especially among the men of the ton.

And she would rather maintain her fantasy of what a perfect love ought to be than risk having it spoiled—and her heart broken—by allowing herself to get caught up in a romance that might not last. She knew she could not bear it if she were disillusioned, so it was better to go on as she was, reading about true love and grand passion and happily ever after, sure in the knowledge that her books would never disappoint her.

She was not averse to the idea of matrimony. In fact, she very much wanted to get married. She liked the quiet pleasures of home and family above all else, and if she was one day going to have to fly the nest, she would like to jump sooner rather than later so that she might begin building a new nest for herself and avoid that most dreaded fate of dependent spinster.

All she wanted from marriage was comfort and stability, mutual respect and affection. Affairs might be tolerated so long as they were discreet, but never bad manners or poor personal hygiene. She had resigned herself to a marriage of, well, she supposed it could be called a marriage of convenience, for it would certainly be convenient to keep her heart in one piece.

She hadn't told her family about her plan, of course. They simply wouldn't understand. She was the dreamer, the romantic, the girl with her head always stuck in the pages of a novel, so how could she explain that she didn't want to fall in love? All she wanted was a little adventure, a taste of excitement before she settled down to her nesting.

That was all Lord Sheldon was to her.

All he could ever be to her.

It was for the best.

Sir Charles joined Olivia and her aunt in the drawing room after dinner, declaring he had no desire to be left to drink port all by himself. As Aunt Kate wished to work on her embroidery, Sir Charles persuaded Livvy to play piquet. He was an excellent companion, and she relaxed more in his company than she had since arriving at Castle Arlyss.

He was quite in tune with her sense of humor, which could not be said of most of her acquaintances. It seemed incredible she had known him for so short a time; they were soon teasing each other and engaging in the same playful bickering she shared with her siblings.

So easy had she grown with him, she forgot to mind what she said. "You're nothing at all like I expected."

Sir Charles looked up sharply. "I beg your pardon."

Olivia flushed. "Never mind. I didn't mean—"

"Don't trouble yourself trying to spare my feelings. My brother-in-law does so enjoy telling all and sundry what a plague I've been to him."

"No, that isn't it at all!" Livvy protested. "Lord Sheldon hasn't said a word about you."

"He hasn't?" Sir Charles looked surprised.

"When would he? When one eschews the presence of one's guests, one rarely has time to comment on the weather to them, let alone family squabbles."

Sir Charles laughed. "Yes, Jace has become quite the hermit as of late. As long as I've known him, he's been a proud, quiet sort of fellow, but he wasn't always like *this*. Just since . . ."

"Since your sister passed away," Olivia finished for him. "I am so sorry. I know the two of you were close."

Sir Charles nodded, then looked at her suspiciously. "How did you know that Laura and I were close?"

Why was it that she seemed only to have to open her mouth to get herself into trouble? Olivia wondered. She tried to think of some logical explanation.

"Miss Weston?" Sir Charles prompted.

"Oh, I just assumed—" she floundered. "I mean, what with losing your mother so young—"

"You seem to know quite a lot about my family."

"It was a long trip from Scotland," Livvy reasoned. "I confess I asked my aunt to let me in on all the family gossip to pass the time."

Her answer seemed to satisfy the baronet. "Very well, Miss Weston, but I think it only fair that you even the score. Tell me, whatever possessed you to wish to spend the holiday season *here*?"

Olivia laughed. "You make Arlyss sound like one of the innermost circles of Dante's *Inferno*."

"My brother-in-law does bear a striking resemblance to Lucifer, does he not?"

Livvy giggled and wagged her finger at him. "You are bad, Sir Charles!"

"I pride myself on it, my dear, but please, call me by my Christian name. *Sir* Charles sounds like such a prosy bore."

"Very well, but you must call me Olivia, or Livvy, if you like. There's no need to stand on ceremony here, and we are family of a sort."

He clasped a hand to his heart. "Is that how you see me, fair Olivia? Oh, you wound me." His green eyes twinkled.

"I doubt that very much. I suspect you are a terrible flirt. How many broken hearts are strewn in your wake?"

"None at all. I avoid attachments like the Plague." His voice grew somber. "I was very close with my—with a lady. She was everything good and kind in the world."

"Was?"

He gave a curt nod, not meeting her eyes. He stared instead at his clasped hands, stretched out before him on the card table. "When I was just out of university, I wound up in a bit of trouble. Well, more than a bit. I had lost a sizable sum at the tables, and then I stupidly gambled more to try to win back my losses. The greater my debts, the deeper the stakes I played. After a time, I had no choice but to turn to my, er, lady friend. She had helped me in the past. I would to God she had turned me away—" He broke off, his voice anguished.

Olivia guessed the lady he spoke of was his sister. Had he been suffering a guilty conscience all these years? Lord, what a tangle!

Livvy laid a hand over his. "She must have cared for you a great deal, this friend of yours."

"She loved me, the more fool her. She loved me and it killed her."

Olivia drew in a startled breath. "W-what are you saying?" Her voice wobbled.

Charles met her gaze then. His eyes, usually dancing and bright, were bleak and empty. "The day she died, she was going to meet with someone to try to pay off my debts. I am the reason she was out that morning."

Olivia glanced over at her aunt to be certain she was not listening, and was relieved to find she was engrossed in her needlework and not paying them the least mind. Livvy leaned forward and gripped Charles's hands in her own. She spoke forcefully, though she kept her voice to a low whisper. "Listen to me, Charles. Laura's death was an accident."

He jerked as if shot and wrenched his hands away from her. He opened his mouth to speak, but Olivia acted first. "Aunt Kate, Sir Charles has offered to escort me to the library and help me look for something decent to read. Would you mind terribly if we abandoned you for a little while?"

"Of course not." Lady Sheldon smiled. "I was about to seek my bed anyhow. I suppose I am a rather ineffectual chaperone, but I trust you will both behave. I am too old to stay awake patrolling the corridors."

"Really!" Olivia exclaimed, her cheeks heating at her aunt's suggestion.

"Miss Weston is quite safe with me," Charles assured her.

"Yes, I know," Aunt Kate remarked as she got to her feet. "Good night, my dears." She was almost out the door when Livvy heard her mutter: "It's the other one I'm worried about."

She didn't have time to reflect on her aunt's words, though, for Charles had her wrist in an iron grip and was very nearly dragging her along. She was forced to maintain a sort of skipping gait, lest her arm be taken to the library without the rest of her.

As soon as he had shut the door behind them, Charles whirled to face Olivia.

"Who are you?" His voice was ragged.

Livvy frowned at him. "Just who I say I am."

He advanced on her. "You know things about me, about my family. . . ."

Olivia held up her hands. "I can explain."

"Very well, go on."

Livvy turned from him and began to walk around the perimeter of the room, trying to quell the nervous energy racing through her. The library had been built into one of the four half-round towers that marked the area of the original castle. Special shelves had been built into the walls to accommodate the circular room, and aside from the large window opposite the door, rows of leather-bound volumes filled the space from the wainscoting to the ceiling. Olivia had been completely enchanted with the room from the moment she had seen it, but at the moment, even the sight of so many books failed to soothe her.

Enough stalling, she told herself. She had known deep down that there would someday be a reckoning for what she had done. She should be grateful she was facing Charles instead of the marquess.

"Were you aware your sister kept a diary?" Livvy

asked, seating herself on a beautifully carved double-back settee. She shivered. The fire had been banked hours ago, and a chill had settled over the room. But it certainly would not do to ring for a servant to tend to the fire while she and Charles were alone in the room.

Charles saw her discomfort, for the room was clearly illuminated by the light of the waning moon. He went over to the wooden settle beneath the window and lifted the hinged seat. He pulled out a woolen paisley shawl and brought it over, seating himself beside her.

"My sister was forever complaining about being cold. She kept wraps and blankets in nearly every room. I wasn't sure it would still be there—" His voice caught.

Livvy put the shawl around her shoulders and scooted closer to Charles. She wasn't certain he would accept comfort from her, but she had to try. She disliked seeing anyone in pain, but she felt especially protective of the man beside her, almost as if he were her brother.

Tentatively, Olivia reached out and placed her hand on Charles's shoulder. She half expected him to recoil, but he seemed to relax at her touch.

"You asked whether I knew Laura kept a diary. She did as a girl, but I never saw if she had one when she was grown."

"She did," Livvy said softly. "I found it in the library at Haile Castle. I think it must have been shelved there by accident. I don't know if there were others. This one only contained the couple of years before she . . ."

"Before she died," Charles finished for her. "What did she write about?"

"Everything."

The word hung precariously in the ensuing silence, like a vase poised too close to the edge of a table. The merest sigh would cause it to fall and shatter.

Charles finally spoke. "Then you know."

"That you were in debt?"

"That I killed my sister."

"Charles—"

"No, I'm glad you know. After all this time, to finally be able to talk with someone . . ."

"I want you to listen to me, Charles Avery. You did not kill your sister. The riding accident that killed Laura could have happened anytime—"

"But it didn't. It happened while she was trying to help me. She went out that morning to meet with the man holding my vowels. I may not have put a burr beneath the saddle, but I sent her to her death all the same."

She could see him more clearly now, past the masks he presented to the world. The burden of his guilt was slowly taking a physical toll on him. There were tight lines around his mouth and across his brow where there should have been none. What she had thought an affected, jaded ennui was actually an aura of sadness lingering about him. His eyes seemed to have seen too much, but she had assumed this was yet another sign of dissolution. How well he had fooled everyone.

"Charles, it wasn't your fault."

"Wasn't it?"

"No," she said firmly. "It was an accident—a horrible accident—but it could just as easily have happened any other time she was out riding."

He shook his head. "She must have been nervous and distracted. Laura was an excellent horsewoman. She would never have been thrown if she had been focused."

Livvy sighed. It was clearly time to try another tactic.

"Look at me, Charles. Do you honestly think your sister would want you to spend your life feeling guilty and regretting something that can't be changed?"

"No," he admitted.

"She would want you to be happy."

"I don't deserve happiness."

She saw the desolation in his eyes. He truly believed what he was saying. She suspected he didn't lack for feminine companionship, but now she understood why there were so many women. He had said earlier that he avoided attachment. He probably only took up with unsuitable women, women with whom he would never be emotionally involved. He wouldn't let himself find love because he thought he didn't deserve it.

"You and your brother-in-law aren't so different," she mused. "Laura's ghost haunts both of you, so that you hover in some shadow land where you're not truly living. But I don't think it's her who keeps you there. It's you. You won't let her go. Neither of you. She's dead, Charles—"

He flinched.

"—but you're alive. How long are you going to punish yourself for that?"

He shrugged.

"As your sister is not here to blame you, I would think that privilege falls to Lord Sheldon. Since you are here, and have obviously been welcome in the past, clearly he has forgiven you, so—"

"He doesn't know." The words were little more than a whisper.

"I beg your pardon?"

"Jason. Doesn't. Know."

Olivia was startled. "How is that possible?"

"My sister enjoyed riding early in the park before it got too crowded, and from the time we were young she was adept at losing whichever servant was meant to be following her. Laura never liked people hovering over her. She was far easier with more relaxed country manners. That was one of the reasons she loved this place so much."

The clock in the hall sounded the hour.

"It's late," Charles said. "I have kept you up too long."

"No," Livvy protested, but she punctuated the word with a yawn. She relinquished the shawl, which Charles carefully replaced.

"Can you find your way to your chamber?" he asked, lighting a candle for her. "I would escort you there, but I fear it might prove awkward if we were seen."

She nodded her agreement.

He caught one of her hands and pressed a kiss to it. "I must thank you. I feel better for having spoken of this."

"I'm so glad." Olivia squeezed his hand. "I am generally a very good talker and a very poor listener, but I hope we may speak again. Oh, would you like Laura's diary?"

He gave her a funny look. "You brought it with you?"

"I should have left it at Haile Castle, I know, but I also should not have read the diary in the first place. Once I had, I couldn't put it back in the library where anyone might stumble across it. Now I think on the matter, I should have made use of one of the hidey-holes where I found—" She yawned again. "I beg your pardon."

"Then I must ask yours, for you would have long been in bed but for my prattling. As to the diary, I entrust it to your safekeeping. I almost believe she meant you to have it." He shook his head. "I've no idea what possessed me to say that. Apparently I am also in need of sleep. Good night, my dear. Sleep well." He pressed a quick, brotherly kiss to her forehead and padded off toward his room.

Despite Charles's entreaty, once she was in her bed Livvy found sleep elusive. How confused she was. Life was becoming as complicated as one of her novels, but she had no guarantee things would come right in the end. The hero of her story wanted to be written out entirely, which could not be allowed, no matter how he provoked her. She knew he had hero material in his hidden depths, but those depths were proving surprisingly deep and quite well hidden.

Her supporting cast consisted of her aunt, a couple of young children, a few masterful servants, and a pair of enormous dogs. And tonight she had learned the villain of her piece was not a villain at all, but a poor, troubled soul in need of forgiveness.

December 26, 1798
St. Stephen's Day/Gwyl San Steffan

Perhaps it was for the best he had slept through dinner, Jason thought as he dressed the following morning. He would have been poor company. He'd felt black doggish since that moment in the church when he'd found himself desiring Miss Weston.

No, not desiring. He'd suffered that curse from the first. This was a different sort of wanting, and it was far more dangerous.

Just how much, he wondered, did a man have to go through before he learned his lesson? The past had haunted him every day for years. Why should those painful memories choose to desert him now, when he needed them most?

He wished he could remain alone in his room. Avoidance seemed a perfectly good solution. If he could not remove the temptation at hand, he would remove himself. But he could not. Today was St. Stephen's Day, and he would be expected to assist Katherine in the distribution of the Christmas boxes.

Besides, he was starving and he had no doubt that Katherine would forbid the servants to bring him food if he kept to his chamber longer than she deemed acceptable. He also had no doubt they would obey her commands, no matter that he was their master. Bloody ingrates.

He vented his spleen in this manner all the way to the breakfast room, where a cold spread was laid out, as the servants had the day off. Dimpsey had offered to watch Edward and Charlotte, declaring he could imagine no better way to spend the day. On hearing this, Jason decided the man was totally insane, a candidate for sainthood, or utterly devoid of imagination.

"Good morning," his stepmother greeted him. "I trust you slept well."

Jason grunted in response, filling a plate for himself before taking his place at the table.

"I do believe you are the last person up," Katherine continued. "Shall I have Dimpsey take the children out to collect more holly branches?"

"Why ever for?" Miss Weston questioned.

"Holming is the traditional punishment in Wales for the last person out of bed on St. Stephen's Day," Charles answered.

"And what is 'holming'?"

Jason's stepmother explained. "Holly-beating. It's customary in most parts hereabouts for men to slash the arms and legs of their female servants until they bleed. They believe it brings good luck. In more civilized households, only the last one to get up suffers the holming, and then he has to spend the day following the commands of his family."

Miss Weston looked appalled. "But that's barbaric," she protested.

"That is your opinion," Jason countered. "For many, it is simply the custom. As children they watched their parents take part, and now they do so as well. It's all in good sport."

"All in good sport? How can you say that? Do you wish your son to follow your example? To grow into a man who condones this abominable practice of inflicting pain on helpless women?"

"Whilst you reside under my roof, Miss Weston, you will keep a civil tongue in your head."

"That would pose no problem, my lord, if you would but run a household worthy of civility."

"Olivia, dearest, I am afraid you don't understand," Katherine began, but Jason cut her off.

"I have never been tempted to join the day's festivities, as I have always found them distasteful. But if all the women in my life were like you, I believe I could be persuaded. You, Miss Weston, are capable of inciting a man to violence."

"Isn't that just like a man?" she muttered furiously. "Violence is the solution to every problem."

"So you admit that women are, in essence, a problem? And yet however much you plague us, we poor men cannot do without you. Whatever your flaws, women are needed for the continuation of the race ... among other things."

Her face turned quite red. He knew she was untouched, but was her mind innocent as well? Or had she turned to thoughts of other things? Her chest rose and fell quickly in her agitation, and the movement made her breasts bounce in a most delightful manner. Desire pooled low in his stomach.

"W-whatever our flaws?" she sputtered.

"You cannot mean to deny the multitude of ways females are inherently inferior to men."

Her eyes widened and her mouth opened and closed like a landed fish. "You can't always have been like this," she said finally.

What the devil was that supposed to mean? Jason

wondered. Like what? Like a man? Intelligent? Logical? And yet he did not think her assessment was meant to be flattering.

Then, all of a sudden, her demeanor changed. Her face lit into a smile as she wagged a reproving finger at him. "You are being deliberately provoking, and it is too bad of you, my lord. You don't really believe the horrid things you say, but you hope they instill in me such a thorough dislike of your person that I will go out of my way to avoid you for the duration of my stay. It will not work."

"Miss Weston, I have long since ceased to follow this stream of babble. You are a woman, so it is only natural you should wish to defend your sex, but—"

"Say what you like, my lord. Now I am wise to your tricks, I shan't take it to heart. You had me thoroughly fooled for a time, though. I must confess I would have been disappointed to learn you were the sort of man to be threatened by a woman with opinions."

"Your opinions do not threaten me," he growled. "They aggravate me. I begin to believe you communicate so well with children because their naive understanding of the world so closely matches your own."

"Ooooh!"

Jason fought not to laugh. So much for Miss Weston not taking what he said to heart. Her color was high and her eyes were flashing blue daggers at him.

All that fiery passion only made her more bloody desirable. He had no doubt she would be a wildcat in bed. It would be a lucky man who got to tame her, to make her purr....

"That is quite enough, both of you," his stepmother admonished. "As it's a custom you yourself banned here at Arlyss, Jason, I cannot see why you and my niece are arguing about it."

"If I could suggest—" Charles started to say.

"Stubble it, Chas," Jason said tightly.

Bloody hell, he couldn't ever remember wanting a woman this badly. Not even in the early days of courting Laura. . . . The memory of his wife gave Jason the strength to rein in his emotions and cool his blood until his icy reserve was back in place.

"You're right, Katherine. I beg your forgiveness, Miss Weston."

"She is? You do?" she spluttered, baffled by his sudden capitulation.

"Coward," muttered Charles.

Katherine was having none of it. "There's no cowardice in admitting defeat when one is in the wrong. Besides, as of this moment I will not tolerate any quarreling during Christmas. You may resume your disagreement after Twelfth Night if you wish, but I'll not have the holidays spoiled with your bickering. Now if you are finished, Jason, there are tenants to be visited."

As he'd lost his appetite, Jason rose and followed her from the room. That was another grievance he could lay at Miss Weston's door. She had stolen his desire for food and replaced it with another hunger.

An *impossible* hunger, damn her, because it was one he could not sate. He would not be appeased by a visit to a bawdy house or a night with one of the barmaids in the village tavern. No, he wanted Miss Weston, and only Miss Weston. He wanted to kiss that pert nose, dip his tongue into that cheeky dimple, whisper naughty words that would make her blood rush to her cheeks. . . . He wanted to taste every last spicy, salty, saucy inch of her luscious little body and take her in every possible way he could think of. And he could think of quite a few ways to take her, having spent too many sleepless nights contemplating just that.

But it was forbidden without the bonds of matrimony

and, having had firsthand experience of the " 'til death do us part" aspect of marriage, Jason knew without a moment's hesitation that he would rather die of unrequited lust than ever again chance the death of love's bond.

Chapter 9

"Love sought is good, but given unsought is better."

Twelfth Night, Act III, Scene 1

Olivia was not certain whether the marquess was avoiding her in particular or if he was avoiding company in general, but he made himself very scarce over the days following their disagreement. He sat down with them at meals, but he remained withdrawn and excused himself directly afterward, even in the evenings. Aunt Kate sighed and shook her head each time he retreated, but she seemed to sense, as they all did, that he was waging some internal battle, so she let him be.

Livvy had little time to fixate on the situation, for she was busy helping prepare for Twelfth Night, and her free moments were spent either playing with the children or searching through books in the library for some remedy that might help Edward.

How odd it was to think she would be leaving Arlyss in less than a fortnight. She remembered Charles telling her how fond Laura had been of this place, and she understood the feeling well. The castle had all of the modern comforts one could want while retaining its rich history. There was a sort of magic in knowing that families had lived in this same space, walked on this same ground, and breathed this same air for over six hundred years. The castle had stood strong against both human strife and the ravages of time, and it would remain as a safe haven for many generations to come.

Something at Arlyss—and some*one*, she admitted to herself—called to her. Livvy had always supposed she could never love a place so well as she loved Weston Manor, but she had been wrong. Or perhaps she had been away from Weston Manor for so many months—the longest time she had spent away from there in her life—she was learning to think of "home" in other terms.

Was home truly where the heart was, adjustable to wherever a person's loved ones might be? Could a person have more than one home in which he or she truly belonged? Or was a person meant to have just one home, but that home changed over time just as people changed over time? She posed these questions to Charles as he sat with her in the library one day.

"Does it really matter, so long as you have a roof over your head and a comfortable place to sleep?" he asked her.

"Obviously not to you," she retorted, then sighed and set down the book she was looking through. "I beg your pardon. I am a bit out of sorts today."

He gave her a crooked smile. "Fretting over Jason?"

Olivia swallowed hard. "What makes you say that?"

"My dear girl, I'm not blind. The attraction is plain to see. When the two of you are in a room together, sparks practically fly."

"I am sure you are mistaken. We are constantly at odds," Livvy protested.

"You know why that is. You said it yourself the other day. Jason picks quarrels to keep you at a distance. He's frightened of you."

"Of me?" Olivia was incredulous. "Why should he be frightened of me? Aunt Kate is much scarier."

Charles laughed. "True, but he isn't attracted to her."

"He's not attracted to me, either," she mumbled.

"If you don't mind, I believe I will take his word over yours."

Livvy nearly pounced on him. She shoved the book back on the shelf and hurried over to sit beside him. "Do you mean he actually said so? When?"

"The day I arrived. He took me straight to his study and warned me to stay away from you. He was worried you would be unable to resist my charms."

She gave him a pointed look.

Charles grinned. "He may not have used those exact words, but that was the sentiment."

"Why are you telling me this?"

"It is past time for him to be happy again."

Olivia pondered this for a moment. "And you think I am the one to make him happy? He could have his pick of women. Don't you suppose he would prefer someone . . ."

"Someone?" he prompted.

"You know what I mean." She waved a hand at herself.

"Someone taller?"

Fine. She would say it. "Someone *prettier*."

Charles looked at her in confusion. "I don't know what looking glass you've been checking lately, but I suggest you have it replaced."

"There is nothing wrong with my looking glass. I see the same reflection no matter which mirror I find myself in front of. If you could see me standing beside my sister, the difference would become clear. Isabella is a Great Beauty. I imagine your sister was as well." A wistful sigh escaped her.

"Laura was lovely, a true English rose, but beauty is in the eye of the beholder. In any case, Jason would never be content with merely a pretty face. A featherbrained woman would be unable to hold his interest. He needs the sort of challenge you present."

"Someone to argue with, you mean? I doubt such a relationship would make *me* happy. What if *I* don't want *him*?"

"Do you honestly expect me to believe that?"

"All right, I want him," she admitted. "In my defense, you would be hard-pressed to find a woman who wouldn't want him. The man is positively sinful. But I don't want to have my heart broken."

"Why do you think he would break your heart? You must know from reading her diary that he didn't break Laura's."

"No," Olivia said sadly. "She broke his. For all I know, he'll never be able to truly love again."

"You don't believe that any more than I do. I'm not asking you to marry the man tomorrow. I only want you to give him a chance. He is going to fight his feelings every step of the way, but you cannot give up on him. As long as you think there is a possibility you belong together, you have to fight, too."

"I don't know if I want to," she said truthfully. "What if I fight him—fight for him—and lose?"

He thought on that for a long moment. Finally he said, "Can you tell me, in all honesty, that your feelings are not already engaged to some extent?"

She knew she could not. If she did not care at all, she would not be so afraid to lose. She gave a single, jerky shake of her head.

"Then you will wind up hurt either way, so you may as well try. He would be a fool to let you go, and Jason is not a stupid man." Charles put a reassuring arm around her shoulders. "Chin up, love. I'm sure you—"

He broke off as the marquess burst into the library, already talking as he entered.

"Miss Weston, your aunt—" He broke off, scowling as he took in the scene.

Charles had snatched his arm back to his side as soon as the door had opened, but apparently he had not been quick enough. Still, however suspicious the scene might appear, they had done nothing wrong, Olivia reminded herself. She fixed a level gaze on Lord Sheldon.

"Sir Charles has been so kind as to keep me company while I look through countless dull volumes in search of some remedy that might help *your son.*"

She emphasized the last two words in an effort to try to restore the balance of power to herself. It seemed to work, for the marquess halted his tirade and just stood silently, glaring at her. She refused to be cowed.

Let the battle begin.

"You mentioned my aunt?"

"Katherine asked me to fetch you to dress for dinner. She mentioned you tend to lose track of time in a library."

Olivia glanced out the window and saw how dark it had grown. "Thank you, my lord. I confess I did not realize the lateness of the hour."

He took a few steps toward them and held out an arm. "Come, Miss Weston. As we have the same destination, we may as well walk together. We will see you shortly, Charles."

The marquess said nothing as they walked through the castle. Though the window in the haunted tower room had been fixed, Livvy had remained in the Marchioness's Chambers. There had been no suggestion of moving her, for which she had been glad. She liked knowing that she was near in case Edward was sick in the night again.

She also liked knowing that, while she was lost in dreams, the marquess slumbered so close by. Her feelings were quite unmistakably engaged. She sighed.

"Is something the matter, Miss Weston?" Lord Sheldon inquired.

Yes, Livvy wanted to shout at him. *I wanted to help*

you move past your grief without getting involved. I don't want to care. Not about your home, not about your son, and certainly not about you. But now it's too late, and I fear my heart will not escape this unscathed.

She could say none of that, and thinking about it had brought a lump to her throat, so she shook her head in response.

Her answer failed to satisfy the marquess.

"Miss Weston, I should tell you— That is, I hope—"

He fumbled for the right words, more ill at ease than Livvy had ever seen him. Her heart skipped a beat. Had he somehow read her mind? Was it possible he was about to admit—?

"It is only natural, while you are under my roof, that I feel a certain . . . a certain responsibility for you. To that end, I feel I must warn you not to pay too much heed to my brother-in-law's attentions. Flirtation is naught but a game to him, a means of alleviating boredom, and you would be unwise to hope for anything more."

This was his grand confession? Warning her away from Charles? Disappointment made her voice sharp. "I appreciate your concern, my lord, but it is as unnecessary as it is unfounded. Sir Charles has behaved like the gentleman he is, and what feelings I have for him are those of dearest friendship."

He arched one eyebrow in obvious disbelief, which made him look quite supercilious. Olivia mentally added that ability to the list she was keeping of the marquess's annoying traits.

"Men and women are rarely capable of lasting friendship, Miss Weston. Someone always wants something more than the other can give."

Was he speaking from past experience, Livvy wondered, or cautioning her about the future? Unfortunately they had reached their rooms, so she had no time to question him.

"Knock when you are ready," he told her, "and I will escort you downstairs."

Though the question was still very much on Olivia's mind, the marquess seemed disinclined to talk as they made their way to the drawing room, where her aunt and Charles were waiting for them.

"Shall we eat?" Lord Sheldon gestured at the others to get up.

"Well done, Jace!" Charles exclaimed, miming applause. "You've led Miss Weston right under the mistletoe, you sly dog. That's a trick I shall have to remember." He winked at Olivia.

Livvy looked up. Sure enough, she and the marquess were standing directly beneath a chandelier to which was tied a spray of evergreens. A nervous twitter escaped her.

"Don't just stand there, Jason," Aunt Kate chided. "It's bad luck to disregard the mistletoe."

Livvy closed her eyes.

This was it.

Her first kiss.

How long had she waited for just this moment?

Well, her entire life, not to put too fine a point on it.

She had always wanted her first kiss to mean something. She had wanted it to be special. And now she knew it would be. Jason Traherne had set her heart racing from the moment she'd laid eyes on him.

No, before that actually.

Her heart had been aflutter from the instant she had realized what was contained in the scrap of paper she'd found in the library at Haile Castle so many months ago. But what woman would not be intrigued by a man who invented puzzles for his wife's amusement? What woman could remain unmoved by a man who gave his wife jewelry engraved with romantic prose? She thought of the quote on the back of the brooch. "So we shall be one, and one another's all." That was a man who was deeply, irrevocably in love.

A man like that was the sort of hero books were written about. She hadn't believed such a man truly existed. Oh, her parents were devoted to each other, and she knew her sister and her sister's husband, James, had a Great Passion. It was obvious to everyone—well, everyone except them—how much they adored and needed each other.

Still, as much as she loved her brother-in-law, Livvy had to admit that James was a bit lacking in creativity. She had been the one to come up with a plan for James to woo Izzie back after he'd made a mess of things. Of course, he was a man, she had reminded herself, and thus was bound to need assistance when it came to romance.

The existence of Olivia's niece indicated that James had the other side of things well in hand, which was fortunate, really, as Livvy knew she could be of very little help there. Izzie had once tried to show her a book of lurid engravings she had found somewhere in their brother's room, but Livvy hadn't paid much attention, as the subject hadn't interested her at that age. A few years later, when the relations between men and women had become a matter of the utmost importance, the book was nowhere to be found. And her sister had become annoyingly vague and tight-lipped about important details once she was married.

Isabella had said that kissing in real life was even better than it was in novels. Now Livvy was finally, *finally* going to experience it. She would feel light-headed. Her knees would go weak. The world would narrow to the place where their mouths joined. He would grumble about—

No, that was not supposed to happen. He should not

be grumbling. Dear heavens, the stupid man was going to ruin her perfect first kiss!

Her eyes flew open to tell him so, but his face was already descending on hers. He looked quite strange so close up; his eyes seemed to fuse into one giant eye in the middle of his head like a Cyclops. She squeezed her eyes closed, trying to block out the alarming sight, and then she felt his lips touch hers.

A brief pressure, warm and soft, which then turned into ...

Nothing.

That was it.

Her first kiss was over.

She didn't know whether to laugh or to cry or to kick the man who had managed to mess up so simple a thing as a kiss under the mistletoe.

Then an awful thought struck her. Perhaps he hadn't done anything wrong. Maybe that kiss had been quite usual and there was something wrong with her for not liking it.

She opened her eyes as the marquess urged her forward. Her aunt and Charles were up and leading the way to the dining room. Such order went against the rules of precedence that had been trained into Olivia almost from birth, but no one else seemed to mind. So many strange things had happened to her since arriving at Arlyss, she accepted this deviation from the rules without comment.

But she didn't like it. Her sister Isabella enjoyed flaunting convention and making up her own rules. Livvy preferred to follow the rules already in place. She thrived on order, on lists, on planning for every possible contingency. That kiss—that spectacular failure of a kiss—had not fit with her plans.

She was so altogether unsettled, Olivia only half listened to Charles and Aunt Kate's discussion about proper presents to give on New Year's Day. With a start, she realized they would be celebrating New Year's Eve on the morrow. Suddenly, a hint of a plan began to form in her mind.

"Is it customary to exchange gifts here on New Year's Day?" she interrupted.

"Oh, yes!" Her aunt launched into a description of what was indubitably yet another eccentric Welsh tradition.

Livvy paid her no mind. She had her answer, and she knew what she needed to do. Two days hence she would get the answers to the rest of her questions.

New Year's Day/Dydd Calan

Jason looked up from the papers on his desk and scowled at the door to his study. Rather, he scowled at the person knocking on the other side of the door. Hadn't he told Gower to keep everyone away?

His head felt like it had been stuffed with wool. He'd had a touch too much to drink the previous evening, but after a day spent in Miss Weston's presence, his nerves had been stretched to the breaking point. As he couldn't seem to dull his senses against Miss Weston's allure, he had decided his only choice was to ensure he drank so much as to be incapable of acting on his desire.

Damn Katherine. He had warned her that she was being lax in her duties as a chaperone, but she had laughed and said there was nothing but friendship between Charles and Olivia. Jason was not so certain, and since he couldn't trust his stepmother not to leave them alone together, he had stuck close.

Close enough to drive him mad. He'd been without a woman for too long. 'Struth, it was the only acceptable answer.

The knocking grew more urgent.

With a curse, Jason pushed his chair back and moved to open the door. When he saw who was on the other side, he was tempted to shut it.

"Miss Weston, come in." He tried to sound pleased to see her. "To what do I owe this pleasure?"

She came into the room, her expression at once nervous and determined.

"Might I have a moment of your time?"

"Of course." He gestured to the chairs by the fireplace. "Won't you sit—"

She looked at the door, which he had left open for propriety, and shook her head. "May we speak in private?"

Jason knew closeting himself in the room with Miss Weston was a bad idea.

Worse than bad.

More like horrible, idiotic, and bound to get him into trouble.

And yet he found himself nodding and pushing the door shut.

He noticed she kept one arm slightly behind her. "What are you hiding back there?" he asked suspiciously.

"It is customary to exchange gifts today, is it not?"

"Ah, you mean *calennig*. I suppose Katherine taught you the rhyme as well. Do you wish to recite, or shall I just hand you some coins?"

She looked at him as if he'd grown a second head.

"I haven't the faintest idea what you're talking about. I brought you a gift."

"Yes, I know," Jason said impatiently. "Apparently my stepmother failed to explain the custom properly. To begin with, the children who take part are generally a bit younger than you are, but I'll make an exception as you're a *Saesnes* and don't know any better. Now, you say the little verse you've been taught, wish me a happy new year and show me the skewered apple you've got behind your back, and I'll reward you with a few coins.

Come along, then, for I've enough bad luck without you collecting *calennig* past noon."

"A skewered apple? Is that what you wanted? And you wish me to recite? Perhaps I *should* have consulted my aunt."

Jason frowned. "Katherine didn't put you up to this?"

"No." She chewed nervously at her lip. "I'm afraid I hadn't realized impaled fruits were in fashion this year."

He couldn't contain his laughter. When he had himself back in control he explained. "In Wales the traditional offering is called *calennig*, an apple with three twig legs, studded with cloves and stuck on top with a sprig of evergreens. Children carry them from door to door, offering good wishes for the coming year, and in return, they are given a bit of food or some money."

"Well, I imagine it must smell nice," Miss Weston said, "but it seems a silly sort of present. I suppose it's not sillier than mine, though."

She handed him an exquisite watercolor sketch of Edward and Charlotte dressing up the dogs. The excitement and pure childish joy of the moment was captured perfectly on their faces, and yet it was not a sentimental piece. She was a true artist with a remarkable ability for capturing the essence of her subjects.

He could not help but wonder how she would draw him.

"You are very talented. This is beautiful."

"Thank you." She ducked her head as if embarrassed by his compliment. "It's nothing really, just a hobby of mine."

"It is I who should thank you, but I am afraid you have me at something of a loss. I have nothing to give you in return."

Her cheeks turned a glorious shade of crimson.

"There is actually a favor I wanted to ask of you."

He should have known. In his experience, women rarely bestowed gifts without expecting some sort of recompense. He stifled a sigh.

"So you have a gift in mind, do you? Well, what's it to be? The family jewels? No, wait, I know! You want permission to reorganize the library here."

"As a matter of fact, that wasn't at all what I wanted, but if you're going to poke fun at me, I'll be on my way. I'm pleased you liked the drawing."

She marched resolutely toward the door, her chin held high.

Jason caught her slender wrist in his hand and halted her departure. "I beg your pardon, Miss Weston. I'm in an odd mood today, but no offense was meant. Please, tell me what you would like and I will do everything within my power to see that you get it."

She raised her eyes to his. Today they were a stormy gray blue. What shade would they be at the height of passion?

She drew in a breath, then released it, letting the words tumble out of her.

"I want you to kiss me."

Jason took a step backward, shaking his head. That was the problem with letting his mind wander where it should not. For a moment he'd thought she'd said . . .

"I know it sounds forward, asking you to kiss me—"

Oh, dear God, she had said it.

"—but under the mistletoe, that was my first kiss—"

Jason half listened to her, focused more on the odd feeling of pleasure stealing over him. He didn't think he had ever been a girl's first kiss. That was the sort of nonsense women remembered forever. He felt a measure of satisfaction that he had, however unintentionally, left his mark on her.

"—so you must see how dissatisfying it was—"

"Eh?" Jason knew he had missed an important point. Surely she was not still speaking of their kiss.

"Well, it wasn't exactly the sort of kiss one reads about in novels, you know."

He cleared his throat. "I'm afraid I don't."

"Oh." Her disappointment was palpable. "I did so want a real first kiss." She gave a wistful sigh. "Perhaps Sir Charles will know more about it."

Over his dead body, Jason thought. "Perhaps you could explain it to me. I'm not sure how first kisses ought to differ from regular kisses."

"Would you describe the kiss under the mistletoe as a regular kiss? Because it wasn't at all how the books describe kissing. My stomach wasn't fluttery and my knees didn't go weak. I didn't feel the least bit like swooning."

"I see," he mused, wondering how to go about this situation. He was going to have to kiss her. If he didn't, she would go to Charles, and that puppy would never be able to stop with a kiss. Then Jason would have to call him out to defend Miss Weston's honor or (and somehow this seemed the worse scenario) Charles would refuse to fight him and choose instead to marry Miss Weston. No, Jason must be the one to kiss her.

He knew how he wanted to kiss her, but it wasn't how he ought to kiss her. Her first kiss should be sweet and tender. He cupped her face in his hands and tilted her head back.

Her skin was soft as silk under his fingertips. He wanted so badly to run his hands over her body. To trace the lush curves of her breasts, down past the gentle indentation of her waist and over the swell of her hips.

He ached to crush her to him.

To force her to feel the hunger she aroused in him.

To awaken a matching passion in her.

He could do none of those things.

Not here. Not now. *Not ever*, he reminded himself.

She had asked him for a kiss. He was a grown man. A widower. Surely he could handle one innocent little kiss without too much difficulty.

"Close your eyes," he instructed.

Her lashes fluttered closed, forming dark crescents against her pale skin, and she pursed her rose-pink lips as tightly as she could.

He wanted to laugh, but the sight of her, so vulnerable and trusting, made it difficult to breathe. His hands shook with need and lust and other, deeper emotions he wanted desperately to ignore. She was trembling, too.

Was it fear? Anxiety? The same gut-wrenching need consuming him? He was tempted to ask her. All in an instant he wanted to know what she was thinking, what she was feeling. He wanted to know what she'd had for breakfast that morning and whom she had inherited her artistic talent from. He wanted to know how she took her tea and what she was afraid of and every last detail about her, from her favorite color to her middle name.

The thoughts tumbled over each other in rapid succession, overwhelming him. He couldn't handle this. Couldn't handle her. But he couldn't let her go.

He brushed a thumb across her lips. "Easy, now."

He didn't know whose benefit the words were more for. He lowered his head and kissed her. It was like no kiss he'd experienced before. This was like a prayer, a benediction, reverent and holy. His blood heated and energy crackled in the air around them. This meeting of lips was simple and innocent, yet earthy and elemental.

It was . . . sweet.

Her lips were soft but firm beneath his, matching his light pressure. She slid her hands up around his neck, threading her fingers through the hair at his nape, pulling him closer. A little sigh of pleasure escaped her, and he quickly took advantage of her parted lips, gently catching the bottom one between his teeth. He sucked and nibbled, pausing now and again to run the tip of his tongue over the satiny flesh of her inner lip. She tasted like elderberry wine, sweet with a tantalizing hint of spice, and every bit as heady....

Jason wrenched away, breathing hard. He didn't know what had just happened to him, but he sure as hell hadn't liked it. All right, he had liked it. He'd liked it so much his body felt ready to explode, but such a loss of control could not be countenanced.

He would not lose his head over a woman, no matter how desirable she might be. Nor would he lose his heart, or whatever bits still remained of it. And now he was condemned to a torturous hell of wanting and watching but never having.

He didn't fool himself that he'd forget her as soon as she left Arlyss; the memory of that kiss would be seared on his lips and memory for much longer. He hoped it had damn well been worth it.

"Oh!" Her fingers came up to touch her lips. After a long moment, she asked, "Was that a real, proper first kiss?"

"Yes," he said, pleased with his restraint. At least one thing about that kiss had gone right, even if the rest of it had turned his whole world the wrong way up. "That was a proper first kiss."

"Thank you very much then. I had best be going." Her voice sounded a bit wobbly as she turned to leave.

Jason sighed. "Livvy, what's the matter?"

She turned back to face him and he saw that her eyes were bright with tears.

"That's the first time you've called me that."

"Now that we've kissed, using your Christian name seems a fairly light transgression," he remarked.

"No, I like it . . . Jason."

"Won't you tell me what has upset you? I fear I am responsible."

"Oh, no, it isn't you. It's me. I know kissing is supposed to be pleasant, and now I'm worried there is something wrong with me. Maybe I have some sort of defect. . . ."

"What do you mean?"

"I'm afraid I don't enjoy kissing," she exclaimed.

Perfect. While he'd heard choirs of angels singing hallelujahs, she'd felt nothing. She might as well have picked up the letter opener from his desk and stabbed him in the gut . . .

"I don't mean to say that it was *unpleasant* exactly—"

And then twisted the knife.

"—it just . . ."

"—wasn't like the books," he finished for her.

She nodded and wrapped her arms about her middle, looking dejected.

Christ.

"Maybe you aren't attracted to me," he suggested, though the thought was depressing. "Physical desire is surely a required element for one of these book kisses."

"Of course it is, but I am hardly in the habit of seeking out kisses from men I find undesirable."

Her admission was a salve to his wounded pride, but salve was a poor remedy for a knife wound.

"I know it must sound stupid to you," she said, "but I always imagined kissing would be magical."

Whereas he had never really thought much about it. Until today. Until she had shown him how special a simple kiss could be.

"Other people certainly seem to enjoy it," she continued. "I know I have no right to ask, but . . ."

"But?" he prompted.

"Maybe two people have to be in love for the magic to happen."

"I don't think so." No, he *knew* so. Because there was no way he was in love with Miss Olivia Weston.

"But was it different with your wife? Different than kissing me, I mean."

"Yes," he replied truthfully, "but I kissed other women before I was married, and it was different with each one."

"But wasn't it better with her than with those other women?"

Jason forced himself to think of Laura, bracing for the rush of pain that always accompanied such recollections.

"Yes," he said slowly, "but the initial giddiness of being in love enhances all your feelings. And then, by the time that wears off a bit, you've grown used to each other and there's a sort of comforting familiarity. After a fashion, kissing becomes an unspoken language."

"I see," she whispered sadly.

Bloody hell. He couldn't stand another moment of this. He desperately wanted to take her in his arms and prove to her just how pleasurable kissing and all that ensued could be.

It wouldn't be difficult. He could tell she had a passionate nature. If he hadn't stopped the kiss when he had, she would know that about herself. Of course, if he hadn't stopped the kiss when he had, they would also probably have been rolling around naked in front of the fire by now.

He was tempted.

As he'd said, it wouldn't be difficult.

But neither would it be wise.

Mind battled body and for today, at least, mind won out.

He was going to let her go.

But he could satisfy one craving.

"What's your middle name?"

She must have thought it an odd request, but she answered him anyway.

"Jane."

"Olivia Jane Weston." He tested out the feel of it.

"I've always thought Jane suited me better than Olivia," she confided. "Olivia sounds like a rather grand, exotic person. The sort of person one would write novels about. Jane is a more ordinary name. A Jane would read books about the Olivias of the world and dream of having grand adventures."

"Do you dream of grand adventures?"

"I used to. But if there is one thing I have learned in the last year, it's that life is the grand adventure. It is up to each of us to make as much or as little of it as we wish. Holding a new baby in your arms can be as thrilling as riding an elephant. Not that I've ridden an elephant, mind you, but I used to dream of it."

She smiled shyly, seemingly embarrassed by this heartfelt outpouring of emotion. She was just opening the door to leave when he found his voice.

"You're wrong, you know. Olivia suits you. You just don't know yet how extraordinary you are."

"Oh!" She gasped with pleasure.

The sound wrapped around his chest like a vise.

Her hand fell away from the doorknob and she turned back to him. Her eyes, at once cautious and hopeful, searched his face.

"Truly?" Her voice was scarcely more than a whisper. "You aren't just saying that to be kind?"

"Kind?" He let out a little humorless laugh. "Do I strike you as a kind man?"

Jason meant the question to be rhetorical, but Olivia nodded.

"You *are* kind," she insisted. "I will concede you are disagreeable and churlish much of the time, but you are kind, too. Would an unkind man come to the rescue of two mistreated dogs? Would an unkind man tender such care on his son as I have seen you do with Edward?

Would an unkind man have gone to the trouble of finding a great Danish dog for Charlotte? I know the puppy was from you because Aunt Kate would have found a way to put off getting a dog until Charlotte fixed her mind on something else. You care deeply when you let yourself."

Her earnest belief in him was as misplaced as it was unsettling. In her bright, shining eyes, he was some sort of hero, like in one of those rubbish novels she went on about. He ought to tell her there would be no happy ending for him, but he didn't have the heart. And, for just a little while, he wanted to live in her realm of fantasy and imagine that, just maybe, there could be.

Chapter 10

"As the old hermit of Prague,
that never saw pen and ink,
very wittily said to a niece of King Gorboduc,
That that is, is."

Twelfth Night, Act IV, Scene 2

Twelfth Night

He thought she was extraordinary.

Four days later, the idea still thrilled her.

She didn't even mind her kissing defect.

Not much. Thinking back, she was almost certain there had been a moment when Jason kissed her when her knees had felt wobbly. Maybe she just needed more practice.

Even if she never grew faint or felt like her heart would pound out of her chest, Livvy thought she would be happy to kiss Jason Traherne for the rest of her life. Because he made her feel extraordinary.

As she dressed for the party, Olivia was a jittery bundle of nerves. Would Jason like her dress? It was new, and quite the most adult dress she had ever owned.

Aunt Kate had decided that new gowns were in order for the occasion, so they had gone to Haverfordwest one day with Charles. It was too short notice to order custom gowns, but both she and Aunt Kate had found dresses that needed only a few alterations. Livvy's was of fine white muslin with silver embroidery and lace trimmings round the neck and on the short sleeves. The gown was banded under her breasts with a lavender satin sash that tied in a bow at the back.

The bodice was lower than she was used to, but once she was certain that she would not tumble out and humiliate herself, Olivia decided she was quite pleased with the effect.

Aunt Kate had lent her a strand of pearls with a diamond clasp and a matching bracelet. She wore no other jewelry aside from the tiny brooch pinned to her garter. She couldn't leave it off and risk someone finding it, and in any case it had become a talisman of sorts.

The brooch somehow was at once the least of her troubles and the biggest problem of them all. After a passing glance in the mirror had revealed the vacuous grin of a besotted woman, Livvy had admitted to herself that if she wasn't already in love with Jason, she was well on her way there. And why shouldn't she be? He found her extraordinary. Yes, she, Miss Olivia Jane Weston, was extraordinary.

But in realizing this, Livvy also realized she needed to speak with Jason about the brooch and Laura's diary. It was wrong to keep confidences from the man she thought she might love. She couldn't tell him about the diary, though. He might demand to see it, and Charles hadn't agreed to that yet. She understood his hesitation; his relationship with Jason would surely be changed. No, she could not tell him about the diary, but the brooch was another matter. The only person he would be angry with over that was her.

And he would be angry, there was no doubt about that.

She just had to trust her feelings were not one-sided and hope her eardrums could withstand the vocal outpourings of his fury. After he ranted and raged for a bit, he would forgive her transgression. He must, he simply must.

Perhaps in time he might even come to believe, as she did, that Laura had led her to find the brooch and the diary. That Laura wanted happiness for Jason and had somehow brought them together.

She would tell him tonight, Olivia decided, after all the guests had gone. She only had another week before they were supposed to leave. She couldn't guess what would happen after that, and she didn't want the remainder of their time together clouded by secrets.

Her melancholy thoughts were banished by the arrival of her aunt's maid, Alice, who had come to do her hair. Alice had brought Charlotte and Edward with her, since Olivia had told them they might come to her chamber and see her done up in all her finery, as they would not be allowed downstairs.

Charlotte, of course, was not content with watching. Her sharp young eyes found every loose piece of hair that had escaped the pins, every tiny bump where the coiffure ought to be smooth, and she proceeded to point out these flaws. Fortunately, Alice was used to Charlotte. Any other servant, she feared, might have been tempted to commit mayhem with the curling tongs.

Edward, in contrast, sat quietly on the floor looking very glum.

"Are you feeling poorly?" Livvy asked, worried that all the fuss over the party might have triggered the beginnings of an episode.

He shook his head. "I don't want you to go."

"To the party? Why not?" Olivia asked in surprise.

"No, I don't want you to leave. I want you to stay here." With a cry, he launched himself at her and clung to her legs, burying his face against her knees.

Livvy's heart shattered.

She motioned Alice to wait, and then drew Edward to his feet and pulled him onto her lap. He had become so dear to her, this shy, serious little boy.

He flung his arms around her neck and buried his face in her shoulder.

"My mama went away. I don't want you to go away, too."

A lump came into Olivia's throat. She couldn't speak, so she just hugged Edward more tightly.

"Your mama is living with my papa in heaven," Charlotte explained. "It's very far away, so they can't come visit. Cousin Livvy isn't going there, though. She's only going to her home, where my other cousins live, and then she has to go to London."

Edward raised his head. "Why does she have to go to London? Why can't she stay here?"

"Because she's going to get married, of course," Charlotte sang, skipping around the room in her excitement.

Edward looked up at Olivia. "Is that true?"

"I hope so," Olivia said, smoothing his dark curls. "I hope to have a pair of imps like the two of you someday."

Edward's brow knit in concentration. "So you are going to London so you can be a mama?"

"Er, well, yes, I suppose. It's a bit more complicated than—"

"Then you don't need to go anywhere." Edward beamed. He slid off her lap and began to jump about with Charlotte. "You can stay here and be my mama."

Livvy's eyes grew wide at this pronouncement. And because Alice had resumed her task and was shoving pins into the coronet of braids she had fashioned. The maid seemed to view getting the pins to actually puncture Olivia's scalp as a personal challenge from which she would not back down.

"Wait, Edward. She has to be married," Charlotte insisted. "I don't think you can be a mama unless you're married."

"Then she can marry my papa," Edward countered.

Charlotte thought a moment, then slowly nodded. "All right," she agreed. "But she did say she wanted a *pair* of imps. A pair means two and there is only one of you. How will she get another baby?"

Edward frowned. "I don't know," he admitted. "I'm not entirely sure how my papa got me. He got you a puppy, though, and that's a baby dog, so I expect he could get a regular sort of baby."

Olivia choked on a laugh and began to cough. Edward raced over and thumped her on the back. When she could breathe, Livvy decided it would be prudent to change the subject. She raised her eyes, seeking inspiration, and saw the marquess standing in the door frame between their chambers, the hint of a smile twitching at his lips.

She hadn't heard the door open. He might have been standing there for ages. *How much had he heard?* Her cheeks flamed as she replayed the conversation in her head.

Edward followed her gaze and ran over to his father.

Lord Sheldon held up a hand. "No, Edward, we are not going to discuss how you came into existence."

Edward thought a moment. "All right. I don't need to know that anyway. Just whether or not you could get another one of me."

"What? Two Edwards? Heaven forbid. I can barely keep up with the one I already have." He ruffled his son's hair. "See here, Edward. I want you to get it firmly in your head that I am not going to marry Miss Weston—"

"No, indeed," Olivia agreed.

"—or any other female." The marquess shot her a quizzical look.

"They have to fall in love first," Charlotte declared. "People need to be in love to get married."

Lord Sheldon rolled his eyes. "That is the stuff of cheap novels and fairy stories, and you are not to believe a word of it, either of you. People get married every day for reasons other than love."

"But you loved my mama, didn't you?" Edward asked.

Lord Sheldon's face grew distant and shuttered at the mention of his late wife. "Yes, I did," he said softly.

For a moment Livvy glimpsed the strain of years spent hiding the still-raw wounds of his grief. Beyond the sadness she sensed the vicious, bitter anger of an injured animal, unable to tell friend from foe, but ever wary of further pain. Then, just as quickly it was gone and the mask of cool reserve was back in place.

"But marrying for love is not typical," he continued. "I don't know what sort of foolish tales Miss Weston has been telling you—"

"Be careful, my lord, or all this admiration may go to my head," she said dryly.

"I doubt there is room. As far as I can tell, your head appears to be filled with the nonsensical dreams you impart to these children."

He thought she was extraordinary, Olivia told herself. That was the real Jason. This was the cool, defensive facade he presented when threatened. She must not lose her temper. At least, not while the children were around.

Alice tucked some purple silk flowers into the wreath of braids encircling her head and fluffed the curls that had been artfully (and painfully) pinned to frame her face with wispy tendrils.

"There you are, miss."

Olivia surveyed herself in the mirror hung above the

vanity table. She was entranced by what she saw. For once she looked at herself without making comparisons to someone else. The woman who stared back at her was beautiful in her own right. Extraordinary, one might even say.

"Oh, thank you, Alice. I am tempted to live with Aunt Kate forever so that you can work this magic on me every day."

The maid gave her a fond smile. "You look lovely, Miss Olivia. Come, my lambs, it's time you were back in the nursery."

They protested—Charlotte a bit more vocally than Edward—but allowed themselves to be led off once Livvy promised to save some sweets for them to have on the morrow.

Once they were safely out of earshot, she faced Jason. "Was there something else you wished to say to me, my lord? Another insult to get off your chest?"

"Have I unintentionally insulted you again, Olivia?"

"I doubt it was unintentional," she huffed. "You can hardly have thought I would be flattered to hear my head is full of nothing but nonsensical dreams. Besides, the children and I were discussing my upcoming Season. Pardon me if I fail to see how such a subject can be construed as either nonsensical or a dream."

"Because," he drawled, "I am certain you have been spinning stories about how you are going to fall in love, get married, and live happily ever after."

Livvy crossed her arms over her chest. "I have said nothing of the sort."

"But that is what you expect will happen, is it not?"

"I expect I will get married," she allowed. "And what of you? Did you mean what you said to Edward about not wanting to remarry?"

His features grew shuttered. "I did. I have no wish for a wife."

"Not even for Edward's sake? Children of such a young age need a mother's love."

He shook his head. "You have such a romantic view of the world. Not all mothers are possessed of such loving inclinations. A great many children are raised by servants."

"But surely your wife—"

"Oh, my wife adored Edward."

Understanding began to dawn. "Then your own mother was cold?"

"Not deliberately, no. I don't think she had the first clue how to be a mother. She was the youngest in her family and, from what my father said, quite cosseted and spoiled. Theirs was an arranged marriage. My mother was scarcely more than a child when she married, and she bore me almost exactly nine months from her wedding day. I think she tried in her own way, but she wasn't suited to take care of anyone. She needed to be taken care of. She had no wish to dote upon a child; she craved the attention for herself. And she paid the price with her life."

"What do you mean?" Livvy's words were scarcely more than a whisper.

"My mother wanted more attention than my father saw fit to give her. Eventually she sought admirers elsewhere. When I was eight she decided to run off. She and her lover were killed in a carriage accident on their way to catch a ship to the Continent."

Her heart ached for him. "I am so sorry. You must have missed her terribly."

"Not particularly. I've a feeling having no mother is better than having a bad one."

Livvy could tell he didn't mean a word of it.

"Sometimes," she said thoughtfully, "it is easier to live without that which we convince ourselves we do not want. It doesn't truly help, though, does it? The wanting is still there, buried underneath all the fears and denials."

"You sound as though you speak from experience. What is it you secretly long for? Love? A grand, all-consuming passion?"

Olivia struggled to ignore the disdain in his tone and to withstand his barbed taunts. She reminded herself that Jason's hurtful words were his way of fighting his feelings by pushing her away. She assumed what she hoped was an impassive expression and airily declared, "One cannot expect more than one grand, all-consuming passion per generation in a family, and my sister has already claimed it."

"You cannot expect me to believe that you—a young lady who has during our brief acquaintance devoured more ridiculous romantic novels than I knew existed—are not planning to marry for love."

"Believe what you like, my lord."

He cocked his head to one side. "I do believe you're serious. You aren't set on a love match. Why? Do you aspire to be a duchess?"

She shook her head. Just then, she didn't aspire to be a marchioness, either.

"Wealth, then."

"No, but please continue guessing. My character has not been so maligned since last I saw my older brother. This barrage of insults is making me feel quite at home."

"It is not my intention to offend," he said stiltedly.

"Is it not? You, my lord, are a cynic."

"Brava, Miss Weston, you have figured me out."

So she was back to being Miss Weston. It seemed the evening was off to a poor start.

"It wasn't meant with admiration," she informed him crossly.

"I would rather be a cynic and have my feet firmly

planted on the ground than be a hopeless dreamer drifting among the clouds."

"My feet are as firmly planted as yours. Just because I acknowledge the existence of love, the power it holds, does not make me weak and pitiable."

"No," he agreed. "Those adjectives are best reserved for the poor saps who believe themselves in love. Come, we are not allowed to quarrel until tomorrow, remember? Now, if I recall correctly, compliments are in order."

He looked at her, really *looked* at her, his eyes traveling from Alice's handiwork down her body in a slow perusal and then back up again. His gaze caressed her, leaving every inch of her alive with excitement. She was seized with the urge to press her body against his and wondered what it would be like to kiss him now, with her body feverish and yearning for his.

Was she wicked enough to ask him to kiss her again? *Yes.*

It seemed every moment she spent in his presence made her a little more wicked.

How extraordinary . . .

Olivia was looking at him like she wanted to devour him. Jason wasn't sure if he should run away as fast as possible or strip off his clothes and offer himself to her. If the blood rushing south at breakneck speed was any indication, his body enthusiastically voted for the second option. It also indicated that, unless he got himself under control, a body part other than his brain would soon be making the decisions.

She was looking at him expectantly. He clamped down on his desire, willing some blood back up to his brain. Oh, yes, he was supposed to be complimenting her.

What to say? Beautiful was apt, but trite. The word

was also too boring and pallid to properly describe her. Beautiful didn't encompass her sharp wit, her charming naiveté, her compassionate spirit, her compelling vivacity, her maddening persistence, or any of a thousand other remarkable traits she possessed.

Remarkable. The word suited her, but some masculine instinct for survival warned him that "remarkable" was not what a woman wanted to hear in this situation. He was about to go ahead and tell her she looked beautiful, and if she thought him lacking in creativity, so be it, when he suddenly knew just what to say.

"If you ever again refer to yourself as ordinary, Olivia Weston, I will take you over my knee and paddle your backside."

Oh, Lord. He should not have let himself go there. Now he was assaulted by visions of his hands gliding over the firm, satiny flesh of her arse. Her radiant smile was worth every second of his discomfort.

"I believe that is the nicest compliment I have ever received. Certainly the most inventive."

"Telling a woman she looks beautiful slips off a man's tongue without thought. You deserve better than a glib line."

Her smile widened, and she practically glowed with happiness. His breath caught in his chest, and his throat grew tight. His emotions, only held in check by an increasingly frayed leash, slipped free and ran riot.

When he'd entered the room, he had been thrown to see Olivia at the vanity. He was not upset by her presence in the Marchioness's Chambers. Laura's presence was everywhere in the castle, a constant aching reminder, but no more so in this room than any other. When he was married, Laura had always shared his bed. He had a few vague memories of his mother here, but they were such distant echoes, they barely impinged on his conscious.

Any number of people had suggested he leave Arlyss, especially in that first year. He had other estates, places he had never been with Laura, but Jason refused to consider moving. He didn't want to uproot Edward, for one thing. More than that, though, whether it was a blessing or a curse, Arlyss was tied to Laura and he would not—could not—move on. He needed to remember to keep himself from being hurt again.

He needed to harden his heart against the domestic scene he had walked in on. To tell himself that it hadn't felt natural. Unfortunately, he was hardening in other places.

He had been lusting after Olivia since their kiss, but he had braced himself before he'd entered the room. Of course, nothing could have prepared him for what he found. She looked stunning. And she knew it. There was a newfound confidence about her.

"Jason!"

"What?" Damn, he had either lost track of the conversation or said something inappropriate.

"I asked you if it would be equally dissembling for a woman to bestow that compliment upon a man."

"Ah, er, that is, I don't suppose so," he babbled, not really knowing what she was talking about.

"Oh, good. You look beautiful, Jason."

She thought he looked beautiful?

Her eyes were a warm, rich blue, like the sky on a summer evening. He wanted to lie back and stare into them, watching and waiting for the twinkle of a shooting star. . . .

Christ, what in blazes was wrong with him? He had never spouted such twaddle in his life. Not even when he was young, foolish, and in love. Perhaps this isolated existence was adversely affecting him.

"You always look dashing," she continued, "but tonight you are just splendid. Women will probably swoon when they see you."

"I hope not," he grumbled.

"I remember one of Izzie's most devout suitors was prone to impromptu verse. Do you suppose men will compose poetry when they catch sight of me?"

Despite the teasing glint in her eyes, Jason's hands curled into fists at his sides. If he heard so much as a rhyming couplet praising any part of Olivia, he would take the fellow outside and beat him to a bloody pulp. Or maybe he would simply shoot him. One advantage of this relative isolation was that disposing of a body was far less trouble.

"Olivia," he began.

"Won't you call me Livvy?"

"No, in this I shall call you Olivia, or, better yet, by your full name. I want you to listen to me, Olivia Jane Weston. Whatever romantic notions are in your head, I pray you will act sensibly this evening. Duels over a lady's honor are far less thrilling than your books doubtless make them out to be."

She flitted forward and rested her hand on the sleeve of his coat. Her hands were delicate and graceful—an artist's hands. Her long, slender fingers were so white next to the black wool of his coat. What would they look like, what would they feel like against his skin— No. This evening would be interminable if he kept allowing his mind to wander these forbidden paths.

She squeezed his arm. "If I decide to forgo good sense tonight, Jason Traherne, you will undoubtedly be the first to know."

Since his good sense seemed to vanish in her presence, he was somewhat less than relieved by the prospect of Olivia forgoing hers. If neither of them displayed good sense, he had a very bad sense about how the evening was liable to end.

Chapter 11

"He does it with a better grace,
but I do it more natural."

Twelfth Night, Act II, Scene 3

"That is quite all right, Sir George. It didn't hurt a bit," Olivia reassured her partner as he trod on her toes for the eleventh time. It wasn't a lie, either, she thought. Her poor feet had ceased to register pain after their seventh squashing or so.

Sir George was a man who evidently liked his food. He also evidently liked her chest, since his eyes never strayed up to her face, even when he was apologizing for trampling her. She was most relieved when the dance ended and she could excuse herself to the retiring room.

As she had no desire to dance again until her feet were recovered, she made her way to the refreshment table, which had been set up at the far end of the Great Hall, off to one side of the enormous fireplace. She selected some sweets for the children as she had promised, though Edward would be lucky to receive so much as a bite with Charlotte around.

Charles came up beside her. "You look ravishing, my dear. It's a pity you're so stuck on my brother-in-law."

She batted him with the fan in her free hand. "Keep your voice down. Someone will hear you."

He laughed. "With the way you've been watching him

I doubt there's a person in this room in question of your feelings, except perhaps Jason."

"Have I truly been that obvious?"

He regarded her a moment. "No. I suspect I am overly sensitive since I wish those languishing looks were directed at me."

"You're only saying that to make me feel better."

"Is it working?"

She shook her head. "I'm making a fool of myself, aren't I?"

"It's not too late to convince everyone that you're madly in love with me instead," he joked.

Olivia eyed him speculatively.

Charles took a step backward, his palms raised as if to fend off an attack. "I wasn't serious."

"Then you shouldn't have suggested it." She smiled sweetly and placed her hand on his shoulder, gazing up at him with what she hoped was as languishing a look as those she had apparently been bestowing on Jason.

Who was he dancing with now? She glanced around the room in search of him.

"Livvy, my love, your admiration for *me* becomes less believable when you turn to look at *him*."

"I can't help doing so. He hasn't asked me to dance. Wouldn't you want to dance with a woman you found desirable?"

"Maybe he wants to avoid singling you out," Charles suggested.

"Then he's going about it the wrong way," she growled. "I am practically the only female here he hasn't danced with, and I'm meant to be the guest of honor. More of a statement is made by his avoidance than there would be if he danced with me."

"Perhaps he wants to give you the chance to dance with other men. You certainly haven't been lacking in partners. This is the first dance you've sat out."

"But it isn't as if most of these men are prospective suitors. Nearly all are married. Besides, he would hardly be pushing me at other gentlemen if he wanted me for himself," she argued.

"Ah, but if you were attached to another man, you would be off-limits. Then he would be safe from temptation."

"I shall never understand how the male mind works."

He grinned. "We're simple creatures. Our thoughts revolve around women and food." He picked a piece of toffee off her plate and popped it into his mouth.

"Stop that," she scolded him. "These are promised to the children. Do you want me to tell Charlotte you ate her sweets?"

"Heaven forbid!"

"That's what I thought. If my aunt asks for me, tell her I've just gone to place these in my chamber."

"Why not let a footman see to it? We can't have the guest of honor disappearing."

She leaned close. "If you want the truth, the guest of honor needs to make certain Sir George did not break any of her toes."

He laughed and nearly choked on his toffee. "Go on with you, then. I've a fair notion to escape myself."

Once she was in her room, Livvy allowed herself a few quiet moments to relax. She frowned at the thought of the lecherous stares that had been directed at her by Sir George and other men of his ilk. Worse, though, were the even more predatory gazes their wives cast in Jason's direction.

These women were less the swooning sort than the pursuing sort. A pack of bloodhounds that had scented something they liked. Perhaps the setting had incited some ancient compulsion to hunt and conquer; the Great Hall dated back to the days when the mighty

Marcher Lords had sought to subdue the native Welsh. Livvy wanted to tell all of them that Jason was not a tasty bit of meat to be slavered over by a pack of hungry dogs but, if he had been, he was her prize morsel.

It wasn't true, of course. She had no claim on him. Except she couldn't quite persuade herself of that. Ever since she had found that first clue leading to the brooch, Jason had been hers. Her special secret.

She felt she knew him on some higher plane, understood him on some deeper level. This wasn't to say that she didn't find him puzzling and aggravating a good deal of the time, because she did. But she couldn't shake the growing feeling that they had been brought together, and that her coming to Castle Arlyss was all part of some greater plan.

And perhaps she was trying to convince herself that all this was predetermined—that Jason needed her—because she was beginning to fear he was necessary to her future happiness. She had never dared hope she'd find a man able to live up to the hero archetype that had gradually taken shape in her mind. Over the years, with each new novel she read, the ideal had been refined and rewritten, like a palimpsest, until only the very best attributes remained.

Jason obviously didn't entirely fit this image of perfection. He was too knowledgeable about Shakespeare's canon for her comfort, and he tended toward grumpy and withdrawn over gracious and welcoming. She shouldn't, by her reckoning, have been at all tempted by so clearly flawed a specimen. Perfection was her standard, love her divine inspiration.

Was she ready to accept the idea that a perfect love didn't have to be, well, *perfect*? Could she admit that desiring a fallen angel had greater appeal than worshipping one on high from afar? Was it possible for love to be at once sacred and profane?

And why was she bothering to ponder these questions when she had yet to answer the most important one? How would she ever figure out if what she felt for Jason was love or some other confused emotion?

She had never questioned her sister's insistence that James was the only one for her. He was the love of Isabella's life and that knowledge was as much a part of her as her fingers and toes. More so, really, since her sister could survive without fingers and toes, but without James she had lost the will to live. Livvy accepted what was between Izzie and James as a fact of life. Like moths and flames or stars and the moon, they simply belonged together.

But because Isabella had always been so certain of her feelings, Olivia had never thought to ask her *how* she knew James was the man she was meant to be with. And Livvy guessed that even if Izzie was standing right beside her so she could ask, her sister would shrug and say: "I just knew." Which would really be no help at all because Livvy never *just knew* anything.

She didn't have that same trust in her feelings or the ability to leap without knowing where she would land. She thought Jason might be her match, but thinking it wasn't the same as knowing it. There were moments when she *thought* she knew, like when he smiled at something she said although he clearly didn't want to. Sometimes as she watched him with Edward and Charlotte she imagined him playing with a child of theirs and it seemed less like a daydream and more like a vision of the future.

But what if Jason had *known* that Laura was the only one for him? Was it possible to love that deeply more than once in a lifetime? If it wasn't, was she prepared to accept always being second best? And did that mean she was actually jealous of a dead woman?

Yes.

How lowering. Love—or whatever these mixed-up feelings were—certainly didn't seem to be making her a better person. But at least she wasn't a married woman ogling a man other than her husband. She was unmarried and thus well within her rights to ogle. Perhaps if she ogled long enough she would know. That was, if she even wanted to know. She was certainly safer not knowing, but she was having an increasingly difficult time remembering just why she wanted to be safe.

To know, or not to know: that was the question.

Oh, heaven help her, she was quoting Shakespeare, or misquoting in this case. Now she knew one thing for certain. She *knew* she was going mad.

Olivia headed back to the party, taking a shortcut by using the stairs off the solar, which was being used as the ladies' retiring room. She had just opened the door to slip inside when she heard voices and realized the room was not empty. She opened her mouth to announce her presence so as not to startle the other women, when one of them said something that stopped her dead in her tracks.

"You know I hate to speak ill of anyone, but that niece of Lady Sheldon's is really too much. Did you see the way she was watching the marquess?"

Livvy's hand flew to her mouth.

"Jealous, Callista?" the other woman asked.

Callista. That was Lady Vernon, Sir George's wife. Olivia hadn't liked her on sight. Not because she was beautiful, and not even because of the come-hither looks she had cast at Jason all throughout dinner. No, Livvy disliked her because she so obviously thought herself superior to everyone around her.

"Jealous? Of that little innocent? Hardly."

Her barking laugh grated on Olivia's raw nerves.

"In any case, I have no need to be jealous. I'll have Jason Traherne in my bed before the month is out."

"You had best be careful with that one," her companion warned. "He's got the look of a lean, hungry wolf."

"Then he'll need a woman in his bed, not a girl," Lady Vernon declared with no small amount of satisfaction.

"And what makes you think you're the woman he wants?"

"I sat by him during the meal. Believe me when I say I have irrefutable proof of his desire."

Olivia felt sick, yet she couldn't walk away.

There were whisperings back and forth that she couldn't make out, and then a startled gasp.

"No! You didn't! Really? And. . . ?" the other woman inquired.

"A lady can be assured of a good ride with a mount like that."

The two women burst into gales of laughter.

Olivia couldn't stand to listen to another word. She forced her legs to function and rushed back the way she had come. Her eyes were filled with tears, so she did not see the person standing in front of her. She slammed up against a hard masculine body.

Hands came up to grasp her shoulders. Steadying her. Trapping her.

She knew at once it was Jason.

Fate wouldn't be so kind as to let it be anyone else.

Besides, she had been in contact with any number of men that night, and not one of them had produced the sort of thrill that ran through her body when she touched him.

"There you are!" His voice was angry. "I've been searching everywhere for you."

"Charles knew where I was," she said woodenly, keeping her eyes fixed on his shoulder.

"He disappeared as well. Damn it, Livvy, if you've been with him—"

She couldn't believe he had the gall to accuse *her* of

sneaking off with Charles—*Charles*, for heaven's sake— after what she'd just heard. She wrenched herself free of his grasp and took off running.

Cursing under his breath, Jason set off after her. He caught her easily and dragged her into the nearest available room. His emotions were running high, his control frayed so it was hanging by a thread.

"Were you with a man just now?"

Damn, he hadn't meant to sound quite so accusatory.

"I'm not angry with you"—he was bloody well furious—"but I need to know. Who was it? Christ, did he hurt you?"

He reached for her, but she pulled back, shaking her head.

"The only man who has hurt me tonight is you."

She met his gaze then, and the confusion and pain he saw in those blue depths made his heart clench.

"Me? What the devil did I do? I haven't spoken two words to you since the guests began arriving."

"Yes, I noticed. As soon as there were other women around you— Oh, why do you even care? Just let me go. We both know you would rather be with Lady Vernon."

He frowned. Something was definitely not right.

"Why would I want anything to do with that harpy?" he demanded.

Her eyes blazed with indignation. "Then you deny that you are planning to make her your mistress?"

"Hell, yes, I deny it. Who told you such a thing?"

"I overheard her in the retiring room. She seemed quite certain of your intentions. She told the woman she was with that she had proof of your desire."

Jason groaned. Callista had always been a brazen hussy, but she had gotten worse since she'd married old Sir George. She had managed to seat herself next to him at dinner, and when he had ignored her suggestive whispers, she had decided, under the cover of the table, to make a very literal grab for his attention.

She had indeed found "proof of his desire," as she put it, but it hadn't been for her. He had been bored past bearing during the meal. Callista disgusted him, and the woman on his other side, a Mrs. Griggs, had been so awed at finding herself next to a marquess, her dialogue was limited to repeating, "My lord," after every single bloody thing he said.

Was it any wonder his thoughts had strayed to Olivia, whose clever, cutting remarks elevated conversation to an event akin to a fencing match? He found her remarkably agile brain every bit as fascinating and lust-inducing as her lush body. A verifiable pocket Venus sent to tempt this poor mortal. He didn't know how long he would be able to hold out, especially if his son persisted in bringing up matters of the flesh.

Edward's questions had brought an uncomfortably arousing image to Jason's mind. He envisioned Olivia lying beneath him, her lips parted and her face flushed with exertion. He imagined thrusting into her over and over, hard and fast, their bodies slamming together as they both reached for release. Her hips would rock up to meet him, forcing him deeper. In his mind he heard her breathless pants against his ear, and then little mewling cries when the pleasure finally overtook her. Her hot sheath would contract around his cock and he would forget everything, losing himself in her as he planted his seed in her womb.

Heaven help him, he'd nearly come there at the table just thinking about it. Unfortunately Callista had heard the small moan he'd been unable to suppress and had attributed it to her crude innuendoes. He had thought, however, that he had made his lack of interest in her clear when he'd removed her hand from his crotch and warned her never to touch him again. The lady was persistent, he would grant her that.

"And this is why you've practically thrown yourself at every man here tonight?" he asked incredulously. "You were trying to pay me back in my own coin?"

"You can't be serious. I don't need to stand here and listen to you insult me." She started to walk out but he caught her arm.

"Christ, Livvy, I'm sorry. I didn't mean that the way it sounded. You're driving me mad. I wanted to smash in the faces of every man in there you danced with and smiled at. You needn't torment me by flirting with other men. Whatever desire Lady Vernon may have noticed, I swear it was only for you."

He could see she didn't believe him. He ought to leave it there. To walk away. He shouldn't be telling her any of this, but the raw pain in her eyes compelled him to press on.

"I have been aching since the moment I walked into your chamber and saw you in that damnably low-cut gown. No, longer than that. I've wanted you since you fell at my feet your first day here."

"I did not fall at your feet. I merely landed there after your dog tried to kill me," she corrected him, her reserve beginning to melt. "Did you truly desire me then?"

"I am only a man, and you are quite lovely. As much as I didn't want to want you, I should have been worried for the health of my, er, manly self if I had not."

"It's my sister who is the great beauty in the family."

He shook his head in disbelief. "So you say."

It amazed him that she didn't recognize how beautiful she was. It was true he'd never seen her sister, but he could not imagine her looks held a candle to Livvy's inner light. At first, he had thought her merely pretty, but the word didn't do her justice. She reminded him of a wood nymph, able to blend in with her surroundings when she wished, but the magic about her—the spirit she could not dim—gave her away. And once you noticed Olivia Jane Weston, it was difficult to forget her.

She spilled over into the castle, her delight in the place forcing him to view his home in a new light. In *her* light. Her scent lingered in the rooms, that tantalizing combination of soap and roses and Livvy.

He hadn't been lying when he said he didn't want to desire her. After Laura's death, he hadn't thought he would ever want another woman. He'd begun to believe, had almost hoped, that part of him had been buried with her.

But he hadn't counted on Livvy, with her sunny smiles and her way of coaxing him out of a foul temper. Not that she didn't have a temper of her own, but he only liked her more for it. There was no point in denying she affected him. She pestered him during the day and plagued his dreams at night.

It wasn't just lust, either. Pure, simple lust he could handle. No, he cared about her, and he knew he shouldn't. He shouldn't let her get any closer. She was too close as it was. Dangerously close. It would be better—safer—for both of them to maintain a distance. But she kept inching closer and, God help him, he didn't have the strength to keep pushing her away.

As long as he kept it to caring he would be all right, he told himself. Caring and wanting. That was where he drew the line. He would not cross over into loving or needing. *Never again.*

He looked into her eyes, and then drew her up against him.

"I want you. Only you, Livvy."

"Truly?" she whispered.

"Truly."

"I want proof."

She wanted proof? He imagined Livvy's fingers on his cock and was instantly hard.

"Livvy—"

"Don't 'Livvy' me. If that Callista woman saw some proof of your desire, and you claim that desire is for me, I should be able to see the proof as well."

Christ.

She was going to be the death of him.

"The proof is there," he said through gritted teeth. "You're just too innocent to know it."

She pouted.

The sight of those full berry pink lips was his undoing.

He took her hand and held her palm over his pounding heart, then guided it down over the buttons on his coat to the falls of his breeches. His erection jerked and leapt against her palm as if it could break through the fabric barrier separating them.

Jason dropped his hand.

By some miracle, hers stayed put.

"Is that proof enough for you?" he demanded hoarsely.

"This means you want me," she breathed.

It was part statement, part question.

If he answered her truthfully, there could be no going back.

He closed his eyes, praying for the strength to push her away yet again. It would be for the best.

But when he opened his mouth, he found himself saying, *"Yes."*

Chapter 12

"Wherefore are these things hid?"
                    Twelfth Night, Act I, Scene 3

He wanted her.
   Her.
   Olivia Jane Weston.
   It was almost too much to believe. And yet the proof was in her hand. Lord, but she felt wicked. It didn't feel bad, either, this wickedness; it felt glorious.
   She ran her hand up the hard length of him, marveling at what lay beneath the fine wool of his breeches. Unaccountably, touching him seemed to affect her body as well. She could feel her nipples jutting out, pressing against her corset. And the place between her legs throbbed.
   Jason stood as still and stiff as a marble statue. He seemed scared to move for fear she would stop touching him. Foolish man. She did remove her hand, which made him groan in disappointment, but she wanted to touch the rest of him. She smoothed her palms over his shoulders, feeling the heat of his body through the layers of clothes. She began sliding her hands down over his chest.
   "Olivia," he rasped.
   "Livvy," she instructed.
   "Livvy, you need to stop."
   She didn't listen. Her hands trailed lower, deliber-

ately avoiding the hard ridge of aroused masculine flesh, to play on his muscled thighs.

"Olivia, stop!"

Her arms dropped to her sides, and she stepped away from him, stung by his dismissal.

He caught her hands in his.

"No, love, you misunderstand. I want you to touch me. I want it more than I want to breathe, but this is too public."

Love.

How was it that a casually uttered endearment could be so thrilling?

Love.

How many times had she read, heard, said the word without thought. On his lips, those four simple letters combined to form something new.

Something holy.

Something she prayed was just a little bit true.

"You— You don't think I was too brazen?"

He looked like he was in pain, but he managed a chuckle. "Despite what tales you were told in the schoolroom, I cannot believe there are many men who object to brazen women. So long as that brazenness is restricted to one man, that is."

"I suppose, as I have already begun, I shall have to restrict it to you, my lord."

"Jason," he corrected her.

"Jason," she sighed in agreement. "You know, I don't think I want to touch you after all."

"Have you decided to be sensible, then?"

She shook her head. "Not unless you have. That wasn't quite what I meant to say. I do want to touch you, but first I want to draw you."

He inhaled sharply.

She rose up on her toes and whispered in his ear. "All of you."

His hands tightened on hers.

"Are the guests leaving yet?"

"Not for a while. It's not yet midnight."

He swore. "Now will you admit that guests are a nuisance?"

His impatience made her feel like the most desirable woman alive.

The thought gave her pause. Why had she felt the need to add the bit about being alive? Was she trying to remind herself that she would never be able to compete with Laura?

She strove to keep her tone light. "I should be insulted. You will recall I am a guest."

"Very well," he agreed. "All guests are a nuisance except those who want to draw me."

"I don't know. I think most of the women here would draw you, given the chance."

"You are a provoking minx. I amend my statement. All guests are a nuisance save those who want to draw me and are named Olivia. Are you satisfied?"

She shrugged. "If you are."

"I am not satisfied in the least, but we must return to the party. If we have not already been missed, we soon will be." He wound her arm through his and they began walking toward the Great Hall.

"Will you dance with me?" she asked, hoping he wouldn't notice the slight begging note in her voice.

He shook his head. "I don't dare. I might lose control and ravish you right then and there. And even if I somehow managed to restrain myself, everyone in attendance would know in a moment that I wished to do so."

"I don't think my aunt would be pleased by that." She laughed.

He didn't join her. Instead, a pensive frown clouded his face.

Oh, there went her stupid mouth again. Why had she

brought up her aunt? She had been so close to a marvel-
ous adventure, and now she had given Jason the perfect
reason to back out.

She knew he didn't care for her in the way she had
come to care for him. It hurt, no denying that, but he still
had a long way to go in terms of opening his heart again.
And as much as she'd wanted to be the magic woman
who healed all his hurts and helped him love again, that
was the stuff of romantic dreams.

Jason was real. He was not one of the perfect men in
her novels. And yet, in many ways, she thought he was
a hero.

She could easily see why Charlotte and Edward—
and even Charles—looked up to him. He was strong,
but he was kind and caring, too. He tried to hide these
noble qualities, of course, but he likely believed showing
emotion was a sign of weakness. She knew from observ-
ing the men in her life that they were often possessed of
such ridiculous notions.

She dug in her heels.

"Jason Traherne, if you are having second thoughts,
I'll— I'll—"

"Shh." He pressed a finger to her lips. His hand moved
to toy with one of the curls at her temple, twisting it around
his fingers. "I passed second thoughts ages ago. I've lost
track of how many times I've fantasized about you and
the equal number of times I've told myself not to."

"As the female in question, second and all other numbers of thought are my prerogative. If I am not having
them, neither can you."

"If you say so, it must be true." He ran his knuckles down her cheek. "In any case, you still have time to
change your mind."

She shivered with pleasure at his touch. "I am quite
resolved. I plan to draw you until you are satisfied with
the results."

He groaned. "Now look what you've done. I can't possibly go back to the party like this," he said, gesturing at his tented breeches.

She giggled at the sight, and he swatted her backside in retaliation.

"You are a cruel, lusty wench," he bemoaned, "but it is probably all to the good for us to go in separately. You go ahead. I'll rejoin the party shortly."

"But what about our plans?" she asked.

"Our plans? For what?"

In addition to being ridiculous, men were also infuriatingly dense creatures with memories in proportion to the smaller size of their brains. It was fortunate they made such excellent drawing subjects.

"For tonight," she hissed at him. "Where are we to meet? And when?"

"You seem to have forgotten that our chambers adjoin. We shall have little trouble locating each other. Come to me once you have dismissed your maid."

"In your chamber?" she squeaked.

No, no, no. She refused to share his bed with a ghost.

"I suppose I could be troubled to walk the few steps to yours, if you wish," he offered.

In Laura's room? That would be even worse! She thought quickly. "A bedchamber just seems so . . . so ordinary."

He didn't bother to hide his amusement. "Heaven forfend we should be ordinary! Where would you prefer, my little adventuress? The library?"

He was joking, she knew, but it sounded perfect to her.

"Yes, the library. What time?"

"Once the guests have gone, I will wait there for you. Come to me when you are able." He pushed her forward. "Now take yourself off before I decide to challenge myself to a duel."

*   *   *

Once she had gone, Jason headed for the nearest washroom. He was so aroused from his encounter with Livvy and the prospect of what might happen later that night, he only needed a minute for things to come to a head, as it were. He just hoped his efforts would be enough to keep his desire in check for the remainder of the party. If he was lucky, and if by some chance his sanity returned, maybe it would be enough for the evening and he could forget these fantastic notions of a late-night rendezvous in the library.

And perhaps he needed to stop fooling himself. This thing with Olivia was not going to go away just because he found lusting after her inconvenient. But he had told Livvy the truth. He was having serious doubts as to the wisdom of all this. He had always thought himself a man of honor and morals and scruples. Was he willing to abandon a lifetime of virtue for a bit of pleasure?

Absolutely.

There you had it.

How low the mighty had fallen.

He would not allow her to become fallen, though. He could have pleasure of her, and she of him, without her getting ruined. She would just go to her marriage bed a little more informed.

The thought of Livvy getting married sent a bolt of white-hot rage racing through him. The violence of his reaction left him shaken . . . and ashamed.

As he had told Edward earlier, he had no intention of getting remarried, not just to Livvy, but to any woman. If he wasn't going to put his ring on her finger, was it really fair for him to begrudge her finding some other man to do it? No, of course it wasn't fair, but he did all the same. At the moment she belonged to him, and Jason was not a man who shared what was his.

He entered the Great Hall, his eyes involuntarily

seeking her out amongst the crowd. She was not hard to find. Most of the women present were married or widowed, and Livvy's light-colored dress stood out amongst the deeper hues of their gowns. A beacon of her innocence.

He quashed down on the guilt that rose up in his throat. It wasn't as if she didn't want his attentions, he reminded himself. And in any case, she would still be innocent when she left Arlyss. She would have a much clearer idea of the relations between men and women, but she would remain a virgin. On that point he remained firm.

An unfortunate choice of words. He was already beginning to feel the flutterings of arousal. Damnation. He was as randy as a goat. And he was not happy to see that Charles had been Livvy's partner through the dance. The two of them were too close for his liking. Would Olivia turn to him once she and Jason were through? Assuming, of course, that they ever actually began. It was not a thought he wanted to dwell on.

He forced his mind—and his gaze—in another direction and saw Callista determinedly making her way to him through the crush. Bloody perfect. He hoped she had enough common decency not to grope him publicly with her husband nearby. Then again, if Vernon ran him through with a sword or put a lead ball in him, he would have to take to his bed until Olivia was safely gone.

"My lord," Callista simpered, batting her lashes at him. "I had begun to believe you had disappeared."

No such luck, he thought glumly.

He bowed. "Lady Vernon."

"So formal with an old friend?" she chided.

To make a scene or not to make a scene, that was the question. He wanted to tell Callista that not only had they never been friends, they never would be. How the mild-mannered vicar and his meek mouse of a wife had produced such a hellcat for a daughter was beyond him. She had been wild as a child and had only become worse with age.

Her marriage to the elderly baronet had elevated her position in Society, and she had become so proud and bold as to believe the rules of polite society no longer applied to her. He decided then that he would not give her the dressing-down she so richly deserved. She would bring about her own downfall soon enough with her grand airs and her loose tongue.

"Was there something you wanted, *my lady*?"

She sulked at his insistence at formality.

"You haven't yet asked me to dance, my lord," she said, lowering her gaze to his groin. "I'm certain we would both find the activity *invigorating*."

She took his hand and began leading him over to the other dancers.

Jason spoke in a voice low enough that only she could hear. "I will dance with you, Lady Vernon, because there would be talk if I turned and walked away from you now, and I don't want to cast a blight on my stepmother's party. I told you earlier not to touch me again. As this was not a particularly complicated request, I must conclude that you are either abysmally stupid or, more likely, you have deluded yourself into thinking you are irresistible. In either case, I trust I will not have to tell you again."

Her eyes blazed with anger as the musicians began to play a cotillion. At least he'd be able to keep trading her off to the other men who'd had the misfortune to join their set.

He bowed.

She curtsied.

They joined hands and stepped toward each other.

Or rather, he stepped toward her. She gave more of

a leap and landed on his toes with as much force as she could muster. Damn, but that had hurt!

Jason shot her a warning glance.

Her eyes were fixed on his crotch.

He sighed.

It was going to be a long night.

Olivia crept to the library, her heart pounding so loudly she couldn't hear if she was making any noise. Over the sound of the beating drums was her mother's voice spouting phrases like "most improper" and "ungrateful child," and "banished to your room forever." If her mother ever found out what she was doing ... She shuddered, refusing to finish the thought.

Her mother was not the type to understand about adventures. She would understand about falling in love, though, and maybe about needing to grab what you could while you could.

There, she had admitted it.

She was in love with Jason.

When she'd overheard Lady Vernon, she had been devastated. Her worst fears about allowing herself to care and ending up heartbroken had seemed to be crashing down on her. But she had worried for nothing. She had been right to trust Jason with her heart. He wouldn't hurt her, at least not intentionally.

Livvy had no illusions that Jason was going to suddenly fall in love with her before she left. And as he certainly wasn't going to be in London for her Season, once she left, she could not look back. But she knew she would and she wanted to be able to do so without regret.

Life was short. In the past year she'd nearly lost both her sister and her brother-in-law. She didn't know if she would ever fall in love again. Maybe someday, if she could see her way to somehow falling out of love with Jason, but there was no knowing for certain.

The future was hazy.

The present was clear.

She was prepared to live in the moment and take whatever Jason would give her.

She took a deep breath and opened the door to the library. She swallowed hard. Jason lounged on the wooden settle beneath the window wearing the red silk banyan she'd seen him in the night of Edward's episode. Only the faintest sliver of moon remained in the sky, and the only light in the room came from the golden glow of the fire and the few scattered candles Jason must have collected and lit.

She had thought him beautiful in the moonlight, like a fine marble statue of antiquity, but by firelight he was perfection. The flickering flames cast dancing shadows on him, gilding the olive tones in his skin and highlighting the sable undertones in his raven hair. On his chest, in the vee of flesh exposed by his robe, she saw dark, crisp curls, the same color as the hair on his head. Her mouth nearly watered at the sight of that naked skin; at the knowledge that she could reach out and touch him with no barriers to get in the way.

He rose in one fluid motion and walked over to her. His feet were bare, as were his muscled calves. This time he wasn't wearing anything under his banyan.

Knowing how he felt about her hideous monstrosity of a wrapper, she had dismissed her maid once her gown and corset were off, telling the girl she would finish undressing herself. She wore only her chemise, stockings, slippers, and a shawl she'd wrapped around her shoulders to ward off a chill, though the last seemed a foolish precaution, as she was burning up inside. She should have felt shockingly underdressed. But faced with Jason in that loosely belted silk robe—really, she could undo the knot at his waist with little more than a tug—she felt as though she was wearing a ridiculous amount of clothing. Which probably accounted for her sudden desire to strip it all off and launch herself at him.

"You came." He sounded pleased and not a little surprised.

"I told you I would," she responded breathlessly.

He smiled and inclined his head. "So you did."

Silence filled the space between them.

Livvy fought the urge to burst out in nervous chatter. She didn't think inane babble was going to make her more alluring, but if he didn't say something in five seconds, she wasn't going to be able to stop herself.

Five . . . four . . . three . . .

"Lock the door, Olivia."

The sound of his voice, low and rough, did something funny to her insides. She turned around and fumbled with the lock, her hands shaking, and when she heard the bolt slide home, she knew her fate was sealed.

She turned back to Jason and froze. He had shed his banyan and was now totally, gloriously nude.

And he was perfect.

Far more beautiful than the prints of classical sculptures she'd discovered in her father's library. He was hairier, too. And the male part of him—the part that was proof of his desire for her—did not look as if it could possibly be covered by a fig leaf.

Breathing became difficult. She stumbled her way to one of the settees, never taking her eyes from him.

He placed one hand on his hip. "How shall I pose for you?"

"I—" She licked her lips. "I'm afraid I forgot to bring my drawing materials."

He dropped his arm. "And here I was set on having my glorious male self immortalized," he teased.

Olivia gave him a shy smile, beginning to get into

the spirit of the game. "I can work from memory, but I'll need to perform a close study." She rose somewhat unsteadily, leaving her shawl behind. How had she ever thought this room draughty?

Jason held out his hand to her and she grasped it, needing his warmth. She might be prepared to embark on an adventure, but that didn't mean she wasn't a little bit afraid.

"It's still me, Livvy," he said, as if he sensed what she was thinking.

"More of you than I'm used to."

"We can take as long as you need. The last thing I want to do is pressure you into something you're not ready for." He bent down to reach for the robe pooled around his feet, but she stopped him.

"I'm ready, Jason. I want this. I want *you*."

He reached up with his free hand and cupped her cheek in his palm. "Then I'm yours."

Chapter 13

*"O! what a deal of scorn looks beautiful
In the contempt and anger of his lip."*
                                   Twelfth Night, Act III, Scene 1

I*'m yours ...*
    Livvy's heart clenched. If only it was true. It *was*
true, she told herself. In that moment, for this night, he
was hers and, though he didn't know it, she was his.

She nestled her face into his hand. "Will you kiss me?
I know I didn't like it much before, but—"

He placed a finger against her lips, quieting her. "It
will be different this time."

He threaded his other hand through her loose hair to
cradle the back of her head. With a gentle tug he tilted
her head back, angling her to receive his kiss.

Her eyes fluttered closed.

She gasped in surprise when he pressed his lips to
the base of her throat, right in the curve where her neck
met her shoulder. The next kiss fell on her forehead. The
one after that in the sensitive hollow just below her left
ear. On and on he went with these surprise kisses, never
quite landing where she wanted him.

Her lips parted of their own volition.

"Jason," she pleaded.

Her knees didn't feel weak; they felt as though they
had turned to liquid. And she wouldn't be surprised if
she swooned, as she was having a difficult time remem-

bering to draw breath. She clutched at his arms, needing support but not wanting to open her eyes for fear this was all a dream.

His lips brushed over hers in a feather-soft caress, so tender and reverent, tears stung beneath her closed eyes. He kissed her like she was made of porcelain, delicate and fragile. She took a step closer to him, twining her arms around his neck.

He ran one of his hands down her back until it was resting lightly on her bottom. She gasped in surprise and he seized the opportunity to slide his tongue into her mouth.

Oh, my. She had never imagined anything like this. She tentatively touched her tongue to his, trying to learn him as he was learning her. He tasted of the wassail, that delicious hot mixture of winter ale, apples, cinnamon, and cloves, which had been served in keeping with the holiday spirit.

Alongside the wassail was a dark, masculine flavor that she knew was Jason. She wanted more. She pressed herself up against him, reveling in his heat and his strength. And in the urgency of his desire, which she could feel clearly against her belly.

He groaned, and she wriggled her hips, trying to get closer still. She wanted to melt into him, into his skin—into his very soul. So this was the reason people risked everything for love. This was the divine madness that obliterated all sense and logic.

He kissed her the way she had dreamed of being kissed. Like she was extraordinary. Like he couldn't live without her. Like she was a heroine—*his* heroine.

His hand came up to cup her breast, and her head fell back. He pressed hot, openmouthed kisses along the column of her throat as he gently squeezed and kneaded first one breast, then the other, through the thin lawn of her chemise. He lightly nipped her earlobe with his teeth as he pinched the hard bud of one nipple.

"Jason!" she gasped, her knees buckling under the onslaught of such intense pleasure.

He sank down to the floor with her.

"Livvy, are you all right?"

"Again," she commanded.

He laughed and toppled her onto her back.

"Do you have any idea what you do to me?"

She arched her hips up against him. "Oh, I think I have some idea," she purred, peering up at him through lowered lashes.

He regarded her with amazement.

She didn't know how, but she knew just what to do and say. Perhaps she had always had this seductress inside her, lying dormant, waiting for a man like him. A man who would encourage her to act on her every last naughty desire. A man who would want her to be a little more wicked.

He had shocked her with his nakedness. For all her bold talk about drawing him in the nude, she had never expected him to actually allow it. But he had somehow known what she needed before she did. She had been touched that he had offered himself up to her and made himself vulnerable, perhaps the only way he knew how.

She had been freed by his gesture as well, because by doing something so totally unexpected he had wiped away any preconceived ideas she'd had about the way things ought to be. She wasn't overthinking and fretting that this wasn't the way things were done in her books. She was free to give herself over to feeling.

"What is that smile for?" Jason asked, tracing the curve of her bottom lip with his index finger.

"I was just thinking that nothing like this ever happens in my books."

"Thank God," he teased her. "The last time I was

weighed against that standard I came up sorely lacking."

She lifted her head and bit the tip of his finger. "You have redeemed yourself. I am actually beginning to feel a little sorry for all those heroines. They have no idea what they are missing."

He gave her a light, tender kiss. "There's still plenty more to come. But this is better than your books, then?"

"Oh, yes!"

He gave her a lazy, mischievous smile. "And you're certain you never read about this?" He tweaked her other nipple.

Her back arched up off the floor. "No, never. Blast you, don't stop."

His smile deepened. "Then I feel fairly positive they never did this, either."

He untied the drawstring of her chemise and pulled at the fabric until her breasts were bared to him. "So beautiful," he murmured appreciatively.

Was that the sort of compliment one was supposed to respond to? It didn't make much sense. Breasts were breasts. Every other person had a pair—more if you counted portly men like Sir George. If hers pleased Jason, she supposed it was all to the good, but she really wished he would stop staring at them and go back to touching them.

Before she could voice her request, Jason bent his head and licked her breast, circling his tongue around her nipple.

Oh.

Then he gently worried the aching, hardened nub of flesh between his teeth.

Ohhhhhhhh.

When he began to suckle, she dug her fingers into the hard muscles of his shoulders.

"Oh. My. God." The words emerged on a strangled moan as pleasure rocketed through her body.

He raised his head. A lock of hair fell forward onto his brow, making him look particularly roguish. Or maybe that was the extremely satisfied grin he was sporting.

"Again?" He cocked an eyebrow.

"Forever," she told him, drawing his head back down. She felt his smothered laughter against her breast, and then there was only the pull of his mouth stirring up the most wicked, wanton, wonderful sensations.

She couldn't stop touching him. Her hands roamed restlessly over the smooth, broad planes of his back. She had never imagined what immense joy could be derived from the simple act of touching and being touched.

But it wasn't enough. With every new height he roused her to came the growing need for something more. She felt empty and achy inside, and she craved the fulfillment she sensed he could give her. Her hips rocked instinctively beneath him as if trying to direct him to the part of her that throbbed, demanding attention.

He took her mouth again, his kiss hard and passionate and frantic, as if he wanted to consume her. She understood. She wanted to devour him. To bind him to her. To drive him as insane as he was making her.

"God, Livvy," he groaned, raining kisses over her face. "I want to be inside you so badly."

His hips bucked against hers and she shifted, spreading her legs, guided by some knowledge as old as time.

He ran one hand along her side, tracing her curves. He didn't stop until he reached the hem of her chemise.

"Shall I show you what else is missing from these books of yours, Olivia Jane?"

Her eager nod was all the incentive Jason needed.

Lord, he had guessed she would be passionate, but her response to him was beyond his wildest imaginings.

And when it came to Livvy, his imaginings had been wild indeed.

He eased one hand beneath the hem of her chemise and slowly trailed his fingers up her calf. He felt his way around her garter, seeking the ribbon ties, and then wrenched his hand away at the sharp pain the action caused. He looked at his finger and saw a bead of blood welling up.

She rose up on her elbows. "What's the matter?"

"You stabbed me."

"I beg your pardon?"

He showed her the blood on his finger, and then popped it into his mouth to soothe the hurt. Even though his lips were nowhere near her, Olivia's entire body arched up as though he were sucking on her.

His eyes darkened in response.

"There must be a bloody pin somewhere. Come, let me find it and take it out before you hurt yourself on it."

Olivia scrambled up, shaking her head. "No, you tend your finger. I'll get it."

She looked almost . . . afraid?

"I am quite able to remove a pin, you know. And I shall take care not to prick my finger a second time."

"I really think it would be best if I did it," she said.

What the devil was she hiding?

"Don't be ridiculous," he told her. "I'll have done in a moment."

When she saw that he was quite determined, she laid back and flung an arm over her eyes.

In a moment, he understood why.

Though he hadn't seen it since he'd hidden it away all those years ago, Jason knew the brooch at once. He'd have to be blind not to, since the damned thing held his profile.

"Where did you get this?" he demanded angrily.

She scrambled away from him, fumbling to draw her chemise back over her breasts.

"Come, Miss Weston, don't you think it is a bit late for maidenly modesty? Now answer me!"

"I found it when I was in Scotland. W-when I was organizing the library. I took all the books off the shelves and your note fell out. I knew it was wrong, but I had to find where the clues led. I can't be sorry that they led me to you."

"And you said nothing, not a single word the whole bloody time you've been here. It's all been a lie."

"No!" she protested. "Please, Jason, you must listen to me. I wanted to tell you, honestly I did."

"Then why didn't you?"

"When? You weren't exactly a model of understanding and compassion when I arrived. If I had told you then, you would have tossed me out on my ear. And then ... Then, I just couldn't. I was too scared you would hate me," she whispered.

"What makes you think I don't?"

"Don't say that," she begged. "I know it seems like I've trespassed on your marriage. I never meant to try to take Laura's place. I only wanted you to be happy again. I know you loved her, but how long will you punish yourself with this unending grief?"

Jason rose slowly and donned his banyan in silence. He wanted to rant and rage, but doing so would allow her to win. He called on his former icy reserve. "I fear you've been laboring under a misapprehension, my dear. I am not mourning my late wife."

Her brows drew together in puzzlement. "You— You're not?"

"Women aren't worth grieving after. As you and Callista have both so thoughtfully reminded me this evening, you're all lying, manipulative bitches."

She gasped and took a step back as if he had hit her.

Her eyes were huge in her face, bewildered and bright with tears. Despite knowing she had lied to him from the start, Jason wanted to draw her close and kiss her until that look was once again one of dazed passion. Until she was lost to anything and everything but his touch and the passion that flared between them.

But more than anything he wanted to punish her for making him feel all those tender, protective feelings, even though she had betrayed him . . . just as Laura had betrayed him.

"Do you know where my wife was going the morning she was killed?" he demanded. "She was leaving me."

"What?"

It was his turn to nod, and he took no little delight in her complete horror at his revelation. The bitter truth had been bottled up inside him so long that he took a sick pleasure in releasing it, in spewing the acid venom at someone else.

"It was no accident that Lord Verney found her body. He was supposed to meet her in the park that morning. They were lovers."

She stared at him, totally aghast. "I believe you're mad."

"Cursed is the more popular theory, though I must confess it's their brides, rather than the Trahernes themselves, who seem cursed. They're the ones who wind up dead, after all."

The anger in her eyes astounded him. She was livid.

"Does that not suit your romantic longings? It's the sort of tripe that might have come out of one of those gothic novels you're so enamored of."

"What proof can you give me that your wife was involved with Lord Verney?" she demanded furiously.

Jason crossed his arms over his chest. "I don't need to defend myself to you, though I must admit to being surprised by your belief in my wife's innocence. I thought women were always eager to think the worst of each other. Of course, I suppose it must be galling to hear that another of your gender failed to uphold her marriage vows, but you may as well come to terms with the matter. Women simply can't help themselves. Eve herself was too weak to resist the serpent's temptation."

"I— You—" she spluttered.

His eyes narrowed. "Miss Weston, did you ever meet my wife? Is there some past connection that I am unaware of?"

For a moment he thought she was going to answer in the affirmative, but she shook her head.

"No . . ." she said slowly. "I may not have known your wife, but my aunt knew her. The staff here and at Haile Castle knew her. Servants talk, and I have never heard a hint of gossip about your wife to suggest she was anything other than loving and devoted to you and your son." She braced her hands on her hips. "You wonder why I am so ready to believe in your wife's innocence? I wonder why, as the husband who loved her, you are so quick to find her guilty?"

Something inside Jason snapped. He grabbed her shoulders. "Do you think any of this makes me happy? Do you think I was pleased to realize my wife was leaving me? To learn that even if she no longer cared for me she didn't love our son enough to stay and be a mother to him?"

He punctuated each question with a small shake.

"But this is life, Miss Weston, and facts have to be faced, even if they don't work out into the happy ending you wish them to." He let go of her. "I advise you to stick to your books. No relationship will ever measure up to the pretty portrait of perfection you've painted in your head. But I think you'll find books to be cold comfort when you lie awake at night, remembering the pleasure I gave you tonight—"

She slapped him.

The little hellcat had actually slapped him.

"I want you out of here," he told her.

"I don't particularly want to be here," she spat, "but I don't see another alternative."

"Then look harder. I don't care what lies you have to tell Katherine, but you are no longer welcome to reside under this roof. I have some business to attend to in Cardiff. I was planning on putting it off until you left, but I'll leave in the morning. I will be away for two nights, possibly more. I expect you to be gone by the time I return. Is that clear?"

She shook her head, swiping the back of her hand at the tears coursing freely down her cheeks. "Nothing is clear anymore." She gave him one last searching look and then bolted from the room.

He watched her go, unable to shake the feeling that he had somehow failed her.

Damn her.

Damn the treacherous hearts of women.

He headed for his chamber to pack. The sooner he got away from here—from her—the better.

He needed to leave before she could look at him again with those big, beseeching blue eyes. Before she made him feel things he didn't want to feel. Before he was tempted to turn and look back.

Chapter 14

"What is love? 'tis not hereafter;
Present mirth hath present laughter;
What's to come is still unsure:
In delay there lies no plenty;
Then come kiss me, sweet and twenty,
Youth's a stuff will not endure."
Twelfth Night, Act II, Scene 3

Olivia ran straight to her aunt's chamber. Her heart was breaking, and she wanted her mother, but her mother was in Essex at Weston Manor. Aunt Kate was the next best thing.

Her emotional state had further deteriorated during the minutes it took her to get to the other side of the castle, so by the time her aunt opened her door, Livvy threw herself into her arms, sobbing.

"Good heavens, darling, what's the matter? Are you ill?" Her aunt ushered her into the room.

Olivia shook her head.

"Come sit near the fire. Let me fetch you a dressing gown before you take a chill."

Her aunt wrapped her in a cozy quilted robe, and then sat beside Livvy, rubbing her back until her sobs quieted to sniffles and the occasional shuddering breath.

"I suppose you must be wondering why I woke you," Olivia said. "I'm sorry, but I didn't know whom else to—"

"Hush. Clearly something has upset you. I would be hurt if you felt you could not come to me, no matter what the hour. As to what has caused this upset, I trust you will tell me when you're ready."

"I am afraid something has come up. I need to leave here as soon as can be arranged."

"I see." Her aunt looked at her, assessing. "And might this 'something' have to do with my stepson?"

"It might," Olivia allowed.

Aunt Kate took her hand. "I can tell you care for him, and I believe he cares for you."

She ignored Livvy's snort of disbelief.

"Do not let him scare you off. Beneath that gruff exterior is a man who needs love and is quite capable of giving it in return."

"I'm not being scared off so much as I'm being run off the premises. We had a . . . a bit of a disagreement this evening. He—" She took a deep breath. "He doesn't want to see me again. Ever. He's planning on leaving as soon as possible, and he will not return until I am gone from this place."

"That seems most extreme. This argument must have been quite serious."

Olivia twirled a lock of hair around her finger.

"I wouldn't call it an argument precisely." Unable to meet her aunt's gaze, she rose and walked over to the bed. She climbed up and sprawled on her back, hugging a pillow to her chest. She stared at the intricately embroidered bed curtains as she searched for the right words.

"I am still finding it hard to believe. The change was so sudden. Everything was going so well, I thought—" Her throat swelled. "Well, regardless of what I thought, I feel certain he was making progress."

"You are speaking of Jason, I take it, but progress toward what?"

"In moving past his grief," Olivia explained. "That was one of the reasons why I wanted to come here, you know."

"I confess I did not. You told me that you wanted an adventure."

"I did, but I wanted to help Jason, too. I suppose he was to be part of my adventure in a way. For all the novels I've read, I never really believed in divine plans and the like, but I know I was meant to come here." She rolled over onto her side so she could see her aunt. "Fate sent me. Or perhaps it was Laura."

"Laura?" Aunt Kate sounded startled. "Do you mean Jason's wife? What could she possibly have to do with your coming here?" She gave Livvy a worried frown. "I know I said the Marchioness's Chambers had a ghost the first day we came, but I didn't mean it literally. I only mean that the memory of her is still very strong here."

Olivia sighed. "Yes, that's just the problem."

"My dear child, I am afraid you have quite lost me. I think perhaps you had best start at the beginning."

"It might take some time," Livvy warned her.

"Then you had best begin now, had you not? I can hardly help you without understanding the situation."

"I suppose it all truly began while I was reorganizing the library at Haile Castle. I pulled one of the volumes off the shelf and out fell a bit of foolscap, folded and sealed with a dab of wax."

"Why do I doubt you had the fortitude to put it back unread?"

"It might have been important. In any case, the wax needed to be removed. It was making a terrible mess of the endpapers."

"Your concern for the endpapers prompted you to read a private correspondence?"

"Well, I might also have been the tiniest bit curious as to the contents."

"I confess I would have been as well. Come now, do not keep me in suspense. You cannot dangle a juicy morsel like that without expecting me to bite." She moved to sit with Livvy on the bed, and for a moment Olivia felt as though she were home, sitting up late to gossip with her sister.

"It was a riddle to a hidden treasure!" Even in the retelling, Livvy could not help but get excited.

"How intriguing! Were you able to solve it?"

"I know I shouldn't have even tried, since the treasure wasn't meant to be found by me, but I couldn't help myself."

"Well, did you find a treasure?"

Livvy nodded. "It was a little brooch with a shadow portrait. The back had a bit of engraving on it, so tiny I needed a magnifying glass to read it." She quoted the verse that had become etched upon her heart: " 'So we shall be one, and one another's all.' "

"Shakespeare?"

Livvy rolled her eyes at her aunt's guess. "I should hardly consider *that* a treasure. No, the poet is Donne. The final clue was hidden in a volume of his verse."

"Donne," Aunt Kate murmured. "He was William's favorite poet. Jason's, too, I think. There were many evenings when he and Jason took turns reading aloud from one of his books while Laura and I worked at our embroidery. . . ." Her eyes widened and she looked at Olivia in dawning horror.

"When you said that you knew that the treasure wasn't for you, were you being hypothetical or did you know whom the treasure was actually meant for?"

Livvy licked her dry lips. "There was a name on the paper that fell out of the book," she whispered.

"Laura." It wasn't a question.

Olivia jerked her head in assent.

"I trust that is the whole story?"

Olivia shook her head. "Not quite. I was fascinated by Jason. Any man who took such time and care planning a surprise for his wife must have loved her very deeply. From what little you had said of him, I suspected he grieved as deeply as he had loved. It sounded as if his grief was destroying him. I wanted to help him in some way, though I hadn't the faintest idea how to go about it. I meant everything I said about wanting an adventure as well. When I asked to come to Wales with you and Charlotte, I thought to accomplish both. I just hated the thought of him languishing here."

She wiped at her eyes. "And then, just before we were to leave, when I was putting the last of the books away in the library, I came upon a diary. Actually, it was Izzie who found it, but as soon as I realized whose it was I wouldn't let her read it."

"And whose was it?"

"Laura's," Livvy whispered. "What clearer sign could there be? I felt more certain than ever that someone or something wanted me to come here."

"I take it you read the diary?"

Olivia stared at her, as if to say, *Do you really need to ask?*

"And Jason knows all of this?"

"Oh, no! I suppose I should be quite dead if that were the case. He only knows that I found the brooch . . . and the clues. The brooch was hidden behind the frame of an old painting, so he would never believe I just happened upon it."

Her aunt pressed her index fingers to her temples. "But how would he know you found the brooch in the first place? You wouldn't be so stupid as to tell him!"

"Of course not!" Olivia said scornfully. "But I don't think you really wish to know how he found out."

Aunt Kate looked at her blankly.

"I kept the brooch pinned to one of my garters. It

seemed quite safe there, as it was imperceptible underneath my dress and petticoats. You never noticed it, did you?"

"Obviously not, but if the brooch was, as you say, imperceptible, then how did Jason see it?"

Olivia bit her lip. "He didn't. See it, that is. Not at first. Unfortunately one of Jason's fingers met with the point of the pin, and . . ." She shrugged.

Her aunt closed her eyes. Perhaps she was praying. A miracle was most definitely in order.

"Of course," Livvy added, unable to stop herself, "if Jason had not been trying to untie my garter, he would never have found it, so this is really all his fault."

Aunt Kate let out a strangled groan.

"Fine. Mostly his fault," Olivia conceded.

"I am less concerned with whose fault it is than how much damage has been done. How much do you know of the relations between men and women?"

"Izzie was wretchedly closemouthed, though she did warn me about being alone in a closed carriage with a man. And I have, of course, read a great deal."

"I see," her aunt said, with the voice of someone who did not see at all.

"In fact," Olivia continued with a satisfied smile, "though you must never, ever tell my parents, I was the one who planned Izzie's compromise."

She really was pleased at how well that had worked out. Granted, there had been a few moments when she hadn't been at all sure she'd been wise in urging her sister to follow her heart in such a bold fashion, but it had all come right in the end. And if questioned, Livvy would swear up and down that she had known it would all along.

Aunt Kate was staring at her with a mixture of awe and horror.

"Oh, don't look at me like that. I knew from the very start that everything would turn out for the best."

"Mmm-hmm."

"I did," Olivia protested.

"Regardless," her aunt said, "your sister's compromise is not the issue at hand at present. Yours is."

Livvy looked at her in surprise. "Mine? But I've not been compromised."

"Are you entirely certain?"

"Entirely, no. Mostly, yes. Not that it matters. I wouldn't marry him if he asked."

At least not without some abject groveling. What was she thinking? She could never marry a man with such a low opinion of her sex. And then there was the lamentable fact that he was insane....

But you love him, some inner voice whispered. *Underneath the anger and hurt, there is love.*

No, whatever she had felt for him, it had not been love. She had fooled herself into believing it was love because she had been swept up in the adventure of it all. The fact that she had wanted to comfort him even while he raged at her simply meant she was an extremely compassionate human being.

"Dearest, it is understandable that Jason was upset about finding the brooch. It must have been a shock to him and—"

"I understand that," Olivia snapped. "And I apologized. Would you believe, I even apologized to him the very first night we were here? I had an idea that Laura's chamber was some sort of shrine to her memory, and I felt I was trespassing." She gave a bitter laugh. "How stupid I was!"

"I don't understand."

"He's not grieving," Livvy shouted, then she lowered her voice. "All this time he hasn't been grieving for

Laura. He doesn't need help mending his heart. Do you know why? Because he hasn't got one. Do you know what he thinks Laura was doing the day she died? He thinks she was having an affair, that she was running away with her lover."

"My God." Her aunt looked shaken. "No, I cannot believe she—"

"Of course she wasn't. She was helping Charles by paying off his gambling debts to Lord Verney. *That* is why she was meeting him that morning. She was afraid to tell Jason what she was doing because he'd forbidden her to help Charles out of another scrape. It's all there in her diary."

"And have you spoken to Charles about any of this? You two became close friends rather quickly."

"As you know, I have a dreadful propensity for blurting out whatever is on my mind. It was only a matter of time before I made some suspicious comments, and then I had to explain about the diary."

"Was he angry?" Aunt Kate inquired.

"Relieved. He's spent all this time believing himself responsible for his sister's death. Being able to talk about it, about her, has gone a great way toward easing his mind."

She saw her aunt had started to cry. She sat up and placed a hand on her shoulder. "Aunt Kate—"

"Oh, that poor boy!"

"Charles will be all right, truly he will," Olivia assured her.

"I know, my dear." She wiped at her eyes. "I was speaking of Jason."

"*Jason?*" Livvy was outraged. "I don't see why you should feel sorry for *him*!"

Aunt Kate took Olivia's hand. "I know you don't, love, but there are still many things you don't know about him. No, before you ask, I am not going to tell you. You will have to wait for Jason to do that. But know that while his accusations regarding Laura are upsetting, they have very little to do with her and a great deal to do with a very old hurt."

"His mother, you mean?"

"You know about her?" her aunt asked with no little surprise.

"He told me she'd been killed in a carriage accident while running off with her lover."

"It's true. Naturally, both families wanted to avoid a scandal, and they might have done had not one of the servants found a note stating, in no uncertain terms, that the marchioness and her lover were running off together." She shook her head in disgust. "Whomever it was that found the note must have made a tidy sum off it."

"Oh!" Livvy gasped. "You don't mean—"

"The contents of the note were reprinted in the *Daily Post*. The ton loves a scandal, and this was the most shocking affair since the Duke of Lansdowne's daughter ran off with his stable master. Well, you know how gossip spreads, and it wasn't too long before the boys at Harrow got wind of it. From what William told me, Jason got into terrible rows trying to defend his mother's honor. He refused to believe she was running off when she was killed, but then what child wants to believe his mother consciously deserted him?"

Livvy's heart ached for that little boy. She could envision him clearly, for he must have looked very like Edward. She remembered Edward's stoicism during the asthma and imagined Jason putting on the same brave face while daring the larger boys to repeat the slander. What she wouldn't give to go back in time and comfort that lost, angry little boy.

"William had no choice but to tell Jason the truth about his mother. After that, Jason never spoke of her,

and he ignored all of William's attempts to discuss what
had happened. William was never convinced Jason had
moved past his mother's abandonment. Though Jason
was already a grown man when his father and I wed, I
vowed to look after him. It seems I've muddled that."

Her expression became thoughtful.

"But perhaps it is not too late to make things right,"
she mused.

She met Olivia's eyes.

"Do you love him?"

Livvy didn't realize she was crying until she tasted
the salt of her tears. She nodded miserably, unable to
speak.

"Oh, my dear!" Aunt Kate pulled her into her arms.
"Don't cry. It will all work out, you'll see. Now lie down
and close your eyes. You must get some rest. We've a
busy day tomorrow, what with packing and planning
how to bring my stepson to his senses."

The plotting began at the breakfast table.

"I think the first thing we must decide is where we are
going," Aunt Kate told Olivia. "Remaining here would
be a wonderful act of defiance, but I don't think it would
do much good. He can't miss you if you never leave. Do
you want to go home to Weston Manor?"

Livvy sighed. "It's silly, but I feel as though going home
would mean the adventure is over. Besides, Mama is sure
to realize something isn't right and she'll persist in ques-
tioning me. I'm afraid I'll tell her everything, and—"

Her aunt held up a hand. "Say no more. We'll go to
the town house. I'm afraid London will be quiet this
time of year—"

"That is quite all right. I have no desire to see anyone."

She rose and began to prowl around the parlor, pacing back and forth like one of the caged lions at the Tower of London.

Her aunt looked up from her plate and shook her head, a slight smile upon her face.

Olivia frowned. "What?"

"Oh, nothing. I was just thinking it wasn't so long ago that I was sitting and watching your sister try to wear holes in the carpet. You girls certainly know how to keep life interesting for your old auntie."

Olivia went over to her and rested her cheek against the top of her aunt's head. "You're hardly old, Aunt Kate. Besides, just think of this as practice for when Charlotte is older."

Lady Sheldon reached up and patted Olivia's cheek. "Heaven forbid."

Charles entered the room and Livvy launched herself at him.

He laughed and wrapped his arms around her, patting her back. "Livvy, my love, if this is the kind of enthusiastic greeting I get for sleeping in, I vow never to rise before noon again." He set her apart from him. "Enough of that now. Jason can't be long behind me, and I have no wish to arouse his ire."

"There's no fear of that," Livvy said. "He's gone. That's why I must speak with you."

She waited until he had got some food, and then seated herself next to him.

"Jason and I had a bit of an altercation last night."

"What exactly do you mean by 'altercation'?" Charles asked warily.

"A lovers' quarrel," Aunt Kate supplied helpfully.

Charles's face lit into a grin. "Finally!"

"It was not a lovers' quarrel," Olivia ground out.

"Call it what you like," said Aunt Kate, getting up and moving toward the door. "I'll leave the two of you alone now. I think it's best if you two work out the next bit on your own."

Once her aunt had gone, Livvy faced Charles, her face grim. "When Jason returns, I need you to tell him the true circumstances of Laura's death."

Charles's face grew shuttered. "No. You know as well as I do that he'll not forgive me. He'll prevent me from seeing Edward. What's happened is in the past. As you've said, it can't be changed. There's no reason to revisit it."

"Yes, there is. I learned something last night that changes everything. It's not pleasant, but you need to know." She took a deep breath. "Jason hasn't been mourning your sister all this time."

"I don't understand."

"All these years, it's not grief he's been consumed by, but hatred. Charles, he thinks Laura was having an affair."

It took a few moments for her words to sink in.

Charles pushed back his chair and jumped to his feet. "That's outrageous. No one who knew Laura could ever believe her to be capable of such a thing. That bastard. How dare he think that. She loved him. She would have done anything for him. That's how she was with the people she cared about. That's why she could never say no to me—" His voice cracked and he sat down heavily, burying his face in his hands.

"I'm so sorry, Charles," Olivia said softly. "But you must see that it isn't fair to your sister's memory to have her husband, the father of her child, so mistaken about the circumstances of her death. Aunt Kate believes there is some reason, something that has to do with his mother, which made Jason misconstrue the circumstances of Laura's death. Until he knows the truth, he won't be able to heal. He'll never find peace."

"I'm not certain he deserves it," he said angrily, getting to his feet.

Livvy told herself to be patient.

"I thought so too at first, but what would Laura want you to do, Charles? Isn't it time you grow up and take responsibility for your actions? Jason deserves to know the truth. And if you won't tell him for his sake, do it for mine."

She swallowed past the lump in her throat.

"I love him," she whispered. "I didn't want to fall in love. I never meant to. But I did. And now I'm terrified. He's a good man. I know he is—" Her voice broke on a sob.

Charles pulled her up out of her seat and enfolded her in a hug. "I'm sorry, Livvy. Don't cry. You're right. He's a good man, and it's long past time for me to confess my sins. Whatever my penance, I'll do it. Don't worry, Jason will come around. I always knew I was blessed to have Laura for a sister. Now I shall be doubly blessed, for when you and Jason wed I'll gain another beloved sister."

Olivia sniffed. "Jason is lucky to have you."

"I'll have to rely on you to make sure he realizes it."

"I think he knows. Deep down."

"As in, somewhere between the eighth and ninth circles of hell, deep down?"

Livvy gave a watery laugh as they sat back down. "I am lucky to have you, too. I never thought I should want another brother. You will see why when you meet my older brother, Henry, but if all brothers were as nice as you I should want dozens."

He patted her hair. "I guess I didn't tell you about the time I took the heads off of all Laura's dolls."

Olivia laughed and shook her head. "And so the fantasy ends. Henry did that to Izzie once, but she got him back. I believe Weston Manor is the sole possessor of a headless rocking horse. I shall never forget the way Henry screamed when he woke to find a horse head in bed with him."

"Good Lord! Remind me never to get on your sister's bad side."

"She can be quite terrifying," Livvy agreed, "but I must confess that I was the one who came up with the idea."

"Why doesn't that surprise me?"

Olivia shrugged. "It's a gift."

Charles choked on his eggs.

Livvy got up and pounded him on the back. "Aunt Kate and I have been making plans," she said. "We are leaving for London later today."

"Then I will take my leave as well."

Livvy frowned. "But you have to stay and talk to Jason."

Charles shook his head. "You'll have to get Jason to come to London for that. I suspect my brother-in-law will try to kill me when he finds out, and when he does, I would at least like the chance of someone overhearing my screams for help."

Chapter 15

"O mistress mine, where are you roaming?
O, stay and hear; your true love's coming,
That can sing both high and low:
Trip no further, pretty sweeting;
Journeys end in lovers meeting,
Every wise man's son doth know."
Twelfth Night, Act II, Scene 3

The Marquess of Sheldon's Town House, London

"Are you certain?" Olivia asked, her voice quavering. "You can't just ask me to marry you and then decide to take it all back, you know."

The dark head kneeling before her looked up, nodding. "I love you, Livvy."

Her eyes filled with tears and she brushed at them with the backs of her hands.

"You're not going to cry all the time, are you?" he asked. "Because that wouldn't be very fun."

"I'll try not to," she promised.

"Now you are betrothed," Charlotte pronounced. Then she hissed, "Give her the gift, Edward."

Edward pulled a watch out of his pocket and thrust it at Olivia. She admired it, not knowing what else she was to do with it. It was a fine piece of work, with the family crest engraved on the front and a large ruby set into the clasp. She tried to hand it back to Edward.

"No," Charlotte said, "that's for you to keep."

"It's a symbol of my love and demotion," Edward added.

Livvy fought back a smile. "That's a lovely gesture, Edward, but I have a feeling this doesn't belong to you."

"It will," Charlotte reasoned. "It belongs to my brother, and the things that are his will be Edward's someday. I told Edward he had to give you a present after he proposed. It was the only thing we could find that was small enough to bring. There wasn't that much room, you know."

Oh, she *knew*.

When they had set off three days ago, Charlotte had been insistent that Mister Dog, as she had named the puppy Jason had given her, ride along in the carriage with them. Aunt Kate had said she wouldn't consider it. The resulting tantrum had been so deafening, Livvy had begged her aunt to give in this once and allow the dog to lie on the floor.

When they reached their first stop, Aunt Kate saw the puppy had not only slobbered all over her pink kid slippers but had also managed to chew the satin bow off one foot, and she declared she wouldn't travel another mile with such a horrid, smelly beast. She ordered Dimpsey to fetch the dog's crate, and Charlotte began to howl. Her reason became apparent when Dimpsey returned with Edward instead of the crate.

"It seems we've acquired another pup, my lady. He was hiding in the crate."

Aunt Kate had trained a steely gaze on her daughter. "The crate has to be latched from the outside, does it not?"

"Yes, my lady," Dimpsey answered.

"Then *someone* must have assisted in stowing him away. Charlotte, might you be able to guess who this *someone* is?"

The little girl hugged Queenie to her chest and affected her most innocent look. "No, Mama."

"Do not lie to me."

"I'm not lying," Charlotte said. "You asked me if I could *guess* who it was. I know very well it was me, and you can't guess at something you already know."

Aunt Kate let out a long-suffering sigh. "I begin to understand why some mothers eat their young."

They decided that Edward might as well accompany them to London, where they could ensure he would be properly supervised. They dispatched a groom back to Arlyss with a note for Gower explaining the situation and asking that he notify his master as soon as he arrived home.

And that was how she had come to be in the nursery of her aunt's town house—actually, she supposed the place truly belonged to Jason—holding what was undoubtedly an heirloom (also belonging to Jason) that Jason's son had given her to seal their betrothal. She wondered that she had been so desirous of an adventure. How had she forgotten that heroines were made to suffer dreadfully before the happy ending? They were always crying, complaining of raw nerves and the sense of impending doom.

She could commiserate.

Jason was not going to be happy about this development with Edward.

She looked sternly at both children. "While this watch may be Edward's someday, it is not his now. The two of you cannot go around snatching things that don't belong to you. Stealing is very wrong."

"We weren't stealing," said Charlotte. "We were more . . . borrowing."

Livvy could see she was fighting a losing battle. She sighed and slipped the watch into her pocket, making a mental note to see it was returned.

"Are you mad?" Edward sounded worried.

"No, of course not. I know you meant well."

Her voice wobbled on the last word. She grabbed Edward to her and kissed his cheek. Lord, she adored both of these children. She'd already started thinking of Edward as her own, and she knew exactly what could come of that—heartbreak.

Edward screwed up his face in distaste and rubbed at his cheek. "You're not going to cry again, are you?"

"Of course not," Olivia sniffled.

"You *sound* like you're going to cry," Charlotte said accusingly.

"Be quiet, Char. Isn't it about time for the two of you to go help Cook? No, I haven't forgot about your punishment. What you did was very naughty. But perhaps if Cook gives a good report of your work Dimpsey can take you to Astley's later."

"Oh, Astley's is lovely, Edward. And maybe we can go to Gunter's afterward for an ice." She danced around in anticipation.

"Only after you have helped in the kitchen," Olivia reminded her.

"If I'm going to marry you, I don't think I should be doing work in the kitchen." Edward crossed his arms over his chest.

Livvy thought fast. "You're right. I just had no idea that you were going to take your responsibilities as my betrothed so seriously."

Edward glared mutinously at Charlotte. "You didn't say anything about responsibilities," he hissed. Then he looked back at Olivia. "What sorts of responsibilities?" he asked suspiciously.

"As my betrothed you must stay by my side and pay lots of attention to me. If I want to go somewhere, you must escort me and stay with me until I am ready to leave. You have to play the games I want to play, and you must let me win most of the time."

Edward was appalled. "I'd rather work in the kitchen!" He looked apologetically at Olivia.

Livvy laughed. "Well, I suppose I would be very mean to hold you to our engagement. You are hereby released. I only ask that you think of me fondly the next time you get betrothed."

His relief was palpable.

"Of course, this means you will have to go down and help Cook. . . ."

Edward nodded and grabbed Charlotte's hand. They ran out of the room before she could change her mind.

She went downstairs and sat in the drawing room. She hadn't been there more than five minutes when there came a knock on the door.

Dimpsey poked his head round the door. "Sir Charles to see you, Miss Olivia. Shall I show him in?"

"Too late," Charles said, pushing past Dimpsey as he entered the room. "How are you, my dear?"

"Quite well, actually. And you? Are you ready to bare your soul to the devil?"

"I only have to do so if you manage to get the devil to come to London. The odds of that happening . . ."

"Are not even in question," Olivia told him, her eyes twinkling. "It just so happens that I have something belonging to Jason that I feel fairly certain he'll want to claim. I have no idea how long he actually stayed away for, but as soon as he returns to Arlyss, he'll be on his way to London. He might be on the road this very minute."

"What would he want so badly? Laura's diary?"

Olivia shook her head. "No, but that reminds me. Let me fetch it from my chamber and hand it over to you. After you have spoken with Jason, which will happen imminently, please give it to him. I believe he is the proper person to take possession of it. I'll just be a moment."

She moved to the door and was nearly bowled over by Charlotte and Edward running into the room. "Uncle Chas!" they chorused.

Charles's jaw dropped at the sight of his nephew.

"Told you so," Livvy preened. "Oh, don't look at me like that! It's not as if I kidnapped him. We found him hidden among the baggage at our first stop."

"That was my idea," Charlotte put in proudly.

"I don't doubt it," Charles assured her.

"What are the two of you doing here? You're supposed to be helping Cook. It's hardly a punishment if you're not there to do the work. Off with you, now." She shooed them out of the room. "I admit it is difficult to punish them when their plans have fallen in so well with our own."

Charles gave Olivia a pitying look. "I suppose so. If your plan is to give Jason apoplexy."

As if scripted, someone began furiously slamming the brass knocker on the door. Livvy and Charles looked at each other. It could only be Jason. Moments later their suspicion was confirmed when an angry shout rang out through the house.

"I think that's my cue to hide," Livvy said.

Charles nodded. "And mine to leave."

"But you can't *leave*. You have to talk to Jason."

"Now?" he exclaimed. "Do I *look* like I have a *death wish*?"

The man had a point.

"You don't have to *talk* with him right now, but you must at least talk with him *about* talking with him. Otherwise he'll take Edward and leave London before you get the chance."

"Wouldn't *that* be a pity," Charles muttered.

"Charles . . ."

He held up his hands in surrender. "Very well. I had best get it over with now."

"Yes," she agreed, "you *had*. And I shall be right here listening to make certain you *do*."

Jason was going to do one of two things when he got hold of his son. He was either going to throttle him or he was going to hug him so tightly his ribs would crack. Then again, maybe he would do both.

"Edward!" he yelled as Dimpsey silently divested him of his hat, coat, and gloves.

"Hello, Jace. You made good time."

"Charles! What the hell are you doing here?"

"Katherine sent round a note asking me to call. What a shock to find Edward here!"

"It was more of a shock to find him not at home," Jason said pointedly.

"Yes, yes, of course, but he's none the worse for his little adventure, so no harm done, eh?"

"His 'little adventure,' as you put it, took ten years off my life. Christ, what if he'd had one of his episodes? The doctors warned me about the air in London."

"He didn't have one, so there's no point in dwelling on it, but if he had, I expect Katherine could see to him just as well as you could. Keeping him at Arlyss won't make him safe, Jace, not when it's his own body turning on him."

Though he didn't want to, Jason had to acknowledge the truth of his brother-in-law's words. "You're right. That's the truly damnable part of it all. I can't protect my own son."

"Protection is just another way of expressing love, and Edward couldn't ask for a more loving father, though I have a feeling he'd be grateful if your love extended to getting him off of kitchen duty."

Jason frowned. "What on earth is he doing there?"

"He and Charlotte have both been ordered to help Cook for part of each day as punishment. What say you and I rescue them and take them out for a bit? It seems a shame for Edward not to see London while he's here."

"I had planned to head home as soon as I collected Edward."

"What difference will it make if you wait until tomorrow? I'd like to spoil my nephew a bit and take him to Astley's or to a show of Punch and Judy. We can bring the children back here afterward and eat at White's. I'll hazard a guess you don't want to dine here. I understand something happened with Miss Weston and you all but kicked her out of the house."

"Er—"

"Deuced uncomfortable to have to sit across the table from her." Charles gave him a sympathetic look. "We'll have a meal blissfully free of feminine chatter, and then perhaps you would agree to stop by my apartments. There's an important matter that's come up that I must speak with you about privately."

"Jason?" His stepmother's voice carried from the upper levels of the house in unusually strident tones. "I heard you bellowing, so there's no use pretending you aren't there. I shall be down in a moment. We need to have a talk, you and I."

Charles patted Jason on the back. "Don't worry, old fellow. I'll fetch the children. You just step outside and wait for us."

"You have my undying gratitude," Jason told him, heading for the front door before Katherine could catch him.

"I hope you remember that later," muttered Charles.

After a visit to Astley's and a trip to Gunter's for an ice, which Charlotte insisted on, Jason was more than ready for a relaxing evening at his club. He was surprised to realize how much he had missed the rich masculine decor and the low hum of men in conversation. And nothing could compare to the cellars at White's. He was feeling quite mellow by the time they reached Charles's apartments in Bayswater.

"Well, Charles," Jason said as he followed him into the small sitting room. "What's all this about? Don't keep me in suspense any longer. What grave secret have you been keeping from me?"

Charles had begun to pour out two snifters of brandy, but he jumped at Jason's words and the liquid sloshed over the sides of the glass. He fumbled in his pockets for a handkerchief, but before he could find one Jason was already mopping up the mess with his own.

Jason eyed his brother-in-law. "Jesus, man, you look like you're about to be sick. Sit down and put your head between your knees."

"No. I— I've got to get this out before I lose my nerve. I should have told you years ago. I—" He brushed the back of his hand across his forehead, swiping at the beads of sweat that had gathered there. "Lord, I knew this would be difficult, but it's even worse than I feared. How did I let Olivia talk me into this?"

"Olivia! What does she have to do with this?"

"I don't suppose you would be willing to forget I mentioned her name?"

"Not on your life," Jason replied with grim determination. Then he slapped his palm against his forehead. "She told you about our disagreement, didn't she?"

"Yes, but—"

"That little witch doesn't know when to leave well enough alone. I warned her to stay out of my affairs, but did she listen? No, she kidnapped my son—"

"But Edward admitted he—"

"—and now she is trying to destroy this family with unpleasantness better left buried. Lord, I am sorry you had to find out like that. I had hoped to keep it from you.

Or was that what you wanted to tell me? That you've known all along?"

"Not exactly."

"Just sit down and take your time, Charles. If it's waited years, I'm sure it can bide a few minutes longer. Besides, whatever it is, I doubt it's as bad as you believe."

Jason strolled to the window, hoping a bit of distance between them would ease the other man's nerves. What in God's name could he be hiding? There had been real remorse in Charles's face and a genuine glint of fear in his eyes.

Jason's thoughts were diverted by the sudden tumult taking place where a crowd had gathered on the street below. A Runner was wrestling to take custody of a young man, little more than a boy from the looks of it. Two of the hotel porters were holding on to the lad, whose attire, black from head to toe, gave away his criminal occupation.

"I do believe they've caught a burglar out there," Jason remarked. The thief was wriggling and jerking about, trying desperately to free himself, but he was no match for the larger men.

Charles got up and came over to take a look.

"He's putting up a good fight for such a small fellow," Charles said admiringly.

Jason frowned. There was something about the boy that didn't add up. He didn't have the lean, underfed look one usually associated with street urchins. His coat had ridden up during the scuffle with the porters, revealing a most nicely rounded— Jesus, what was wrong with him? Was he really still so hard up from his encounter with Olivia that he needed to ogle any arse that came into view?

He turned from the window and walked across the room to the brandy. He picked up his glass but, on second thought, he set it back down. He'd clearly already had too much to drink if pederasty was beginning to appeal to him.

Christ.

The lad's posture was wrong, too. Even in disgrace, it was dignified, erect. The kind of posture trained into aristocratic children from birth. And there was something about the arrogant tilt of the boy's head, the way he stuck his chin in the air, which seemed horribly familiar.

A very, very bad suspicion took root in the pit of Jason's stomach.

"Charles, tell me quickly, does this important matter you have to discuss with me concern Olivia?"

"Yes, in a way. I already let it slip that she was the one who talked me into meeting with you."

"And did she know we were meeting here?"

"I suppose so. She was listening in the drawing room when we were discussing our plans for the evening. Why?"

"I think she tried to listen in here, too." Jason strode back to the window. The police cart was gone. *Damn.* He braced his shoulder against the frame and heaved the window open.

"Hey, you there," he called out to a peddler woman. "Can you tell me what happened just now? There's money in it for you." He drew back a moment and instructed Charles to fetch some coins.

"They caught a thief," the old woman said. "A Runner come an' took 'im off. Only 'im what were the thief said 'e weren't an 'e at all but a *she*." The crone's cackle revealed a mostly toothless grin. "An' *she* said she were the daughter of a lord, no less. They'll be takin' 'er, I mean 'im, or whate'er it was straight to Bedlam if'n they knows what's good for 'em—"

"Charles?" Jason held out a hand.

"I don't have anything smaller than a crown," he complained.

"Then I suppose it is this woman's lucky day." He took the coin and tossed it down to her. He didn't wait to hear her thanks; he was already shutting the window.

"Get your coat," he told Charles, "and be quick about it."

Charles looked at him with horror. "She couldn't mean that the thief who was taken off was . . . It's not possible, I tell you. It's just not possible. It's like something out of one of those cheap novels Olivia is always— Oh. Oh, no." .

Jason's expression was grim. "My thoughts exactly."

Olivia was furious. And cold. And, though she hated to admit it, a bit frightened. She had never thought the truth might be thought so outlandish as to be impossible. Surely, she had pleaded with the constable, one or two young ladies of respectable upbringing had been caught sneaking about the streets of London. Meeting a lover, perhaps. He had allowed this to be true, though never on his watch, but a lady of quality would never, he intoned, roam about dressed like a boy.

Olivia wished she could tell the man that stealthy business was much better conducted in breeches than skirts, but she doubted it would help her cause.

This was all Charles's fault. He must have known she'd want to listen in, and he'd gone and set the meeting at his bachelor's quarters, that wretch! Didn't he realize he wouldn't be speaking to Jason at all if she hadn't clued him in to what was going on? Excluding her was the very height of rudeness!

If there was one thing Olivia hated (well, there were a lot of things she hated; forty-seven, according to the last list she'd made), it was being excluded. She'd been excluded by her parents and older siblings for being too young, and she'd been excluded by the younger ones for being too old. She'd been excluded because she was female, and she'd been excluded because she was unmarried.

She'd decided that this time she wasn't going to stand for it. Not when her future happiness hung in the balance. She needed to know how Jason responded to Charles's confession. She felt she couldn't trust Charles's observational skills with a matter of this delicacy and importance, and she really hadn't wanted to wait for those observations until the following day. And, foolish though it might be, Livvy needed to be close to Jason when the blow fell. He wasn't the sort of man to admit he needed comfort, but she wanted to be near enough to provide it all the same.

She'd vowed to spy on the men and listen in on their conversation if it was the last thing she did. And it might be. Stealing was a hanging offense, and the constable interrogating her thought she was a thief.

Olivia wanted to bang her head against the wall, but it looked dirty and sort of . . . crawly. She shivered. When she'd slipped Jason's pocket watch into her jacket, she'd thought herself remarkably clever. She would be able to keep track of the time and, heaven forbid she found herself in trouble, she'd have an expensive bargaining chip. Now it might be the noose around her neck.

"Now, missy," the constable said sternly, "even if I did believe you were out to meet a lover, which I don't, there's still the matter of this watch." He pulled it out of his pocket, where he had placed it for safekeeping, and inspected it in the dim light. "You've confessed to it not being yours."

"Of course it isn't mine. What use would a woman have for a gentleman's pocket watch? But I didn't steal it."

"Then how did it come into your possession, eh?"

"Well, that's a bit more complicated, but if you would just see reason, you would realize I could not have stolen Lord Sheldon's watch from the hotel because he isn't staying there." Olivia gave the constable her most winning and, she hoped, convincing smile.

"So the watch belongs to this Lord Sheldon, does it?"

"Yes," she agreed, wondering if she was digging herself into a deeper hole, "but the marquess isn't staying at the hotel—"

"The *marquess*? Odsbodlikins, an' this could turn into a fine mess! And how would you know where he's staying? Been tracking the cove's movements, like?"

The constable's speech, Livvy learned, deteriorated when he was upset. Of course, she had been watching Jason, but she decided the good constable didn't need to know that. She shook her head emphatically. "When he is in London, Lord Sheldon resides in Mayfair. As I told you earlier, my aunt was married to the current marquess's father, and I have been staying with her at Lord Sheldon's town house."

"Well, an' if that's the case, I should see you home. We'll go pay a call on her ladyship right now, shall we?"

Olivia shook her head violently, horrified by this suggestion. Her reputation would be ripped to shreds if anyone saw her being hauled like a common criminal before the front door of the town house. And someone *would* see her, no matter the late hour. The residents of Mayfair thrived on scandal, and so did their servants. Within minutes a crowd would be gathered to witness her disgrace. Come to think, that had already happened once tonight but, by the grace of God, she hadn't been recognized.

If word of this escapade got round she would never be able to hold her head up in Society, not that she would ever again be allowed out of her room once her mother caught wind ... She swallowed hard at the thought.

The constable smirked. "Changed your mind, have you?"

"Not for the reasons you suspect," Olivia sniffed. "I don't wish to bring scandal down upon my family, and your presence in Mayfair would cause nothing but trouble. It doesn't follow that I came by the watch dishonestly."

"Aye, and I suppose you'll next be telling me that the marquess himself made you a present of it."

"No. Not exactly." The situation was so ridiculous, hysterical laughter began to bubble up inside her.

The constable frowned. "This isn't a laughing matter, miss. What do you mean, 'not exactly'?"

A nervous giggle escaped her. Then another. "I'm terribly sorry," she trilled. "The marquess did not give me the pocket watch."

The constable scribbled something in his notebook.

"His son, Edward, presented me with the piece just this morning. It was a small token of his affection in light of our betrothal."

"Now see here. Are you telling me you're engaged to Sheldon's son?"

"No," Olivia sighed, "I am afraid not. Lord Bramblybum decided we wouldn't suit, no matter how good my bedtime stories were."

The constable closed his notebook with a sharp slap. "If you think I'll be gammoned into some Banbury tale about a *Lord Bumblebun*—"

"Bramblybum," Livvy corrected.

"I don't know what game you think you're playing at, miss, but it's my guess that a night here won't do you any harm and will make you a mite more cooperative and inclined toward making sense."

The air left Olivia's lungs in a whoosh.

"No, please, I'm sorry. Edward did give me the watch this morning, truly he did. And he really is Lord Bramblybum. I know it sounds ridiculous, but it's true. I was at the hotel tonight because I wanted to eavesdrop on a conversation between the marquess and his brother-in-law. I know I must seem stupid to you—indeed, I wonder at my own foolishness—but it is very difficult being shut out of things, and these sorts of plots always seem to work in books. I used to know where the stories in books ended and real life began, but lately everything seems so confused that I can't quite tell the two apart the way I ought."

She was so miserable, so utterly appalled at the situation she'd got herself into, she put her face in her hands and began to cry. The night had started out so exciting. As she'd sneaked out, dressed in a motley ensemble of dark clothing she'd somehow cobbled together, Livvy had thought how she was more like her older sister than she had imagined. She was supposed to be the rational sister. The one who planned and made lists. And to some extent she still was, since she could have easily made a list of all the reasons why she shouldn't be doing what she was doing, but she was still doing it. Caution and common sense had deserted her.

At least Izzie'd had an excuse when she'd sneaked out. She'd done it to save James's life. Livvy's only excuse was morbid curiosity. Izzie had also been going from their home in the country over to the neighboring estate, while Livvy planned to set off into London.

Charles's quarters were in a fairly fashionable neighborhood, so it wasn't as if she was heading into a slum, at least not if she didn't get lost, but there was no arguing that the city was a far more dangerous place. Her sister's purpose—seduction—had smacked more of impropriety than Olivia's plans to eavesdrop but, perhaps because she was acting on selfish curiosity, Livvy had felt what she was doing was a little more ... wicked.

Jason Traherne seemed to have that effect on her.

Of course, the more Livvy had thought about everything that could go wrong, the more tempted she'd been to abandon the plan and spend the evening safely curled up with a novel. But even if she could have trusted Charles to give a good account—which she couldn't—and even if she had been certain Jason would not need consoling—which she wasn't (she was only certain he wouldn't be vocal about his needs)—Olivia believed she had the right to be present at this meeting ... or to listen in, at the very least.

She had come too far and had given too much of herself to sit quietly while someone else decided what to do. For the first time in her life, instead of reading about heroines, Livvy had been determined to finally act like one and see her adventure to the end. In hindsight, she would have done well to remember the discomfort and despair heroines experienced for the better part of each book.

Disappointed in love? Yes.

Raw nerves? Most definitely.

Sense of impending doom? Absolutely.

In all truth, she didn't want to be a heroine ... or a thief, for that matter. She just wanted to be Olivia Jane Weston. She fumbled around in the pockets of the jacket. "Oh, bother," she hiccuped. "I should have known he wouldn't keep a handkerchief in his pockets." She looked up at the constable, allowing all her emotions to show on her face. "A man with no feelings wouldn't have need of one, would he?"

"You're telling the truth, aren't you?" The constable handed her his handkerchief. "At first it was too ridiculous to be the truth, but now it's too complicated to be anything else."

Olivia nodded.

"Look, Miss—"

"Weston," Olivia supplied.

"Look, Miss Weston, I'm willing to let you go, but—"

"You will?"

Oh, thank heaven! There was still time for her to get back home before anyone realized she wasn't actually in bed with a headache.

"*But* I don't like the thought of you going about on your own. It's late and the streets are no place for a lady."

There was a loud crash in the outer room and a man began to shout.

"See what I mean?" he said. "London is full of ruffians. Heaven only knows what this one's done. Better stay back, miss."

Livvy gulped. She knew that shout. . . .

"I'm afraid that's not a ruffian, sir," she told the constable. "It's a marquess."

Chapter 16

"These most brisk and giddy-paced times."
Twelfth Night, Act II, Scene 4

Jason was frantic with fear as he burst into the police office. He was absolutely furious, too, but he would deal with that once he knew Livvy was safe. He and Charles had gone straight to Bow Street, but Olivia wasn't there. The magistrates and constables on duty had been greatly amused by their tale, but their laughter had faded when Jason had given one of them a black eye. He had never in his life been so glad to be the Marquess of Sheldon. It had been the only thing preventing them from locking him up.

He and Charles decided it was possible that they had beat Olivia to the magistrate's court, but after a time it became clear that she was not going to show up. Jason had been sick with worry. Had she managed to get away and was now wandering the streets of London? Had the Runner who'd taken her realized who she was and decided to hold her hostage? Scenarios flashed through his mind, each more gut-churning than the next. He'd sent Charles back to the town house to wait for a ransom note.

He didn't know what else to do. This feeling of helplessness was becoming distressingly familiar. As he got up to leave, one of the constables approached him.

"What?" Jason snapped, perfectly willing to hand out

another bruiser to the next person who thought the situation funny.

The man, a dark, wiry chap, was not cowed by Jason's foul temper. Of course, given his profession, that was likely a good thing.

"I only mean to help you, my lord. I've been thinking of this servant girl what you told us about."

With a thought toward Olivia's reputation, Jason had claimed he was trying to find one of his servants who had been wrongly mistaken for a thief when she'd tried to meet up with him at his brother-in-law's apartments for a spot of fun. No great harm would come if it got bandied about that the Marquess of Sheldon was tupping one of his maids.

"You said the girl was taken outside the hotel. There aren't any places catering to the Quality that I know of around here."

"No," Jason agreed. "My brother-in-law's apartments are in Bayswater."

"Then she won't be brought here," the constable said. "She'll have been taken to the office on Great Marlborough Street."

"Great Marlborough Street." Jason repeated the words as if they were a lifeline and he a drowning sailor.

"More like she's there than here, leastways," the man said. "Number twenty-one, it is."

Jason could have kissed the man, but he restrained himself, as he thought such an action might result in his being locked up in truth. He bolted outside and hailed a passing hackney. After telling the driver he would double his fee if he got them there quickly, Jason was treated to a bone-jarring, tooth-rattling, profanity-filled jaunt across the city, though the profanity could not be blamed solely, or even mostly, on the driver.

After paying the driver more than the man probably

earned in a year, Jason ran up to Number 21 and banged loudly on the door. Something else he was getting used to.

A bleary-eyed porter led him into an undecorated room where a group of men lounged around at desks, each clearly doing his part to ensure the safety of the citizens of London.

No Livvy in sight.

"Where. Is. She?" he growled.

The men gave each other knowing looks.

"That's a guinea you owe me, Potts," one man said, rubbing his hands. "I told you the fancy bit would have some sort of rum cove protector. You *are* here for that pretty little bird Yardley brought in?"

"I am," he bit out.

"Must be a tough little nut," mused the man. "Yardley don't hold with no nonsense, and the interrogation has been going on for ages."

Interrogation?

"Damn you," he yelled, lunging for the man, "what have you done to her?"

The man scrambled out of his chair, knocking it to the ground in his haste to get away from Jason. "You nobs are all mad," he muttered. "I haven't done anything to her." He jerked his head toward a door at the far end of the room. "She's in the back."

Jason charged in the direction of the door the man had indicated. God help him, if this Yardley bastard had touched a single golden brown hair on her head . . .

He threw open the door.

Livvy.

Thank God.

She did not, he noted, look particularly pleased to see him. In fact, she almost looked angry.

She crossed her arms over her chest. "What are you doing here?"

What was he doing there?

Jason's eyes narrowed.

That was it. He was, quite simply, going to kill her.

"Oh, the watch," she said suddenly. "Of course. I didn't realize they'd sent for you. Look, my lord, I understand you're none too fond of me just at present, and I know you didn't actually see Edward give me the watch, but I hope—"

"What the devil are you talking about?"

She frowned. "Aren't you here to charge me with theft?"

"Why would I do that?"

The constable who must be the no-nonsense Yardley came forward. "I believe this is yours, my lord," he said.

She'd stolen his grandfather's pocket watch?

"I have no intention of pressing charges. Miss Weston has an unfortunate tendency to pinch valuables, but only those belonging to me."

He could practically hear Livvy grinding her teeth.

"I am endeavoring to break her of the habit," he continued, "but having her criminal tendencies made public would likely ruin her."

"I understand, my lord."

"I don't," Olivia said angrily. "I'm still trying to figure out what you are doing here."

"I'm here to rescue you."

Her eyes had lightened to the stormy color they turned when she was vexed.

"Why would you want to rescue someone you despise?"

Jason kept a tight rein on his temper. Of course, if he just went ahead and strangled her here, he'd save the constables a trip later.

"There is no need to be dramatic, Miss Weston."

"And there is no need for you to rescue me, *Lord Sheldon*. The constable has agreed to release me." Up went that chin into the air.

"Well, that isn't quite true, miss."

"But you said you would let me go!" she protested.

"You didn't let me finish. I told you I didn't want you out wandering the streets alone. I will let you go, but *only* if you are accompanied."

Jason took a very good opinion of Constable Yardley.

"I am happy to release you into Lord Sheldon's custody now, or you can send for someone else if you like."

"I'll send for Sir Charles," she said after a moment's pause. "This is his fault."

"Do you know where Charles is, Miss Weston? He's waiting at the town house hoping to receive a ransom note."

She licked her lips nervously. "Is he so angry he wants me to be held for ransom?"

"*No!*" Jason thundered. "When we didn't find you at Bow Street, there was no knowing what had become of you. If you fell into the wrong hands . . ." He swallowed hard. "If you were to be ransomed, they would leave you alive and untouched. *That* is why Charles is hoping for a ransom note."

"Oh," she said in a small voice.

"My brother-in-law has a great many stupid exploits to his name, but I'll not allow you to pin this on him. Perhaps he should have known. . . . No, even I would never have believed you capable of this had I not seen it with mine own eyes, and I am far better acquainted with your scheming."

Her eyes, so distraught only moments before, now glinted with fury. "My scheming, as you call it, was done to help you. You're right; this isn't Charles's fault at all. This is your fault."

"*Mine?*" Jason exploded.

"Yes, *yours*. I sneaked out to overhear your talk with

Charles, but you and Charles wouldn't have been having that talk if you weren't such a heartless beast!"

She spoke everything in one breath, getting progressively louder so that she was almost shouting at the end.

Jason took her arm in a firm grip. "I am taking you home," he said in a low tone. "If you struggle, I will toss you over my shoulder and carry you out. In that position I could quite easily administer the swats to your backside you have earned with this outlandish stunt. I doubt very much that any of the men here will object to my actions. Do you understand? Very well, I shall take your silence as consent. Thank you, Constable, for keeping her safe. She won't bother you again."

"You'll see to it she keeps out of trouble, then? I can't say I envy you such a task."

"Oh, I assure you it won't be difficult."

The constable laughed. "Going to lock her in a dungeon, eh?"

"No," Jason said, his voice serious. "After what she's put me through tonight, I am going to kill her."

To her amazement, Olivia managed to hold her tongue while Jason hailed a hackney and for the duration of the ride from Great Marlborough Street to Grosvenor Square. She wanted to speak, but Jason was so stiff and silent beside her, she feared if she said anything he might be tempted to make good on his threat. Instead she focused on the coach, which was decidedly shabbier than the one she had taken earlier. It had probably belonged to a nobleman at some point, but the silk upholstery was shattered, revealing clumps of horsehair padding that was no doubt host to all manner of disgusting vermin. She shuddered at the thought, grateful for the mask of darkness. If she could not see the nasty creepy-crawlers, then, she decided, they simply were not there. Fortunately, the ride was short, and she survived without being murdered by the marquess or nibbled to death.

The elegant square was quiet, as nearly all of its well-heeled inhabitants had departed for their country estates some months earlier. Jason must have told the jarvey to go around to the back, for they rumbled past the Sheldon town house, which was easy to pick out, as it was the only one with lights in the windows. It wasn't until she was alighting from the coach, when she reached for skirts that were not there, that Livvy remembered she was still dressed as a boy. She stood by while Jason paid the driver and suddenly, now she was home safe, the enormity of what she had done sank in. Trembling, she sank to the ground, buried her face in her knees and began to cry.

The driver cracked his whip and drove off in a loud clatter of hooves on cobblestone. Jason cursed under his breath, then picked her up and carried her up the steps to the back door. He juggled her weight to one arm to rap on the door, and Olivia buried her face in his shoulder, too ashamed to meet the curious eyes of whoever let them in.

"Oh, thank heaven you found her!" Aunt Kate cried as Jason strode inside. "Olivia Jane Weston, of all the harebrained notions you've taken into your head ... You might have b-been k-killed!"

At the sound of the break in her aunt's voice, Livvy broke down. Self-loathing filled her as she thought of all the distress she had caused with her selfish, reckless conduct. Of course, she knew Aunt Kate would forgive her, and, somehow, that only made her feel worse.

"Just like a woman," Charles remarked. "Only crying once the time for tears is in the past. Come along, there's no point in standing in the hall when there's a nice fire waiting in the drawing room."

Livvy recalled what Jason had said about Charles

waiting here, hoping to receive a ransom note so he would know she was alive. . . . She curled her fingers into Jason's coat and pressed her face harder into the wool, trying to muffle her sobs.

"Miss Weston's scolding will be postponed until the morrow," Jason said as he followed the others up the stairs to the ground floor. "Ah, Dimpsey, I should have known you would be waiting with the others. Help your mistress to her room and tell her maid to make up a sleeping draught. I'm taking Miss Weston to the drawing room. She needs to warm up and take a dram of brandy before bed; she's trembling like an aspen leaf. Charles, I trust you can show yourself out."

"Very good, my lord," Dimpsey voiced his approval. "Shall I come back after to assist you with Miss Weston?"

"That won't be necessary. I doubt she'll get into more trouble tonight. I don't know where Katherine has you sleeping, but there should be a small bedroom close to the nurseries you can make use of. I want someone near the children at night."

"Of course, my lord. As it happens, the marchioness was of the same mind and placed me in that very room. Here, my lady, take my arm. . . ."

The conversation faded to incoherent mumbling as Jason carried her down the hall to the drawing room. She eased her head from his shoulder to peek at him. He might have been carved from stone, so firm and unyielding was his expression. The arms holding her were also stiff with coiled tension. He might have sounded calm and controlled to the others, but his fury hadn't abated in the slightest.

He set her down in a chair by the fireplace before walking over to the sideboard. He poured what had to be several drams of brandy into a crystal tumbler but, rather than bringing it over to her, he tossed back the

contents without pausing for breath. He splashed a tiny
bit more liquor into the glass, then looked over at her.
He muttered something unintelligible, then shook his
head and turned back to the decanter.

Again he filled the tumbler and quickly drained it,
tilting his head back to swallow the last drops of liquid. Livvy's eyes were drawn to his large Adam's apple,
which moved up and down with each contraction of the
strong muscles of his throat. He radiated masculinity
and power and—she flinched as he set the glass down
with unnecessary force—anger. She could easily imagine this man as her Mad Marquess, prowling the moors
and terrifying the maids.

He turned to face her, but still he said nothing. He
simply watched her behind hooded eyes that gave her
no indication of what he was thinking. She shivered and
hugged her arms close about her. She had nothing to
be afraid of, she reminded herself. After all, Constable
Yardley hadn't taken his murderous threat seriously.
But, as the silence dragged on, her nerves stretched
closer and closer to the breaking point.

Just when she thought she could bear it no longer, he
started toward her. Before she knew what he was about
he had lifted her in his arms once more. She opened her
mouth to tell him she was perfectly capable of walking
and could see herself to bed, but he stopped her with a
sharp shake of his head. Given his current mood, she
decided it would be wise not to argue. If he wanted to
carry her up another two flights of stairs, who was she
to object? She did think, however, that such a desire
indicated an unbalanced mental state, for she was not
nearly as light as the proverbial feather. But he made no
complaint as he carried her, nor was he the slightest bit
out of breath when he paused at the landing. Livvy was
about to tell him not to worry, that she could manage
the next bit on her own, when he abruptly turned away

from the stairs and began walking down the corridor. Her breath caught in her throat as she realized he was taking her to *his* chamber. . . .

He shifted her weight as he opened the door, and then slid her down his body until her feet touched the floor. Oh, my! It was quite impossible to mistake his arousal. Was he planning on having his wicked way with her before he killed her? Lord, she hoped so!

She opened her eyes as he moved away to shut the door. There was something in the set of his shoulders that told her the evening had been as difficult for him as it had been for her.

He came forward to face her. "Well, what do you have to say for yourself? It had better be good because I am as close to beating a woman as I ever have been in my life."

She said nothing, but wrapped her arms around him, pressing her body against his.

He stood rigidly in her embrace.

"I'm sorry," she whispered.

His arms came up, clasping her to him so tightly it bordered on painful.

"Do you have any idea how worried I was? Hell, it was pure chance that I recognized you as the thief being carted away. What if the constable hadn't been an honorable man? I sent Charles back here to wait for a bloody ransom note."

She began to cry again as she nestled her head into his chest. "I'm sorry, Jason. I'm so sorry."

With a strangled groan he pressed a kiss into her hair.

"Don't ever scare me like that again, Livvy. Do you hear me? You are never to try anything so foolish again. My God, when I think what could have happened to you out there alone . . . I'll lock you up. I'll barricade you in the Old Tower at Arlyss and—"

She slid a hand up to cup his cheek. "Shhh," she soothed him. "I'm safe."

"Damn you, Livvy, you will not placate me so easily. Tonight was easily the worst night of my life."

Oh. With everything that had gone on she'd forgotten that he'd spoken with Charles.

"Would it help to talk about it?"

He shook his head, and part of her was relieved.

"What's done is done," he said. "I don't want any more recriminations or accusations tonight."

"W-what do you want?" She tried to sound seductive, but she couldn't keep the worry out of her voice. She needed him. Here. Now. If he refused her . . .

"I want you, damn it."

Her mouth met his eagerly, as desperate for the taste of him as he was for her. Her hands crept up to circle his neck, and her fingertips traced lazy circles on his nape. She felt those circles on her own body, on her breasts, and lower, at her very center. She stood on her toes and pressed herself into Jason, loving the way his hardness provided the perfect counterpoint to her softness.

His breathing was ragged.

"Stop me now, Olivia."

"I don't want you to stop." She rubbed herself against his length.

He groaned. "I'm trying to be noble, damn you."

She shrugged. "All the heroes I read about are noble."

"Then you appreciate my restraint?"

She pulled away from him and began unbuttoning her coat. Well, it was really *his* coat. . . .

"You stole my coat as well?"

"It wasn't stealing, exactly," she said, remembering Charlotte's defense. "It was more borrowing. And Edward and Charlotte were the ones who took the watch. Edward gave it to me when we got engaged this morning."

"I beg your pardon? Did you say you are engaged to my son?"

"Not anymore. He decided working in the kitchen was preferable to marrying me."

"Smart boy," Jason said approvingly.

"Knave." She threw the coat at him. "What happened to being noble?"

"The fact that you're not already naked in my bed is a great testament to my nobility," he responded.

A delicious shiver ran down Livvy's spine.

"It occurs to me," she said, "that the heroines in my books might have a great deal more fun if the heroes were a little less noble and a little more ..."

He threw the coat aside, and took her hands. "More what?"

"A little more wicked." There, she'd said it.

He looked amused. "You want me to be wicked?"

She leaned up and planted a kiss on the underside of his jaw. "Only if I can be wicked with you."

The amusement faded and was replaced with hunger. "God, Livvy, you're going to be the death of me."

She reached down between their bodies and ran her fingers along his hard arousal. "You feel very much alive to me."

He grabbed her hand, stilling it. "You want wickedness, my little adventuress?"

"Yes," she breathed.

"You're certain?" he asked.

"Jason?"

"What?"

"I told you to stop being so damned noble."

She felt his laughter against her mouth as he kissed her. His hands swept up to cup her breasts. "What have you done to yourself?" he muttered. He pulled her shirt out of her breeches and lifted it over her head, and then glared at her bound breasts.

"Never again," he chastised her.

"No," she agreed. "It's most uncomfortable."

"Damn," he cursed. "I can't get the knot untied."

"Let me—"

But he had already bent down and ripped the cloth with his teeth. She found the primitive gesture unbearably arousing.

He took hold of one end of the linen bandage and gestured for her to spin. She raised her hands above her head and began to turn. He watched her intently, like a child carefully unwrapping a present, taking as much pleasure in the act of opening the gift as in the gift itself.

Well, perhaps he took a little more pleasure in the gift, she thought as he began to fondle her, smoothing away the lines left by the bindings. She tugged at his hair, wanting his mouth on her again.

"Slowly, my sweet."

He chuckled as he looked at her velvet knee-breeches, which were more like just-below-the-calf-breeches on her.

"I must say these are quite fetching on you. Wherever did you find these relics?"

She blushed. "Yours were too big, and Edward's wouldn't fit over my hips. I found these in the attic."

"They must have belonged to my father . . . or maybe my grandfather."

"I'm afraid I got them filthy when I sat down outside."

He moved to inspect her backside. His nose wrinkled. "I think you brought the worst part of the mews inside with you. Take them off at once."

She shook her head. "Then I'll have nothing on except my boots and stockings."

"My dear, the general idea is that soon you'll have nothing on at all. You didn't mind taking off your shirt."

"You've already seen those parts of me. You haven't seen the, um, lower bit yet."

"I promise I will like it just as much as your upper parts," he vowed. "I thought you wanted to be wicked, Livvy."

It was a challenge she couldn't resist.

Her hands moved to the falls on her breeches. Her face felt fiery as she slipped the buttons from their holes, but she met his gaze as she let the breeches fall to the ground.

He stared at her, his eyes hungry.

Discomfited by such scrutiny, she picked up the breeches and held them in front of her. *Ugh*. They really did smell.

"I don't think so," Jason said, pulling the clothing from her grasp. He walked over to one of the windows. "Let's give the street sweepers something to talk about." He raised the sash and dropped the breeches outside.

Livvy felt ridiculous wearing only her stockings and leather half boots, so she quickly took them off while Jason dealt with closing the window. And then she was standing there, naked as the day she was born.

Jason turned and saw her. For a long time he just looked at her. When he finally spoke, the words sounded as though they were being wrenched from his soul.

"After all the years I have doubted, you make me believe there is a God after all. Only He could create something so perfectly divine."

Tears filled her eyes. "I love you, Jason Traherne. You don't have to say it back. I know you need time to adjust to everything. But even if you never say it, I will still love you."

"Livvy—" His voice broke.

"It's all right, Jason. What is not all right, however, is the fact that you are still fully dressed."

"You've seen all there is of me to see. I want to admire you."

"I am really not sure how much there is to admire," she said, suddenly self-conscious.

"Plenty," he declared, prowling toward her. "Shall I start from the bottom? Your toes are quite tantalizing."

"My toes?" She laughed. "Honestly, Jason. What's next? My ankles?"

"If I skipped to your ankles, I would be neglecting the very attractive arches of your fair feet." He knelt before her and ran a finger along her insole.

She giggled and danced away from him.

"Ticklish, are you? How delightful."

Livvy shrugged. "My brother has always thought so."

"I have a very different agenda than your brother." He pulled her back to stand before him. "Now, shall we continue?"

"If we must."

"Oh, we must. I am a supplicant at the feet of my goddess. I need to pay homage to your alluring ankles, your comely calves, your kissable knees. . . ."

His hands moved up her legs in accordance with his words, and her knees received the kisses that were apparently due to them.

"My kissable knees are feeling a bit unsteady," she told him breathlessly.

He rose to his feet, scooped her up and carried her to the bed. A maid had turned down the red velvet coverlet, which Livvy thought a pity as she imagined the velvet would feel quite sinful against her naked skin.

She watched in fascination as Jason stripped off his clothes, each discarded article revealing more muscle and man. Someday, when she could manage to keep her hands off him, she would draw him thusly, but she didn't see that day arriving anytime soon.

He climbed onto the bed and stretched out beside

her. He cupped her face in his palms, smoothing the pads of his thumbs over her cheeks. "This is your last chance to escape, my little adventuress. I still have the strength to let you go, if that is what you want."

Livvy sensed the unspoken meaning in his words and wondered if he was having second thoughts. She didn't want to ask him and risk breaking whatever spell had bewitched them. Neither of them knew what the morrow would bring, but she couldn't bring herself to care.

She wanted him.

Wanted them.

Wanted this night.

She was going to spend the rest of her life being safe; tonight she wanted to experience passion. She turned her face and pressed a kiss to his palm. "And if I don't want to go?"

He rolled on top of her and kissed her until her toes curled.

"In that case, I think I'll stay," she gasped when he lifted his head.

He nibbled at her throat. "You must tell me if there is anything you don't like."

"I doubt there's much chance of that."

"Says the woman who didn't like kissing."

"Temporary insanity brought on by too much book learning," she pleaded.

A devilish gleam came into his eyes. "Then we had best stick to activities that were not in your books. If I recall correctly, you said there was no kissing here."

He placed light kisses on first one breast, and then the other.

She pouted. "I hardly think those count as proper kisses."

He moved off her.

"I didn't mean you should stop!"

He laughed. "Don't worry. I'm not stopping, just readjusting."

He leaned some pillows on the headboard and sat back against them. He guided her to sit astride his hips, and then brought up his knees to support her.

"I can feel your man part poking my behind," she told him. "I don't like it. Make it stop."

Evidently she had said something hilarious, because Jason laughed until there were tears in his eyes.

"I don't like you laughing at me, either," she informed him. "I believe I will go now."

She began to climb off him, but his hands clamped around her waist.

"You are not going anywhere. I'm sorry for laughing, pet, but I don't think your books were very informative. Unfortunately I can't make my man part stop poking you. It's his, er, way of showing affection, and believe me when I say he feels a tremendous amount of affection for you. I think I can distract you enough that you won't mind him so much. All right?"

She nodded.

He drew her head forward and placed light, teasing kisses on her forehead, her cheeks, and the tip of her nose, before taking her mouth in earnest. Her blood heated as their tongues tangled together in some primal dance. She couldn't get enough of him, of his taste, his smell, his touch.

She grabbed his hands and brought them up to her breasts. He squeezed and kneaded the sensitive flesh, rubbing her nipples with his thumbs. Livvy instinctively spread her thighs wider and arched her back, giving him better access.

He groaned and broke their kiss, eagerly drawing her breast into his mouth.

She threw her head back as he suckled, lost to everything but the pleasure he was giving her. Her fingers tangled in his hair, holding him captive. Her love slave. Now there was an idea for a good book. . . . She gasped as he caught her nipple between his teeth, and then obeyed the urge to rock her hips against his.

The movement seemed to ignite a fire in Jason. In a flash he had rolled them over so that she was on her back and he was on top of her, still settled between her thighs.

He kissed her temple. "It's time for you to become acquainted with my, er, man part," he said against her ear.

She nodded. Anything to make the ache inside her go away.

He reached down between their bodies and fitted himself against her opening. He began to push inside her.

"Oh, Jesus," he moaned. "So hot and wet."

"I don't like this," she whispered.

He pushed in a bit farther.

"I said *I don't like this*," she hissed. "You're hurting me."

He froze above her, looking desperate. Then he kissed her and worked his hand between them, finding a spot that sent streamers of pleasure unfurling through her body. Her entire focus seemed to narrow to that one point between her thighs.

His fingers found a rhythm that made her cry out, and her hips arched up, driving him deeper inside her. To her surprise, it didn't hurt anymore. She wriggled her hips experimentally.

He sucked in his breath.

She did it again.

His hips flexed, and then he was in her all the way.

Filling her.

Completing her.

He pulled out of her and thrust back in, and suddenly it was all too much.

She went spinning into space, adrift on a wave of pleasure so intense she couldn't breathe. She hovered there for an endless moment before crashing back down. As soon as she fell, the pleasure started building again.

She heard someone panting and pleading, urging Jason to let himself go. Then she realized that someone was her. She returned to herself just as Jason cried out, his hips jerking wildly as he shot his seed within her. Those last thrusts were all she needed to fly back over the edge, this time with him.

He collapsed on top of her, his heart racing and his lungs working like bellows. After a few minutes, he pushed himself up and rolled onto his side.

"That," he said, "was incredible."

She grinned. "I was going to say extraordinary."

"Better than your books?"

She nodded. "I find there is quite a bit missing from my books. Now I know, perhaps I ought to write a book to address the issue. I am certain other young women would find these missing bits most enlightening."

"Heaven help us."

He tucked her against him so that her back was to his chest. She had never felt so safe, so sheltered as she did surrounded by the warmth and strength of his body.

"Jason?" she whispered.

"What is it, pet?"

"Upon closer acquaintance, I think I like your man part," she whispered.

He laughed. "Believe me, sweetheart, we are both excessively relieved to hear that."

Chapter 17

"I may command where I adore."
Twelfth Night, Act II, Scene 5

Jason yawned and stretched, and then came instantly awake as his hand brushed across what felt like a breast. His eyes shot open as the events of the previous evening rushed back to him. He turned his head to look at Livvy.

She was still sound asleep, curled on her side in a little ball. Her lips were parted, which would have been tempting but for the little snuffling noises coming from her mouth. He had exhausted her but good!

Jason folded his arms behind his head and settled back with a satisfied smile. He had no regrets about what had happened last night. No, this wasn't exactly how he'd planned his life, but there were certainly benefits to marrying Olivia. Marriage to Olivia. The thought wasn't as terrifying as he had expected it to be.

He had known what he was doing by taking her innocence, and he was willing to accept full responsibility. God knew *someone* needed to take responsibility for her. The chit needed a keeper, and he figured he was as good a man to keep her as any. He wasn't sure he believed that she loved him, since women were prone to exaggeration in these matters, but he felt certain she cared for him. She wouldn't have given herself to him if she didn't.

Then there was his son to consider. Edward was devoted to Livvy, and she had displayed a maternal warmth and tenderness toward him from the very first.

As for him, he enjoyed her companionship, both in bed and out of it. She made him laugh, she made him think, and she sure as bloody hell made him lust. And this time, when he stood at the altar and spoke his vows, he would do so with the understanding that love had nothing to do with it.

Olivia seemed the loyal type, and he doubted she would stray, but then he had thought the same about Laura. He had come to accept that women were fickle creatures incapable of fidelity. It was best not to expect too much. That way, one couldn't be let down. As long as he didn't mix up lust with love, he would be fine.

He kissed her shoulder, breathing in her scent of roses and warm, sated woman. Just the smell of her got him hard. He hated to wake her, but there would be trouble if she was found in his room. He'd been lucky to wake when he did and not to the startled shriek of one of the maids.

"Livvy, sweet, you need to get up."

She made an indistinct yet definitely negative sound.

"I know, pet. You can go back to sleep once you're tucked safely away in your own bed, but the servants will be up soon, and there's going to be trouble if anyone finds out you spent the night here."

She flopped onto her back and opened up her eyes. That morning they were the color of a jay's wing. When she saw him, her face lit into a smile. Then she yawned. "Good morning," she said sleepily.

"Yes, it is a very, *very* good morning."

He bent down and kissed her, unable to help himself. She opened her mouth to him at once, a little sigh escaping her. He wanted nothing more than to spend the morning making love to her, but that was not to be. He reluctantly raised his head.

Olivia pouted and reached an arm up to curl around his neck, dragging him back down to her. He chuckled as he gave in and kissed her again. She brought her other arm up and trailed her fingers down his back in a feathery caress. He couldn't hold back a moan of pleasure.

"Livvy, I must see you back to your room before you are missed."

She sighed. "I wish we could be like this always."

"I think we'll have to leave the bedchamber every now and again, pet."

"No," she said. "I mean you and me. Like this. Waking up together."

"I have no issue with sharing a chamber. When I get old and fat and begin to snore, you may change your mind, but we can cross that bridge when we come to it."

"I don't understand. Aren't you going back to Arlyss with Edward straightaway?"

"That had been my plan, but I thought you would prefer to get married here—"

"Married!" she exclaimed, shock written all over her face.

"Damn it, Livvy, I knew what I was doing when I took your innocence."

Well, that wasn't entirely true. He had been out of his mind with lust. He just hadn't been displeased with the consequences come morning.

"Did you think I would seduce you, and then abandon you? Is your opinion of me really so low?"

"No, of course not," she said hastily, "but you didn't really take my innocence so much as I gave it to you. I never meant that you should be tied to me. I guess I didn't give much thought as to what would happen."

"No, you didn't. While it's unlikely, you could already be carrying my child."

Her radiant smile told him the thought clearly pleased her; she practically glowed with excitement.

"You'll be an excellent mother, Livvy. Both to Edward and any other children we might have."

"I want to believe this is all possible," she said slowly. "More than anything I want to marry you, to bear your children, to raise Edward as my own. I want to go to sleep in your arms every night and wake up there each morning. . . ."

"But?"

"But this all seems so sudden. Just days ago you were convinced women are inherently incapable of fidelity—"

He still thought that, but it seemed prudent not to say so.

"—and now you want to get married?"

He shrugged and simply said, "Last night changed things."

Her expression was thoughtful for a moment, weighing his words, but he must have allayed whatever reservations she had, since she flung her arms around his neck.

"Oh, Jason, I love you so much! I didn't think it was possible for a person to be this happy!"

She began running her hands over his body and pressing kisses to every part of him she could reach. "I don't know what's the matter with me. I can't get enough of you."

He stroked her hair. In the early-morning light the color was more like wild honey than chestnut. She looked every inch the wood nymph he had once imagined her. Her skin was as creamy white as snowdrops, and her rosy mouth was sweet as wild strawberries.

Pure magic.

And somehow she was his.

"If it makes you feel any better, I feel the same way," he told her.

She moved restlessly on the bed. "I feel I've an itch, but I can't get at it to scratch." Her face screwed up in frustration. "Is this wanting as uncomfortable for you as it is for me?"

He nodded solemnly. "Having you in my house has been a constant torment."

"Oh," she said in a small voice.

"Goose! I was teasing you. Though I will admit I've had to ease myself in the washroom a great deal more often since I met you."

"Because you have been drinking more?" she asked slowly, her expression puzzled.

It took him a moment to understand her meaning, and then he had to fight to hold back his laughter. "While your presence has doubtless increased my consumption of spirits, I wasn't using the washroom to relieve myself."

She regarded him blankly.

"A man can, ah, ease himself if need be," he explained. His cheeks burned and he had a horrible suspicion he was blushing like a green lad in the presence of a pretty girl.

After a moment he saw the flash of recognition. Her blue eyes gleamed with excitement. "How?"

He shook his head. "This isn't the sort of thing that young ladies are supposed to know about."

"Don't you dare turn all staid and proper, Jason Traherne. I am not some dainty creature to be protected and coddled."

"What if I want to protect and coddle you?"

Her eyes narrowed. "If you don't tell me, I'll ask someone else. Perhaps Charles will tell me."

Jason nearly choked envisioning his brother-in-law's face upon hearing such a question.

"You wouldn't," he said. Then he looked at the very stubborn set of her jaw and sighed. "You would, wouldn't you? Very well, a man can relieve his, er, frustrations with his hand."

"I don't understand. Women have hands. Why is it only men who can do this?"

"I can't believe we're having this conversation," he grumbled.

The worst part was how aroused he was getting from such bawdy talk. She was insatiably curious. Or perhaps she was simply insatiable.

"Women can do it, too," he gritted out, trying hard not to think about her touching herself. Not, he was certain, that she would ever think of doing so. "It's just easier for a man."

"That doesn't seem fair." Her tone was peevish.

"Life rarely is," he agreed.

"Would you show me?"

He swallowed hard, struggling for control.

"Livvy, this is not the time for this conversation. You must get back to your own chamber."

She squinted at the clock on the mantelpiece. "Pooh, it's only a little after four. Even the most diligent servant won't be up until half past five." She looked at him appraisingly. "It doesn't take longer than that, does it?"

He tried to laugh, but it was difficult. He was so hard he hurt. "My sweet, given the stimulating talk we've been having, I would probably last a couple minutes at most."

"Show me," she demanded.

"I—"

He nearly shot out of the bed as her hand snaked under the sheets and curled around his cock.

"Oh, God," he croaked.

"You've become quite the believer of late," she noted, running her fingers up and down his length.

"Jesus Christ," he hissed.

She grinned wickedly up at him, before removing her hand.

"*Show me,*" she commanded.

Jason knew there were reasons why he shouldn't give in, but quite frankly he couldn't think of a single one. Probably because there wasn't any blood left in his head. It had all rushed south the moment she'd touched him.

There was something important he'd needed to do. He frowned, trying to remember.

Livvy noticed his frown and tensed. "I'm too wanton, aren't I? I've disgusted you."

"*No!* No, pet, I adore your curiosity. It just makes it difficult for me to think."

"Really?" She nervously chewed her bottom lip.

Oh, what the hell . . .

He was going to give in to her eventually. He might as well do so with good grace. If this was something she wanted, he would have to be a complete idiot to refuse her.

"Here, give me your hand. While my hand can do the job, yours is much nicer."

He wrapped her fingers around the base of his cock and placed his hand over hers. He guided her hand up and down, showing her the speed and pressure he liked.

"God, Livvy. Feels so good," he told her between ragged breaths.

Jason took his hand off of hers and lay back to watch her. He realized she was concentrating so hard on maintaining the exact rhythm he had set that she wasn't enjoying herself.

"You don't have to do exactly what I showed you.

This isn't a thinking sort of activity. You have to let yourself go and just feel."

Her worry was palpable. "I don't know what you want me to do."

He reached out and cupped her cheek. "I will enjoy whatever you do. Your touch drives me wild. But this is like making love; you have to figure out what you like, what makes you feel good. Trust me, it all feels good to me, but it feels even better when the pleasure is shared."

"So I can touch you here?"

She released his sex and trailed her hand down to the heavy sac between his thighs.

"Yes," he gritted out.

She jerked her hand back. "You don't sound as if you liked that."

"I liked it too much."

"Oh." She considered this. "Should I do it again?"

He groaned. "Livvy, we're going to be here all morning at this rate. Give me your hand again. I'll guide you."

He gazed into her eyes, watching the desire flare. He started slowly, but he knew he wouldn't last long. His hips soon began to thrust in time with their strokes.

Olivia let out a small moan. "Your ache might be getting better," she complained, "but mine is getting worse."

"All in good time," he panted, moving her hand faster beneath his. "Oh, God, Livvy, I need you to let go now." Jason didn't break eye contact as he pumped into his fist. With a low cry he felt his seed spurt forth, landing on his stomach. He collapsed back on the bed.

"Are you all right?" Olivia asked with concern.

He managed a grin. "Better than all right." He raised himself up on his forearms and glanced at the clock.

"Let me get washed up and we'll see what we can do about that itch of yours."

Olivia jumped off the bed and ran to bring him a damp cloth from the washstand. He got up and cleaned himself off quickly, delighted by her eagerness. He had guessed she would be passionate, but he hadn't thought it possible her sensual appetite might match his own. His lips curved. Yes, his faith in the Almighty had undergone a remarkable restoration.

He turned and saw she was waiting for him. She was leaning back against the bedhead, her face flushed, her eyes dark with desire. He wished he had her artistic ability; if he could, he would paint her just like this.

She held out her arm, and he climbed onto the bed, taking the proffered hand. When he tried to release it, she thrust it back in his face and waved it around.

"Here's my hand," she said.

Jason had no clue what to make of her statement. "Er, yes, that is your hand."

"Well, don't you need it?"

"Need it?" he echoed.

She looked at him as if he were a simpleton, which was ironic as she was the one who had clearly lost her wits.

"Yes." She gave an exasperated sigh. "You said women could ease themselves with their hands. If I knew how to do this, I would hardly have waited for your assistance. Therefore I am giving you my hand so that you can instruct me."

She said this with such a combination of earnestness and annoyance that Jason could not contain his mirth.

"No, sweet, I'm not laughing at you. Well, I am, but only because your innocence is so charming. All you need to do is touch yourself and learn what you like, but I think in the interest of time, I'll help you feel better in a different way."

"How?" she asked suspiciously.

Jason grinned. "I think it's time I become better acquainted with your female part."

Livvy clapped her hands over her breasts.

Jason shook his head. "Your other female part."

Her heart started pounding. She felt the throbbing beat echoing through her body start to settle at the juncture of her thighs.

"I th-thought you got acquainted with that p-part last night," she stammered nervously.

He leaned closer. "Not," he whispered, "with my mouth."

She was going to faint. He wanted to kiss her *there*? And did that mean she could kiss his man part?

He mistook her silence as hesitation.

"I thought you wanted to be wicked with me."

No man should be allowed to have a voice that seductive. He was like a masculine version of a siren. She was powerless to resist the lure of that low, husky tone.

"All right, but you'll stop if I say I don't like it?"

His smile was unabashedly smug.

"Of course, but I don't foresee that happening."

Livvy didn't either, but what he was suggesting was so scandalous she felt she ought to put up at least a token resistance. She owed it to all her mother's years of trying to instill a sense of propriety in her children. So far she had been spectacularly unsuccessful.

The rules of propriety didn't seem to apply to boys in quite the same way as they did to girls, but even so, Henry was, well, *Henry*.

Isabella had always been a bit wild, but the events leading up to her marriage had been outrageous even for her.

And now *she*, the hitherto good child (or at least the not-quite-as-bad child), was acting like some shameless hussy and loving every sinful second of it.

She reached for Jason, pulling him on top of her. She loved the weight of him pressing her into the bed. She began to notice other little pleasures she had missed the night before, like the way the dark hairs on his chest tickled and teased her breasts.

He took her mouth in a slow, lingering kiss. Her blood had been simmering, but now it began to boil.

"Jason," she pleaded, digging her fingers into his shoulders, trying to convey her urgency. She felt wretchedly full, yet somehow empty. The tension between her legs went from uncomfortable to unbearable.

She arched her hips up against him, trying to relieve the ache. Her frustration mounted. He had been all but rushing before, so why this slow torture?

He must have sensed she had reached her limit, since he began sliding down her body, kissing the column of her throat, nipping lightly at each breast, and then licking a path down to her navel.

"Open for me," he commanded, urging her legs apart.

A wicked chill ran through her as she obeyed. She had never guessed that being so bad would make her feel so good. And Jason was about to make her feel even better.

Her breath rushed out of her in a shaky exhale as he settled between her thighs. Oh, Lord, he hadn't even started and she was already so close to that magical place he'd taken her last night.

"Jason," she begged, as he rubbed his face against the inside of her thigh. The scratchy growth of his beard abraded her tender flesh. She moaned and let her head fall back against the pillows. She was going to explode if he waited much longer.

"All right, pet." His voice sounded rough and he was breathing hard. "I think you're ready."

She was going to kill him.

He only just now thought she was *ready*?!

All this endless, exquisite agony was because he thought she wasn't *ready*?

She opened her mouth to tell him just how *ready* she was, but it turned to a silent scream as he licked her.

One sweep of his tongue was all that it took.

The rhythmic contractions started deep inside her and spread all over. She was shaking and crying, overwhelmed by the intensity of her release.

Jason came up beside her and pulled her onto his lap, cradling her in his arms. "Sweetheart, please, tell me you're all right."

She nodded, collapsing against him with a shuddering sigh. A warm golden glow was spreading over her body, and her limbs felt like they had lead weights tied to them. She yawned and tucked herself into his chest. This seemed like a very good place to go to sleep.

"Do not fall asleep now, Olivia Jane Weston," Jason said loudly against her ear. "You can sleep for the rest of the day if you like, but it has to be in your bed."

Livvy grumbled, but she knew he was right. She allowed herself to be pulled from the bed. A rust-colored stain marred the snowy linens.

Jason pulled the sheet off the bed and shoved it into a wooden trunk by the foot of the bed.

"I'll dispose of it later," he said.

"But won't the maids think it odd that the sheet is missing?"

"I am a marquess. I am allowed to be odd."

She laughed, and then frowned. "What am I to wear? You threw my breeches out the window last night."

"The shirt you were wearing last night should cover you adequately," he said, gathering up her boots, stockings, and garters. "I suppose you had best take my jacket as well. Dimpsey is acting as my valet and nothing gets past him."

They made their way upstairs in absolute silence, encountering no one. After one last kiss, Olivia went in her room and climbed into bed. Although she had slept alone for years, after just one night with Jason the bed felt big and empty.

It wouldn't be empty much longer.

She still couldn't believe she was marrying Jason. She had been worried by his sudden change of heart regarding the matrimonial state, but he had set her mind at ease when he'd told her that last night had changed everything. Obviously he was referring to his talk with Charles.

Oh, she had known, she had just known, that once he learned Laura had been true, his faith in love would be restored. She didn't even mind that he hadn't told her he loved her. The words would come in time, and until then every kiss and tender look that passed between them assured her of his affections.

How foolish it seemed that she had once believed she would be content with marrying a man so long as his manners and hygiene were tolerably good. Jason's manners still had some room for improvement, but he was clean. And she loved him.

She had never allowed herself to imagine that she would find a man to love. That was the stuff of novels. Of course, her life was playing out rather like a novel of late.

She fell asleep with a foolish grin on her face, and when she woke several hours later, a glance in the mirror showed that it was still there. She tried to frown, but the muscles in her face refused to obey. She skipped down to the drawing room, where she found her aunt and Jason in conversation. They broke off when they caught sight of her, and Aunt Kate came forward to embrace her.

"Oh, my dear, I am so delighted for you both."

She pulled back and took a long look at Livvy's face, and then turned to Jason. "I see you gave me an expurgated version of the events last night."

Heat rose up in Olivia's cheeks, proclaiming her guilt.

"Ah, well, you are to be married, so there's no great harm done." She rubbed her hands together. "I can't begin to tell you how excited I am to begin planning. I was most put out to have missed your sister's wedding, though it was not the happy occasion this will be. Oh, I can already see you coming down the aisle of St. Paul's."

"Actually, I would like to be married at home," Livvy said. "If that is agreeable to Jason, of course."

He sent her a heated glance. "I don't care *where* it is, so long as it's *soon*."

"My dear boy, these things take time," Aunt Kate began.

Jason held up one finger. "You may have a month. *One*."

"But—"

"If I had my way it would be one week," he said. He took Livvy's hand. "Is a month enough time for you to do whatever it is women do before weddings?"

"I think so. My mother arranged my sister's wedding practically overnight."

"Good." He squeezed her fingers. "That's settled then. Now, here is what I propose . . ."

Chapter 18

"Many a good hanging prevents a bad marriage."

Twelfth Night, Act I, Scene 5

Weston Manor, Essex
Three Weeks, Six Days Later

The day before her wedding, Olivia found herself sitting in the front parlor, keeping close watch for a gentleman other than her intended. She had not seen Charles since that fateful night, and she had felt his absence keenly. She had said as much to her aunt a fortnight ago when they, along with Livvy's mother and three of her sisters, went to Chelmsford to shop for new gowns for the wedding. They were looking through the gowns the *modiste* had on hand, for the woman, in a terribly dramatic and dramatically terrible French accent, assured Livvy's mother, "For zee right price, all zat is in zee shop can be had and altered in time for zee happy occasion."

Aunt Kate called her over to see an exquisite white muslin chemise dress with flowers embroidered in silk and gold around the bodice and hem. Olivia agreed that the gown was beautiful but, she said, "It's a man's opinion I need now. I don't want to look pretty so much as I want to look irresistible and ravishing. It is too bad of Charles to have gone off without a word to anyone."

"Perhaps it is for the best," Aunt Kate suggested gently. "Now, come have a look at—"

"You seem rather calm about his disappearance," Livvy noted, eyeing her aunt with suspicion. "You wouldn't have had anything to do with it, would you?"

"I merely sent round a note about your upcoming nuptials."

"And did this note suggest Charles keep his distance for a time?"

The flush staining her aunt's cheeks had answered for her.

"Oh, Aunt Kate, how could you, especially given all he has done to see me and Jason happy?"

"My dear, has it not occurred to you that Charles's presence would likely rouse painful memories both for him and for Jason? This marriage is a great move forward for my stepson, but not a particularly easy one, I think. In order to take this next step, he had to force himself into a position of having to do the honorable thing, which tells me he has not yet come fully to terms with his feelings for you. Do not misunderstand me, for I truly believe Jason wants to marry you. He would not have compromised you otherwise, nor would I have allowed him to do so—"

"I— You— *Allowed?*" Olivia sputtered.

"Yes, I knew what was going to happen. When a man in the grip of violent emotions insists on carrying the woman who riled those emotions up to her room, there are exactly two possible outcomes: Either he is going to blister her ears and backside before making love to her, or, if the woman is clever, she will find a way to make him forget the first and get straight to the lovemaking."

"You might have shown a bit more concern for my backside," Livvy muttered.

"I should hope any niece of mine would be clever enough to divert a man's interest." Aunt Kate winked.

"Sometimes love just needs a nudge in the right direction."

Olivia frowned. "He hasn't said he loves me."

"Give him time," her aunt urged. "Men are a bit slow in that regard."

Her mother had come over then, effectively putting an end to the conversation, but the thought continued to nag at her. Jason's being so far away hadn't helped matters, but he had needed to see to estate matters, while she had wanted to go home and see to wedding preparations, so they had agreed to separate on the understanding that Jason would join her, special license in hand, at Weston Manor no later than a week before they were to wed. Aunt Kate and Charlotte had traveled with her, and to her surprise, Jason had agreed to her aunt's suggestion that Edward accompany them. Not only would it mean less tiring travel for Edward, she had pointed out, but it would also give him and Olivia more time to get to know each other before she became his stepmother. Livvy's heart had swelled with the knowledge that Jason trusted her with his son. She knew how difficult it was for him to relinquish any sort of control, and giving Edward over into her care could not have been easy.

Her family had taken to Edward immediately, and he to them. Livvy had feared he might be overwhelmed by the general chaos of Weston Manor, but Edward had quickly adapted to his surroundings. Within a few days, it had become as normal to hear him shouting and running about as any of the other children. She had cautioned everyone that if Edward displayed any signs of being unwell or out of breath, they were to turn to quieter pursuits. She was also armed with oxymel of squills, coltsfoot water, and syrup of ipecac, for while in London she had sent to an apothecary for some of the remedies suggested in the various herbals and treatises on pharmacy she had read at Arlyss. Naturally, she had no need of them—one never did when one was prepared.

Aunt Kate's idea to have Edward accompany them was a wise one, for Edward's great popularity had certainly predisposed her family to like Jason. Livvy had been present earlier that week when Jason had formally asked for her hand. Her father had said yes, of course, but he'd also said that the time he'd spent with Edward had told him everything he needed to know about Jason in order to give them his blessing.

Aside from wanting to hear three little words from Jason, life was nigh perfect. Well, except for the fact that Jason was staying at Sheffield Park, the neighboring estate belonging to her sister Isabella and her husband. Whenever Jason visited at Weston Manor they were surrounded by her family, which put a definite damper on random acts of ardor.

She had spent the first three weeks she was home anticipating what she would do when she saw him. That had been trying enough. To have to wait another week, especially when he was within ravishing distance, was torturous. Jason was faring little better. He had told her yesterday that as soon as the vicar pronounced them man and wife, he was taking her upstairs and making love to her until they collapsed, and the guests could go hang. Her cheeks hadn't stopped flaming for hours.

Only one more day, she told herself.

Though Jason had not yet given her the words she most longed to hear, he had brought other news that warmed her heart and filled her with delight. He had asked Charles to stand up with him at their wedding. She'd been worried Jason wouldn't be able to forgive Charles for his part in the weeks leading up to Laura's death, but he hadn't said a single bad thing about his brother-in-law.

Perhaps, Livvy thought, Jason's remorse over thinking Laura an adulteress had softened him toward Charles.

At least, she supposed he was remorseful. They hadn't discussed the situation. She hadn't had the time—or the inclination, if she was truly honest—to talk about it. Now Charles was coming, she could ask him just what had been said that night.

Now where *was* he?

Jason had said Charles was to ride up from London today, and though he would be staying at Sheffield Park with Jason, she had left strict instructions that Charles was to come visit her directly he arrived. As it was the day before the wedding, Jason was to stay away on pain of death.

She heard the faint thunder of hoofbeats just before Charles's curricle appeared at the end of the drive. Olivia hurried to the front door, yelling to Caldwell, their butler, that he needn't bother getting up.

Charles had just handed the reins to a groom when Olivia pounced on him. He returned her enthusiastic hug. "Hello, my soon-to-be sis! Miss me?"

Olivia led him inside. "At the moment I can't imagine why, but I actually did. Do you realize I haven't seen you since, well, that night."

"If by 'that night' you mean the night you were caught trying to enter my building, mistaken for a thief and tossed into gaol . . ."

"Keep your voice down," Olivia hissed. "My mother has been so focused on the wedding she hasn't found out about that yet, and I would like to keep it that way as long as possible!"

"Olivia, dear," her mother's voice came floating down to them from a floor above. "Is that Sir Charles I hear with you?"

"Yes," Olivia responded as Charles called up, "Hello, Lady Weston."

"Did I hear something about a thief and gaol?" she asked from the landing of the stairs.

"No." Livvy's voice was firm. "You heard nothing of the sort."

Charles began to laugh, but he quickly covered it with a cough. "Ah, no. I'm afraid you must have misheard me."

Her mother appeared before them with a quick wink. "I doubt it. Welcome to Weston Manor, Sir Charles. I am very pleased to meet you. I'm sorry my husband isn't here to greet you as well, but he and Henry, my oldest nuisance, are out dealing with a situation that's come up."

"Nothing too serious, I hope," said Charles.

"No. At least, I don't think so. They never did say what it was. Truth be told, they might have made the whole thing up as an excuse to get out of the house. Men are so wonderfully missish about weddings. My sister tells me you're not yet wed. There will be some lovely girls here tomorrow. Miss Merriwether is such a sweet—"

"Mother!"

"Oh, come. You are going to be married tomorrow. You of all people should be preaching the joys of wedded bliss."

"As far as you are concerned, I haven't the faintest notion what wedded bliss is or how one comes by it," Livvy muttered.

"Olivia Jane Weston!"

Livvy grinned and kissed her mother's cheek. "Don't worry. After tomorrow I'll be someone else's problem. And with regards to Miss Merriwether, we both know she only has eyes for one gentleman."

"And your brother hardly knows she exists." Her mother sighed. "On the one hand, I hope Jason knows what he's getting into. On the other, I pray he doesn't find out until it's too late."

"I think it's safe to say he's had a fair taste of her, Lady Weston," Charles assured her.

"More than a taste," Olivia muttered under her breath.

"I will pretend I did not hear that, dearest." She turned her attention back to Charles. "We've come to know your nephew over the past month, and he's quite one of the family now. I hope you will make yourself at home here as well. We don't stand on ceremony, though I have tried to instill some sense of propriety in my children. Not that I imagine you've seen any evidence of it in this one. I know she looks the quiet type, but if there's some sort of trouble, my Livvy is usually in it up to her neck."

A choking, strangled sound emerged from Charles. "You don't say."

Olivia could tell Charles was only just managing to hold back his laughter, so she put her hands on her hips and faced her mother. "Have I any other character flaws you wish to point out or may I show our guest around?"

"Oh, by all means. You might take a walk and enjoy the sunshine, for I doubt it will last. Caldwell tells me his knees anticipate a storm. Caldwell is our butler, Sir Charles, and his knees have been predicting the weather with startling accuracy for well over a decade."

"Then we had best go now," Livvy remarked. "Come, we can go out to the gardens through the study."

"Your mother is frighteningly perceptive," Charles said once they were outside.

"Tell me something I don't know," she muttered as they began to walk through the meticulously tended formal garden.

"Very well. I doubt you know that your husband-to-be is the subject of much speculation, having ordered a frightful number of gothic novels from Hookham's."

"He didn't!" she gasped.

"Indeed he did. There's a wager in the betting book

at White's over whether he is in love or whether he has descended into madness."

"I am scared to ask which side you put your money on."

He clapped a hand over his heart. "You wound me. The man is most assuredly mad—"

"Charles!" she exclaimed.

"—madly in love."

"He is not," she protested, even as her heart raced at the thought.

"Head over heels," he insisted. "I must thank you, by the way. I am still shocked that Jason asked me to stand up with him. When he showed up at my apartments last week I thought he was coming to call me out, but he never said a word. Whatever did you say to him?"

Olivia frowned. "What do you mean?"

"Well, you obviously broke the news gently, seeing as how well he's taken it."

She froze. No, he couldn't mean ...

"What are you talking about?" she asked in a quavering voice.

"Has love addled your wits? About Laura, of course."

"There is no 'of course' about it." She strode rapidly to a nearby marble bench and sat before her knees gave out. "Are you saying that you never spoke with Jason that night?"

"I was just about to tell him," he said, seating himself beside her, "but then Jason recognized you as the thief and I didn't have the chance. I had planned to come around the next day to speak with him, but when I received Katherine's note, I figured the two of you had set things straight."

Olivia felt her world tilt on its axis.

"He doesn't know," she whispered. "What am I to do?"

"I hardly think now is the time to tell him. Everyone seems to be in good spirits, and that's bound to put a damper on things."

"He doesn't know," she repeated brokenly.

Charles looked at her askance. "Livvy, are you all right?"

"No," she snapped. "I am not all right. You *told* me you would tell him."

"And I would have, but I didn't plan on having the evening interrupted with a mad race to Bow Street." His tone softened. "Look, does it really matter if he knows? He's happy now and—"

"Do you know what he said to me?" she demanded. "He told me women are incapable of fidelity."

"Well, unless I am much mistaken in your character, you'll prove him wrong in fifty years or so."

"Don't you see? I don't want to have to *prove* anything. I need him to trust me. How could I possibly marry a man who believes that, at some point, I will betray him? Without trust, there can't be love. I thought he just needed time—" Her throat clogged with unshed tears.

Charles handed her his handkerchief.

Perhaps she could use it to bandage her heart.

This was why she hadn't wanted to fall in love. She'd known it would end in disappointment, but oh, how it hurt to be right. She had let herself get swept up in the excitement of being in love, forgetting the basic law of gravity. She had spent the past month transported to the heights of happiness, and now she had to face the painful fall back to reality. A reality where the man she loved didn't love her. Might never love her.

And she was supposed to marry him on the morrow.

She wasn't sure she could bear it.

She shot to her feet and began to pace. Panic flooded through her, making her frantic. "I have to go away. If he sees me, he'll know something is wrong. I can't talk to him. He'll find some way to convince me to go through with it. I know he will." She knew she was babbling hysterically, but she couldn't seem to stop. "You don't know what it's like. I have no defense against him." She raised her hands to her face and began to weep.

She felt Charles's hands on her shoulders, guiding her back to the bench. She sank down wearily, exhausted by the violent outburst of emotion.

"Come, Livvy, you need to calm down or you'll make yourself sick."

She drew in a shuddering breath, fighting for composure.

Charles squeezed her shoulder. "There's a girl. Now, what's this talk of going away?"

"I can't stay here. I know it's wrong and selfish, but I can't bear to face everyone. Especially not Edward. He won't understand."

Charles eyed her warily. "Tell me you're not saying what I think you're saying."

"I can't marry him. Not like this. Not while he doesn't trust me not to betray him. Without trust, there can't be love. You know I love him. I love him with my whole heart, but his heart is still too broken to love me back. Learning the truth about Laura might help heal his heart, or it might not, but I can't marry him until I know if he'll ever be able to love me back. You have to tell him, Charles."

He took his hand from her shoulder, shaking his head. "I'm sorry, Livvy, but I'm not going to break off your engagement for you."

"Doesn't it matter that I wouldn't be engaged if you had kept up your half of the bargain and told Jason the truth?"

"And so I would have if I hadn't been interrupted by a mad dash to Bow Street."

"So this is my fault?" she demanded angrily.

"I prefer to think of it as a misunderstanding, but if you insist on pointing fingers, then yes, you are as much to blame as anyone for the current state of affairs."

That wasn't fair. Jason had lied to her. He'd said— She paused, thinking back to the morning he'd told her they were to be married. He hadn't asked her, she realized, but she supposed he could be forgiven that presumption given the circumstances. But he'd told her his feelings had changed because of Laura, hadn't he? She grasped at the fragments of conversation lingering in her memory.

No, she realized with dawning horror, he hadn't said anything about Laura. All he'd said was that the previous night had changed things. She had assumed he was referring to learning the truth about Laura because that was what she'd wanted to hear. When she'd voiced her concerns about his claim that women were incapable of fidelity, he hadn't said he'd changed his mind. All he had said were four words that might have referred to any number of happenings, but which she suspected were intentionally vague.

Last night changed things.

Four meaningless words.

No, not meaningless. She'd given them meaning—the one she wanted to hear. She hadn't pressed the matter because his words suited her. Charles was right. She had no one to blame but herself.

Charles sighed. "Look, Livvy, regardless of who, if anyone, is at blame, this talk of leaving is nonsense, and you know it. Besides, where would you go?"

The answer came to her in a flash. She needed to be in the library at Haile Castle. Everything there followed a perfect, rational, logical order, which she had created. She was in control there . . . and it was where she'd first started loving Jason. It didn't matter that it was far away.

It was the perfect place to hide, lick her wounds, and try to make sense of her confused emotions. And Jason would never think to look for her there.

"I'm going to Haile Castle." She began marching toward the house, her chin raised high in the air, defying Charles to tell her she couldn't do it.

He didn't disappoint. "To Scotland? Are you mad? How do you think you're going to get there, my girl?"

"I have some money saved up. I can ride as far as Chelmsford, and from there I shall take the stage to Edinburgh. I expect I can hire a post chaise for the remainder of the trip."

"Good God, you're serious, aren't you?"

She nodded. "I know running away is the coward's way out, and I understand if you despise me for it, but I need to go someplace where I can think. I hardly know my own mind anymore."

"All right. You win, Livvy. If you need to go so badly, I'll take you."

"You will?"

He sighed. "I will. Jason will likely kill me for taking you, but he would also kill me if I let you try to get to Scotland on your own. Go get your things while I see to the horses. Be quick about it, mind you, lest I come to my senses and change my mind."

"What do you mean, she's gone? Gone where?" Jason frowned at his soon-to-be father-in-law.

Lord Weston had burst into the drawing room of Sheffield Park only moments before, his son, Henry, close on his heels.

"I mean she's missing." The older man raked a hand through his already disheveled hair.

Olivia's hair. Jason had made a close study of Lord and Lady Weston, trying to puzzle out which parent she had inherited her features from. Her hair and her sense

of humor had come from her father. Her blue eyes and
quick wit were clearly a gift from her mother. That cute,
pert nose seemed to be uniquely her own. And as for her
mouth, well, it didn't matter who had given it to her, as
it was his now.

"Sheldon," Lord Weston barked, "do you follow? I
said *she's missing*! She told her mother that she was going for a walk with Sir Charles, but that was this morning. I'm afraid my wife closeted herself to work on her
book and lost all track of time. Henry and I were out for
the better portion of the day, but we returned in plenty
of time to dine with your brother-in-law. That was when
we realized both he and Livvy had vanished."

"They never returned from their walk?" James
asked. James Sheffield, the Earl of Dunston, was
married to Livvy's sister Isabella. Jason had enjoyed
his stay with them very much, though he had quickly
learned that just because the door to a room was ajar, it
didn't mean it was safe to enter. He had taken to rather
lengthy throat clearings before venturing anywhere in
the house.

"Genni is sure she saw Livvy come inside at some
point," Henry said. "But Sir Charles wasn't with her."

Genni. Which one was Genni? He couldn't keep track
of all of Olivia's siblings. He needed to keep a bloody
family tree in his pocket.

"I've been out to look for them," Henry added.
"They're nowhere to be found."

James cleared his throat. "Did you, ah, check the
folly?"

His lovely wife jumped to her feet. Jason could see
why Livvy's sister was thought a Great Beauty, to use
Olivia's words, for she was a true English rose. But in his
opinion, Isabella didn't hold a candle to her sister. Clas-
sic prettiness was no match against his wood nymph's
enchanting spell.

"Livvy is *not* in the folly with Sir Charles!" Isabella exclaimed. "She loves Lord Sheldon. I *know* she does!"

Warmth spread through Jason's chest at her words. Olivia had said she loved him, but hearing it confirmed was something else entirely. But what would loving him have to do with visiting a folly?

"Some people use the folly for talking, my love," James murmured to his wife, who proceeded to turn bright red.

Jason coughed and feigned interest in the ornate plasterwork ceiling.

Lord Weston shook his head. "James, my boy, that is not something I want to hear."

"I'm going to remember that next time I get you in the ring at Jackson's," Henry said, grinning. Then his smile faded. "I checked the folly, in any case."

"Well, they can't have gone too far on foot," Jason reasoned.

Henry glanced sideways at his father.

Jason felt his stomach turn over. "What aren't you telling me?"

Lord Weston tugged at his cravat. "If they are together, and we don't know they are, they could have covered some distance. Sir Charles's curricle is missing from the stables."

Jason's belly clenched with fear. "You don't think they went for a drive and—" He swallowed hard. "—and met with an accident?"

He noticed all of the occupants of the room were looking at him with a mixture of bemusement and pity.

"No," Lord Weston said slowly. "I don't think that's the case."

"Why would Livvy run away right before her wedding day?" Isabella wondered aloud.

"I nearly did," her husband pointed out, but Jason heard his words as if from a great distance.

Why would Livvy run away?

Livvy. Run. Away.

Olivia had run away.

Oh, God, it was happening all over again.

The realization struck him like a blow to the gut.

"Something must have sent her into a panic," Isabella declared, "but I can't imagine what. She must know how much you love her."

Was he supposed to respond to that? Apparently, since he suddenly had four sets of curious eyes trained on him.

"Er, I, well—" he prevaricated.

Isabella's eyes narrowed as she fixed him with a steely glare. She folded her hands over her chest. It was, Jason thought, the first time he had seen a resemblance between the sisters.

"You *have* told her that you love her?"

Jason flinched under her scrutiny. "No, not exactly."

"But you do love her, don't you?" Henry asked, his tone implying that Jason's answer had better be in the affirmative.

"I care for her very much—"

"That's not what he asked you," Isabella snarled.

"Izzie—" her husband began.

"Don't you dare tell me that this isn't any of my affair, James Sheffield," she shouted. "This is my little sister we're talking about. We wouldn't be together if it hadn't been for her."

James raised his hands in surrender.

Jason didn't blame him. For all that she looked like an angel, Isabella in a temper was clearly a force to be reckoned with.

"I do have to ask," Lord Weston said coolly, "why you are marrying my daughter if you don't love her."

Because I slept with her.

Because I want to sleep with her again.

Probably not the best response, seeing there were three, possibly four, people in the room who looked capable of killing him at the moment.

"As I said, I care for Olivia. We get on well together, and my son adores her. I never intended to marry again before I met her...."

And I can't imagine life without her.

A vast future stretched before him, cold and gray without Livvy's sunshine to brighten it.

Christ.

He needed her in his life.

He *needed* her.

This was not supposed to have happened. When had he crossed the line between wanting and needing? Probably around the same time he had passed from caring to loving.

He loved her.

He loved Olivia Jane Weston.

He loved that part of her that was Olivia, his little adventuress and wicked temptress.

He loved the part of her that was Jane, the magical wood nymph who organized libraries for pleasure and whose bedtime stories put Scheherazade to shame.

He even loved the Weston part of her, even though they all seemed bent on his destruction, because *she* loved them.

He loved Olivia Jane Weston, every last bit of her.

He *would* choose now to figure it out, Jason thought bitterly. Now that she'd left him. It was his curse.

"Look, none of this matters right now," Isabella said. "Livvy isn't thinking straight. She'll be ruined." She looked at all of the men in turn, including Jason. "You must catch up to them and bring her back."

"Izzie, my love, we don't know where they've gone," James said gently.

Isabella thought a moment. "I can't believe Livvy

would go off without telling *someone* where she was headed."

"Your mother asked all of the children, and Henry and I questioned the servants. No one knew a thing," Lord Weston told her.

"Then she must have left a note somewhere or, if she did leave, there must be a list somewhere of the things she would need to pack.... You know how Livvy insists on being organized. You *did* check her room for some sort of clue, didn't you?"

Lord Weston and Henry shuffled their feet.

Jason was just happy Isabella's anger seemed to have shifted off him, at least temporarily.

There was a knock at the door, and a footman in Weston livery entered the room.

He bowed. "My lord, I—"

Isabella darted forward and snatched the piece of paper he was holding out of his hand. "Thank you, Drake."

Jason's breath caught as she scanned the missive.

"What does it say?" James queried, coming up behind her and wrapping his arms around her.

Jason felt the sharp sting of envy at their closeness.

"That she's sorry and she doesn't want us to worry. She's gone to Scotland with Sir Charles. Oops, I probably wasn't supposed to tell Lord Sheldon where she was headed." Her tone left little doubt her error had been intentional.

"Scotland," Jason echoed dully.

She was headed for Gretna Green.

With Charles.

He began to prowl around the room.

"Lord Sheldon loves her," Isabella said to the other men, as if Jason weren't in the room. "He's just too much of a pigheaded man to realize it."

"If that's true, I have a feeling her elopement with

his brother-in-law will help him see the light," Henry responded dryly.

"Well," Isabella began, "she's not eloping—"

"Damn right, she's not!" Jason swore, uncaring that there was a lady present.

He was going to catch up to them, beat Charles to a bloody pulp, and wring Olivia's neck.

How dare she make him need her and then turn her back on him?

She was no different than Laura.

No different than his mother.

How many times would his heart have to be broken before he finally learned his lesson? No, he wasn't going to focus on the hurt. He would transform whatever pain he felt into fuel for his anger.

"I'm going after them," he said determinedly.

"I'm coming with you," Henry said. "She might be your fiancée, but she was my sister first."

Jason didn't particularly want company, but he'd learned to pick his battles. Jason was a match for Henry in height, but the man was built like bloody Jackson, only bigger. A well-placed blow from him could probably kill a man, and Jason had no desire to die. Not yet. He at least wanted to live long enough to beat the pulp out of his brother-in-law.

And as for Miss Olivia Jane Weston . . . Well, marriage to him would have to be punishment enough. He wouldn't let her go. He wasn't sure whether he loved her or hated her, but whatever sort of fool it made him, he didn't think he could live without her.

Chapter 19

"You are now sailed into the north of my lady's opinion; where you will hang like an icicle on a Dutchman's beard."

Twelfth Night, Act III, Scene 2

A few hours into her latest adventure, Livvy realized she had made a mistake.

A very big mistake.

A ruinous mistake, even.

"Charles?"

"What now?"

She couldn't blame him for being cross with her. She had put him in an impossible position.

"I think I want to go home now," she said in a small voice.

"Thank God!" He wheeled the curricle around so quickly they nearly overturned. "Do you suppose anyone will believe that we went for a drive and got lost?"

"I doubt it," she said in an even tinier voice. "Not if they found my note."

"You left a note?" His voice was strained.

"Of course. I didn't want them to worry."

He made a sound that was somewhere between a groan and a laugh. "What exactly did this note say?"

"Just that I was sorry, and that they shouldn't worry. And that I was heading to Scotland with you."

"Livvy! Your family is going to think we're eloping!"

She stared at him, horrified. "No. Surely not. They know I love Jason."

"You've a fine way of showing it," he grumbled, "running off the day before your wedding."

"I panicked. I'm sorry. I promise I'll tell everyone this was all my idea and that you only agreed to go along with it when I threatened to go alone."

"That will only work," he said, "if whoever comes after us doesn't shoot me on sight."

"I don't think that will happen. They'll probably want to beat you first."

"Oh, well, I feel much better now." His voice dripped with sarcasm.

"Don't worry. I'll explain everything before they have time to lay a finger on you. I only meant to reassure you about the shooting bit."

He laughed.

"If you're laughing, does that mean you don't hate me?"

"Of course I don't hate you. I can't say I'm pleased about the mess we're in, but we're in it together. Laura bailed me out of any number of scrapes, and now it's my turn to help you out of yours." He transferred the reins to one hand and patted her knee.

That simple touch made tears well up in her eyes.

"Thank you," she whispered. "Wait, do you hear horses?"

Charles reined in his bays at the side of the road the better to hear. Sure enough, the sound of hoofbeats carried through the silence, and soon two riders were visible.

"Now we're in for it," Charles said glumly. "That's Jason on the chestnut filly. Who's that with him?"

Livvy squinted her eyes against the setting sun. "That's my older brother."

"Wonderful. Now I'll have people fighting over who gets to kill me."

"Don't be ridiculous," Olivia chided. "Once I explain the situation, Henry's more likely to hug you. And in any case, Henry wouldn't kill you. He might beat you until you wished you were dead, but he wouldn't kill you."

They waited in silence until the riders pulled up abreast of them.

"I'm going to kill you, Charles," Jason said in a deadly calm voice as he kicked out of his stirrups and swung down to the ground.

"You can have him once I'm done with him," Henry interjected as he too dismounted. "The bounder ran off with my little sister. It's my right as a brother to pound him into the ground."

"See, I told you he wouldn't kill you," Olivia remarked to Charles.

"I'd prefer he not beat me, either," Charles replied, "so now would be a good time for all that explaining you promised to do."

"Oh, of course. Jason, Henry, neither of you are to lay a finger on Charles. This was all my idea. I panicked earlier, and for some reason the only place I could think of that felt safe was the library at Haile Castle. Charles only agreed to escort me when I threatened to go alone on the post."

"Why did you panic?" Jason asked quietly.

"I'll tell you," she said, "but only if you answer a question of mine first."

"Very well," he agreed.

"Do you trust me?"

"What kind of question is that?" he asked.

"One with a simple yes or no answer. Do you trust me?"

"I don't really think that's a fair question given to-day's events," Jason argued.

"It's entirely fair. If you trusted me, you wouldn't have thought I was eloping with Charles."

"What the hell else was I supposed to think upon hearing that you were headed to Scotland with another man the day before our wedding?"

"I love you. I love you too much to ever leave you, but I need you to love me enough to trust I'm not going to run off one day. I'm not your mother, Jason," she said softly.

A long, uncomfortable silence followed.

"Well," Charles said with forced cheer, "it seems like you two have a great deal to talk about, so why don't you drive Olivia back in my curricle, Jace, and I'll take your horse. Here, Livvy, hold the reins while we change places." He jumped down and went over to Jason. "Don't worry," he said as he passed Henry, "she'll be safe with him."

"It's not her I'm worried about," Henry replied. "A Weston female in a temper is not a pretty sight."

"Oh, shove off, Hal."

"See what I mean?" Henry said. "I ride hell-for-leather to rescue her and that's the thanks I get." He looked at Jason. "See that you don't fall too far behind us. I'm still in the mood to plant a facer on someone." He swung himself back into the saddle and rode off.

Charles followed suit, leaving her alone with Jason.

He climbed into the curricle and sat beside her. His fingers brushed hers when he took the reins, and when he set the horses in motion, she swayed into him. His thigh brushed her skirts and she fought the urge to press closer to his heat.

"Why did you run?" he asked again.

"It's a bit complicated. When I saw Charles this morning, we got to speaking about my, um, adventure, and he told me something I hadn't known. You remember you had gone back to Charles's apartments so he could tell you something?"

"That's right. His horrible secret. Come to think of it, he never did tell me."

"Yes, I know that now, but all this time I thought he had told you that night. Charles should really be the one to tell you this, but I—"

"If it's to do with Charles, is it really important?" he asked.

"It's not just to do with Charles. It's to do with Laura, too. You see, she wasn't running away the day she died."

"Don't start this again, Olivia," Jason warned her.

"I'm not starting anything. I'm ending it. All the lies and accusations. Laura wasn't ever involved with another man. She loved you, Jason."

He shook his head. "How do you explain Lord Verney's visits to the town house the week prior to her death? I wasn't in residence. What business could he possibly have had with Laura? And if she wasn't running off, why was she carrying a small fortune in jewelry along on her early-morning ride?"

"Laura was paying off a debt for Charles. She didn't have enough money to cover his losses, so she asked Lord Verney if he would accept jewelry instead. They agreed to meet in the park early that morning."

Jason was silent for a long time. "How do you know all of this?"

She swallowed hard, bracing herself. If he had been so furious about the brooch, she didn't want to imagine how he would react to learning about the diary.

"When I was reorganizing the library at Haile Castle, I came across a diary. I had already found the brooch by that point, so when I skimmed one of the entries, I recognized that it must have belonged to Laura."

"Clearly you didn't just replace the book on the shelf."

"No," she admitted. "I know it was wrong of me to do so. Even as I read it, I knew I shouldn't. But I was so fascinated by you, I just couldn't help myself.

"I wanted to tell you about the diary the night you found the brooch. Actually, I had been planning on telling you about the brooch that night."

He made a sound of disbelief.

"I was. I already knew that I was falling in love with you, and I didn't want secrets between us. But then things got so out of control that I forgot."

"A likely story," he said scornfully. "Even if it is true, which I very much doubt, you should have told me about the diary once I had found the brooch."

"I couldn't tell you about the diary. Not without talking to Charles first. The knowledge contained within was likely to have the greatest impact on your relationship with him. Charles was adamant that you not be told. He believed himself responsible for Laura's death, and he was certain you would blame him, too. He feared you would prevent him from seeing Edward."

Jason said nothing, so Olivia pressed on.

"At that point, of course, neither of us was aware you suspected Laura of having an affair. Once I learned about your suspicions, I told Charles he had to confess to you or I would do it. I couldn't let you go on thinking Laura had betrayed you.

"And up until today, I thought Charles *had* confessed to you that night. I thought that was what changed your mind about me, about us. That you had realized that you could trust and love again. I realize now that I misinterpreted some of your words, perhaps because I wanted so badly to believe this magic transformation was real.

When I realized it had never happened at all, I panicked. All this time I thought you loved me. You never said the words, but I simply thought two people couldn't be the way we were together without love. But if you still believed all that nonsense about all women being unfaithful, that meant you didn't trust me not to run away someday. And if you didn't trust me, you certainly didn't love me."

Jason sat, unmoving as a statue save for the little flicks of his wrist as he guided the team.

"Please," she begged. "Say something."

"I . . . I don't know what to say. I can barely take it all in."

She nodded, her eyes bright with tears. "I never wanted to fall in love, you know. I never thought I would meet a man like one of the heroes in books, and I was worried I'd end up with my heart broken. This last month has been like a perfect dream. I want you to know that I don't regret loving you, Jason."

When at last they reached Weston Manor, Jason drove round to the stables. As he handed her down, she realized he looked more disheveled than she'd ever seen him, and there was a lost, wild look in his eyes.

And she had been the one to put it there.

Did he hate her? she wondered.

Did he wish she'd never come into his life?

She refused to believe he had been happy, living as he was. If one could even call it living. He had been drifting along, simply existing. But there was no denying his life had been far less complicated before she had come into it.

He was always so strong, so steady, and she found it unnerving to see him so undone now. *Reach out to me,* she wanted to say. *Let me be your support. You don't have to go through this alone.* But he *did* have to face these demons alone. She couldn't heal the hurt inside him, no matter how much she wanted to.

Jason began to walk, not toward the house but out on the grounds. She followed him, knowing there was still more to be said between them. It was painfully cold, but Livvy found she was oddly grateful for the weather. If she focused on the fact that her toes felt like icicles, she wasn't thinking about everything else going on.

Which was really a very good thing, because if she actually thought about everything that had happened that day, about where she had started and where she was headed, she suspected she would look even more lost and confused than Jason did.

Finally he spoke, and she knew from his tone of voice that the man who had been her lover was gone and in his place was the reserved marquess she had first met. It was an effort not to break down entirely.

"I believe I can safely say certain things were brought to light today which neither of us has come to terms with as yet. Your flight, if nothing else, indicates a situation more complicated than cold feet. You want me to trust you, but I am not sure you trust me, or if you even trust yourself."

Olivia heard Jason speaking, but she was having difficulty focusing on his words. There was a blessed sense of numbness settling over her.

"I'm afraid there is no couching this in niceties. Are you in a condition that necessitates we wed tomorrow?"

A condition? Did a broken heart count as a condition? "I'm sorry, but I don't understand."

She wasn't sure she wanted to.

Was he breaking their engagement? After her precipitous flight with Charles, did an engagement even still exist to be broken?

Broken, broken, broken.

Broken trust.

Broken heart.

A broken engagement fit in nicely.

"I shall have to speak plainly," Jason said. "Is there a chance you are with child? Have your courses come?"

Olivia suddenly felt as though she were standing too close to a fire. Despite all the wickedly intimate things she had done with Jason, discussing her courses was too embarrassing. In any case, she wasn't talking to Jason now, but the Marquess of Sheldon.

Her cheeks flamed, but she shook her head. "I am not with child." For the briefest moment, she thought she saw a flash of disappointment cross his face, but that was foolish, she told herself. If anything, he was likely relieved.

"Well," he said, "that *is* a relief."

She gaped at him. She might have guessed he was thinking it, but it was really too much that he had said it aloud.

"I only meant that if you were with child, we should have to go through with the wedding tomorrow as planned. Since you are not—"

"I think I understand you quite well, my lord."

"I don't think you do. I feel I rushed you into this engagement. There are no laws as to how long a betrothal may last. I believe it would be better for both of us to have time to find answers to the questions raised today. It seems rather inauspicious to start a marriage under a cloud of doubts and suspicions, wouldn't you say?"

"I don't know. What exactly are *you* saying? What will happen on the morrow?"

"I think it best we call off the wedding."

"Oh!" The startled exclamation burst from her lips. "I— I see."

"I don't mean we shouldn't ever get married. Only

that tomorrow seems undesirable given the events of today. You need some time to decide what you want."

I want you, she wanted to rail at him. *I want you to love me.*

"You need time as well," she said. "I imagine learning the truth about Laura will affect your view of everything."

"Of course it does, damn it!"

It was the most emotion she'd seen from him yet.

She tried not to be jealous of Laura, because clearly it would get her nowhere.

"Have you realized you're still in love with her?" she asked in a tremulous voice.

"I don't know how I feel, aside from guilty. If I hadn't been such a hardheaded bastard, Laura might still be alive. My son might still have his mother."

Lord, she ought to lock him and Charles in a room together and let them thrash out who was the guiltier party.

"There's no way of knowing that, Jason. Her death was an accident, a horrible accident, but it wasn't your fault."

He shook his head. "No, if she'd been able to come to me with her problems, if she'd trusted me to see things right, she wouldn't have been out that morning."

"Perhaps not that morning, but she would have gone riding again. You and Charles are both so determined to blame yourselves. Both of you made wrong decisions, but such is human nature. And if there is blame to go around, Laura must take her share, too."

"Laura is the innocent party in all this," Jason said sharply.

"No." She held up her hand. "Hear me out. You yourself said that she didn't trust you enough to come to you with her problem. Laura should have trusted you enough to know you would do the right thing and help Charles."

"What makes you so sure?"

"You're a good man, Jason Traherne."

He let out an ugly laugh. "A good man," he repeated. "Would a good man decide his late wife was guilty of adultery without just cause?"

"I admit it was not well done of you, but given your childhood and the somewhat suspicious circumstances, I can understand why you jumped to the conclusions you did."

She pressed her fingers to his cheek. It was meant to be comforting but he jerked away as if she'd scalded him.

"Jesus, Livvy, your hands are like ice. Where are your gloves?"

"I forgot them. I'm afraid I didn't plan anything very well today." She had grown accustomed to the cold, but his actual mention of it seemed to make the numbness disappear. Her teeth began to chatter.

"Little fool." He swore under his breath. He shrugged off his greatcoat and put it around her shoulders. It was warm and smelled deliciously like Jason.

"Come," he said. "Let's get you back home."

And that, Olivia thought, was the problem. Weston Manor wasn't home anymore. Home was where Jason was. He was what she'd been looking for all along. She hadn't been looking for adventure, not really. She had just associated adventure with what she really wanted but had been too scared to hope for.

Love.

A lover. A husband. A hero.

Not the perfect hero she had once dreamed of, but a man whose scars and imperfections touched her soul. He filled the deepest reaches of her heart, and that terrified her, because she wasn't sure Jason would ever be able to find room for her in his.

Chapter 20

"Make me a willow cabin at your gate,
And call upon my soul within the house;
Write loyal cantons of contemned love
And sing them loud even in the dead of night;
Halloo your name to the reverberate hills
And make the babbling gossip of the air
Cry out 'Olivia!'"

Twelfth Night, Act I, Scene 5

Jason spurred his horse on, but he couldn't outrun the demons that lay behind him any more than he could avoid those waiting before him. When he sensed the gelding was flagging, he returned to the castle. Once he'd handed the reins over to a groom, he began to walk, unable to stand the restless energy that filled him. He always ended up in the same place.

He didn't know how many long hours he'd spent sitting in front of his mother's grave. He'd come to the little plot of land attached to the rectory almost every day since he'd returned to Arlyss, sitting for hours in the bitter cold just staring and waiting. He needed a sign, an answer to his problems, but his mother gave him as little in death as she had in life.

It had been three long, lonely weeks since he had left Olivia. Three long weeks of wondering where his life had gone wrong. Three lonely weeks of not knowing how to find his way again.

He looked up as a shadow fell over him.

"Katherine!" He was surprised to see her. He had assumed she would be with Olivia.

"Hello, Jason. You look terrible."

"It's nice to see you, too, but I'm afraid you're a bit early for Christmas."

She laughed. "Am I only allowed to visit once a year?"

"No, of course not." He got to his feet and brushed the dirt and grass off his breeches. "Is Charlotte with you?"

"No, I left her with my sister. I felt that what I had to say to you was best done without her getting underfoot."

"Have you come to berate me, then?" he asked.

"I only want to talk to you. Will you walk with me?"

He inclined his head in assent.

"When I married your father, you were already a grown man, and you clearly didn't need a mother figure fussing over you. But I always felt you could use a mother's love, and when I made my vows to William, I made a vow to watch over you as well. But it seems I've failed you. I didn't realize how deeply your mother's abandonment affected you, and now this business with Laura . . ."

"There was nothing you could have done, Katherine," Jason said gruffly. "Your visits, year after year, when you would doubtless have rather been with your family have meant a great deal to both me and Edward."

"You and Edward *are* my family, Jason. And you're wrong. I could have spoken to you about your mother."

"It wouldn't have done any good. My father tried to get me to talk about her for years, but I refused to listen. Eventually he gave up."

"No, he never gave up. He knew the day would come when you would want to know more. There's a letter he wrote in the bank vault in London, or, if you would like, I can tell you what I know."

"Please."

"You are aware that your parents' marriage was arranged. Your mother was the youngest daughter of the Duke of Repton. She was just fifteen when she wed your father. I'm afraid she was very spoiled, and while William indulged her spending habits, he later realized he had unintentionally denied her the one thing she truly craved."

"Which was?"

"His attention. As the baby of her family, the entire household had doted on her. She supposed her husband would do the same, but William had little interest in her. Things improved a bit when you were born. Your father took a natural interest in you, and having birthed the heir, your mother received attention as well. Unfortunately, as is so often the case, you were soon put entirely in the care of servants.

"I want you to know that your father later regretted not having spent more time with you when you were young. He was raised in much the same way you were, though, and he never imagined a father was supposed to take interest in a child, even his heir, before that child was old enough to assume adult responsibilities. I think, had he lived longer, he would have been different with Charlotte—" Her voice broke.

"I know he would have done things differently. My father became a different person when you married him, Katherine. He began to live and enjoy life."

"I miss him. I know there was talk about the difference in our ages, but I truly loved William."

"I know you did. I never doubted it. And he adored you."

She dabbed at her eyes. "I am sorry to say he never loved your mother, nor did he understand her. He preferred an evening by his own fire reading poetry, while your mother was desolate if she missed a single event of the Season. But the less interest your father paid her, the more she coveted it. She tried everything possible to make him notice her."

"Such as having an affair?"

"I'm not certain. I think by then she might have accepted that your father would never dote on her in the way she wanted. If she could not get attention from William, she must have decided to seek it elsewhere.

"I am only telling you all this so you understand that while your mother was a selfish, spoiled individual, she was also extremely unhappy. I have asked myself time after time how any mother could abandon her child, but the truth of the matter is that your mother was, in most respects, a child herself, and you had already been taken from her long before she ran off."

"I see," Jason said, not knowing what else to say.

"Do you? You are an intelligent man, Jason. You must realize your mother was closer to the exception than the rule. I was never false to William. My sister has never been untrue. And now you know Laura was faithful."

"When Laura died, I thought I would die, too. I hardly remember that first week. I know I drank constantly. And then I wasn't sad, but angry. I was furious with her for dying. The anger was easier to live with than the pain of knowing she was lost to me forever. That was when I started looking for ways to blame her for what had happened. The more I searched, the more I found, and when I laid all of the pieces of the puzzle out, there was only one explanation I could come up with. Now that I know the truth I can let go of the anger, but I've only traded anger for the guilt of having so misjudged her."

"Laura would have understood. She wouldn't want you to torment yourself."

"How can I not? She might still be alive if—"

"You certainly can't know that. Are you going to spend the rest of your life peering into the past, making yourself mad over things that can't be changed? Laura would want you to be happy, Jason. You have to forgive yourself and let her go."

He swallowed against the lump in his throat. "I know."

"Don't you think, if you let yourself, you could find happiness with Olivia? I know it was not well done of her to run off, but can't you see your way to forgiving her?"

"I already have. She's certainly not the first bride to have second thoughts, nor will she be the last. And my reaction proved she had good reason to flee."

"She understands why you acted as you did. She loves you."

"I love her, too." The words were surprisingly easy to say. He had admitted his feelings to himself, but this was the first time he had voiced them. "I love Olivia," he said again, marveling at the rightness of the words upon his lips. "I love her so much I sometimes think I'll burst from it. I realized it when she ran away with Charles, but the feelings were there before that."

Katherine braced her hands on her hips and glared at him. "Then what are you doing here? Why aren't you telling her this? She's been miserable since you left."

"It's nice to know I'm not alone in the feeling," Jason remarked. "But I'm not what she wants. She wants a perfect man, like out of one of her novels. I've already hurt her and disappointed her so many times. If I love her, shouldn't I let her go? She hasn't even had a Season yet. Maybe she'll find a better man."

"And could this better man ever love her as much as you do? Because I have read some of these novels myself, and there's only one trait the hero always possesses."

He was scared to even hope. "What?" His lips formed the word, but no sound came out.

"He loves the heroine with everything he was, everything he is, and everything he hopes someday to be with her by his side."

She patted his arm. "I'm going to go inside to see my grandson. Why don't you take a walk and think on what I said. Perhaps you'll stop back at the rectory on your way home; it's past time you made your peace."

Jason slowly made his way back, contemplating Katherine's words. If what she said about heroes was true, he knew he could make Livvy happy. There would never be another man who loved her and needed her the way he did.

He stood before his mother's grave. On some level it was hard to let the anger and resentment go. They had been a part of him for so long, they almost seemed necessary to his wholeness. He wasn't sure he knew how to exist, how to function properly, without them. But he knew he had to try.

He knelt down to trace the carved letters. Christine Traherne. The name was his mother's, but the person was a stranger. A stranger who had made foolish choices, but he could see now that they'd had little to do with him. He thought of Edward. Of the joy his son brought him. Of the gift of such unconditional love. His mother hadn't understood such love, and he pitied her for that.

He rested his forehead against the cool stone.

"Rest in peace, Mother."

The next good-bye was easier in some respects, harder in others. He stood for a long time, trying to find the right words. He finally settled for what was in his heart.

"I'm sorry, Laura. I'm so, so sorry." He swallowed hard, forcing himself to bring up an image of her smiling face in his mind's eye. "I'm sorry I let you down.

You should have known you could come to me with any problem. You've probably been laughing these past years as you watched over me and Edward. I've been an idiot. But you would have been the first one to tell me that, wouldn't you?"

He felt tears begin to slide down his cheeks and didn't bother to wipe them away.

"God, I miss you, Laura. I miss you so damned much. I always will. You always knew what I needed before I did, though, didn't you?"

He pressed his lips to his palm and then placed the kiss over her name.

"I don't know how you did it," he whispered, "but thank you for sending Livvy to me. Edward and I will take good care of her."

Today was her last day to cry, Olivia told herself, staring out her window at the rain that so matched her mood. Tomorrow would mark a month with no word from Jason, and she refused to shed any more tears after that. Tomorrow she would lock up her heart and throw away the key. She would tear up all the drawings she'd made of him.

Tomorrow she would let him go and begin the painful business of moving on with her life.

It wasn't even as if she could fall back on her plan of a marriage of convenience, where she would satisfy her romantic cravings through her novels. She simply didn't find the heroes appealing any longer. Even though they were perfect—because they were perfect—none could measure up to Jason.

As she had been unable to find a book she wanted to read, Livvy had begun writing one of her own. She had thrown herself into her work, and what had poured out of her was unlike any book she had read. There were no ghosts or ancient curses or forests full of strange and frightening beasts. It was just the story of an unremarkable girl's quest to become a heroine.

The real trouble she was having was with the ending. She had lost the heart to write it as it should be written, with a celebration of Grand Passion. She simply could not seem to think of a way past the lovers' insurmountable obstacles.

She had never before questioned her novels, but had accepted that love was a power strong enough to sweep aside all barriers and clear the way for a happily-ever-after ending. Having experienced love and passion for herself, Olivia had realized that all love did was temporarily blind you to all the obstacles that actually stood in your path, all the little warning signs. Until you came up against one you couldn't get around.

Her heroine had experienced the joy of finding her hero, and now all Livvy wanted to do was to make them suffer as she was suffering. She had *tried* to write a happy ending for them, truly she had, but invariably one or both of them (usually the hero) ended up dead. But she couldn't imagine a happy ending for them any more than she could for herself.

Perhaps Jason had been right when he'd said love was just as destructive as war. She had always imagined romances as ending happily, one of the reasons she'd never understood the appeal of *Romeo and Juliet*, but now she was forced to admit just how much tragedy was involved. She wasn't speaking only of herself, though she did feel rather like a tragic heroine, but of all those who had gambled in the game of love and come out on the losing side.

Of course, even if one came out a winner, that was no guarantee of continued happiness. A thousand things could happen to steal that happiness away. Not that she was going to come out a winner. There was not going to be any happy ending for her. Jason wasn't coming back. She realized that now. All his talk about postponing the wedding until they were both sure it was what they really wanted was just that. *Talk.*

Aunt Kate had gone to see Jason, and to make certain Edward was all right, but she was back in London now, and Jason had yet to appear. At the thought of Edward, Livvy began to weep. She couldn't forget the sight of Jason dragging Edward into the carriage while the little boy kicked and fought and screamed for his "Livvy-Mama." That's what he had begun calling her. . . .

She pressed the heel of her hand against her chest, trying to soothe the ache that never seemed to go away. Everyone had assured her that she would feel better in time. Everyone except Izzie, that was. Isabella and James had been parted for close to a year, and her sister swore the pain never got any better.

There were times when she longed to be an only child.

She supposed Edward would always be an only child. She'd dreamed of giving him brothers and sisters. Grieving for the children she and Jason would never have, Livvy slid down to the floor and sobbed until she thought her heart would break.

For a moment she thought she heard Jason saying her name, but she told herself that was ridiculous.

Then she felt a hand on her shoulder.

She raised her head, blinking against the tears, and found Jason bending over her.

"Are you really here or am I imagining you?" she whispered.

"It's me, pet."

Her heart hammered in her chest. For all that she'd dreamed of him showing up at Weston Manor, now that he was here she hadn't the faintest notion what to do. She scrambled to her feet.

"What are you doing here?"

"Can't a man visit his betrothed without needing an excuse?"

"I didn't realize we were still betrothed," she said stiffly. "I hadn't heard from you in so long I thought you had changed your mind."

He shook his head. "No. I wanted to give you time to think, but I realized that was a mistake."

"What do you mean?"

"I've done a lot of thinking since I left here."

"About Laura?"

"Yes, partly, but—"

She looked down, afraid he would see the tears still in her eyes. Because she loved him. And he was going to tell her that he still loved Laura.

"Wait. I have something for you."

She went to her desk and pulled out a slim leather-bound notebook. "I meant you to have this before," she said as she handed it to him, "but I never managed to give it to you."

"Laura's diary?"

"Yes, I can leave you alone if you'd like to read it."

He walked over to her desk and dropped the diary back into the drawer she had pulled it from.

"You keep it safe. I'm never going to read it."

"Why not?"

"Well, for one thing, those writings were private. I don't mean to judge you for reading them, but Laura obviously never intended for me to see what she penned."

He thought a moment.

"There are good times and bad in every marriage," he explained, "and that diary was Laura's place to express what she felt without worrying it would ever be found by anyone else. I failed Laura when I doubted her. I will not betray her memory by prying into her secret confidences.

"But there's another, more important reason why I'm not going to read Laura's diary. Now I've let go of the ugly suspicions, I can remember the happy times I spent with her. But memories alone are not enough to sustain a man, to fill in the missing pieces of his heart and help him move forward, out of the past and into the future."

He took her hands.

"Laura is my past. You are my future, Livvy. I don't need to read Laura's diary and relive all those old memories because I'm ready to make new memories with you. I love you, Livvy. I realized it when you ran off with Charles, but the feelings were there from the first. I was just too scared and stupid to acknowledge them. I didn't want to risk having my heart broken again. I know pain and loss are always a risk you take with love, but I don't know what pain could be worse than living my life without you. Tell me it's not too late. Say you'll marry me, Livvy."

She knew this was the part where she was supposed to fling her arms around him. To tell him she loved him and couldn't live without him. To kiss him and tell him yes with all her heart.

"I want to, but I can't."

He was silent for a long moment.

"Have your feelings for me changed?" he asked.

"No! I love you. But I'm so afraid."

"Of what?"

"You. Me. Us. Oh, just everything!" She blew out a frustrated breath and swiped at the tears welling up in her eyes. "It's just— What if we mess this up again?"

"Then we'll mend it again."

"But if something has so many problems, so many faults, isn't that perhaps a sign that it isn't meant to be? Shouldn't love be easy?"

"I would think you of all people would know the 'course of true love never did run smooth.'"

"And then there is that appalling habit of yours," she said shakily.

"What? Quoting Shakespeare?"

Olivia nodded and then began to cry, great heaving sobs that rocked her whole body.

Jason drew her into his arms.

"You had b-better not b-be laughing," she hiccuped.

"I wouldn't dream of it," he assured her, patting her back.

"You're smiling. I can hear it in your voice." Livvy pulled away to see his face. "It isn't funny. All that Shakespeare . . . it's a character flaw. I'm not a person who accepts character flaws. And yet your faults only seem to make you more endearing."

Jason's mouth twitched at the corners. "Now that is most upsetting."

"What?"

"Why, that I have faults, of course. I cannot ever recall a person telling me before that I am possessed of any."

"But of course you have faults. Everybody has faults. Nobody is perfect— Oh!"

The truth of her words suddenly struck her.

"Exactly." Jason nodded. "We're none of us perfect. Life isn't perfect and neither is love. You would find it endlessly boring if it was. How many novels do you suppose I would be able to buy for you if love was just two people meeting, falling in love, getting married and living perfectly ever after?"

"That does sound rather dull," she admitted.

"I know I'm not the perfect hero you envisioned, but a perfect man wouldn't need you as I do. I understand it's usually the hero who rescues the damsel in distress, but it was you who saved me. I love you, Olivia Jane Weston, and if you'll agree to marry me, I promise to give you a lifetime of adventures."

"In that case, how could I possibly refuse?"

"You'll marry me?"

"Only if you agree to go lock the door," she said, a wicked gleam in her eyes.

In a flash he'd locked the door and tumbled her onto the bed. They tore at each other's clothes, careless in their need. It had been far, far too long for both of them.

As he braced himself above her, Jason cupped Livvy's face in his hands. "I love you," he said raggedly, stroking his thumbs over her cheeks. "You are my heart, my very heart." And then he kissed her deeply and there were no more words. None were needed.

They spoke to each other in the language of lovers from the beginning of time. Moans and gasps, sighs and cries, gentle, soft caresses and hard, bruising grips—all mingled together as they learned each other, loved each other, soared over the edge and shattered with each other.

Sated, they clung together, preserving the precious intimacy for as long as possible. It was Olivia who finally broke the silence. "Jason?"

"What?" Jason murmured.

"You lied to me. You said that life wasn't ever perfect. After what just happened, I have to disagree."

"That wasn't perfect, pet."

"It wasn't?" A worried frown came over her face.

He kissed the tip of her nose. "No. It was better than perfect."

Epilogue

"Jove and my stars be praised!
Here is yet a postscript."
                    Twelfth Night, Act II, Scene 5

Five Months Later

Livvy clambered up on the ladder and pulled the remaining books from the shelf before hurriedly climbing down. Jason would be furious if he caught her engaging in what he called "strenuous physical activity." She patted the growing mound of her stomach and was rewarded with a vigorous kick. The feeling never failed to make her heart swell with happiness.

Jason entered the library and groaned when he saw her standing by the ladder with a pile of books in her arms. "Tell me you didn't get those books down yourself," he pleaded, coming forward to take them from her. He set the books aside and pulled her back against his chest, his arms encircling her and their child. He dropped his head so his chin was on her shoulder. "How many times do I have to tell you not to engage in any strenuous physical activity?" he growled, tilting his head to nip at her earlobe.

Her head lolled back against him. "If I recall correctly, we both engaged in far more strenuous physical activity this morning, and you didn't complain then."

"That's different." He pressed a kiss into the curve where her neck and shoulder met.

She shivered in response. "H-how is that?"

"The doctor assured me that particular activity was still safe for you and the babe. He said nothing about climbing ladders."

"You do know you can't keep coddling me for the next four months, don't you? I'll go mad."

"I happen to enjoy *coddling* you." His inflection left little doubt as to his meaning.

"You are impossible," she huffed. "But I love you anyway."

"Not as much as I love you," he insisted, turning her to face him. He brought one hand up to cup her face and smoothed his thumb over her cheek. "You are so beautiful," he whispered. "So very precious to me."

Livvy felt tears well up in her eyes, but that happened quite a bit these days. In the grand tradition of Weston women, no sooner had she got with child than she'd become a watering pot.

She leaned into him, resting her cheek against his chest and listening to the beat of his heart. "I love you." No matter how many times she said the words, they never felt trite. They always felt just right.

"I love you too, pet." He dropped a kiss on her lips. "Gower said you wished to see me. Were you climbing the ladder because you are in need of some strenuous physical activity? Shall I lock the door?"

As always, she had only to look at him to want him, but she shook her head. "Not yet. I found something I want to show you. Here, come look at this."

She pulled him over to the small writing desk across the room where she had placed the fragile paper, brittle and discolored with age, but in remarkable condition for a document some four hundred years old. She watched as Jason slowly deciphered the ornate medieval script. When he had finished, he looked up, lost for words.

She knew the feeling. She had read the letter written by Rhoslynn's son to one of his uncles several times now, and she was still scarcely able to believe the contents. Rhoslynn had not leapt to her death, but had left the castle via a priest hole attached to the old chapel. She had traveled on foot to Haverfordwest, determined to see what destruction her family had wrought and to heal whomever she could. The guards told her of one prisoner who had hovered between life and death for days. When she went to tend him, Rhoslynn wept with joy, for Sir Philip had not been killed after all. She nursed him back to health, and they escaped to his family home in Herefordshire, where they had raised a family and lived long, happy lives.

"You realize what this means, don't you?"

Jason had been reading the letter again, but he looked up at her words. "No, what?"

"This proves happy endings really do come true."

Jason pulled her into his arms and kissed her. "But I already knew that, love. I see it every time I look at you."

Read on for a sneak peek of the next book
in Sara Lindsey's Weston series

A Rogue for All Seasons

Available from Signet Eclipse in January 2011

"I still can't believe *Olivia* is *married*," Henry Weston's sister Isabella remarked with a sigh as she poured out tea from a Meissen teapot, which her brother estimated was worth more than his life.

Henry leaned forward to take the dainty porcelain cup, which appeared even daintier in comparison to the size of his hand, which, like the rest of him, could only be described as large. "A mountain of muscled masculinity" was the term his tailor used, much to Henry's disgust. Monsieur Bazalgette was pleased to have the cut of his clothes shown to advantage without the need for any padding, though, he lamented, Henry was simply too *grand comme un éléphant* to wear the most fashionable colors. A *très jolie* jonquil waistcoat was simply out of the question. As Henry had no intention of going about town looking like an overgrown canary, he had threatened to take his trade elsewhere if the little Frenchman ever made such a ridiculous suggestion again. Of course, both men knew Henry's threats of finding someone new were empty. Monsieur Bazalgette was the very best at what he did, and Henry was accustomed to the very best. He accepted nothing less.

"Olivia. *Married*," Izzie repeated for good measure.

"Just imagine how I feel," Henry grumbled. "I still have trouble believing *you* are actually married."

James Sheffield, Earl of Dunston, Henry's best friend

and, as of a little more than a year ago, Isabella's husband, laughed. "This isn't proof enough for you?" he asked, gently smoothing the blond curls of the sleeping child cradled in the crook of his arm. As if she were aware she was the subject of conversation, Bride squirmed against her father's chest and kicked her feet a few times before collapsing back into limp slumber.

Henry smiled at his niece, but his happiness faded as James and Isabella exchanged a fond, intimate look that left Henry feeling as though he'd taken a bite of something unpalatable. It was, unfortunately, served up with distressing regularity.

Henry set his teacup down on a spindly legged table that looked like it would splinter into pieces if he so much as breathed on it the wrong way. He shifted in his chair, praying it would continue to hold his weight. Was there some rule against drawing room furniture being sturdy? He'd heard women complaining that their husbands rarely left their studies, never realizing that the study was probably the only room in the house where the poor bastards could sit comfortably.

Henry eyed James speculatively. "Speaking of your marriage, how's that shoulder feeling, old friend? I believe we're overdue for a round or ten at Jackson's. There's still that little matter of you seducing my innocent, impressionable younger sister."

James grinned. "Wish I could oblige you, but I think my days in the ring are past."

"It's still bothering you?" Henry asked, honestly concerned. "Perhaps you ought to see a doctor."

James had been injured during his brief stint with the navy—a featherbrained undertaking that also made Henry want to beat him to a bloody pulp. At least, that was, when he didn't want to hug him until his ribs cracked just to reassure himself his best friend was still alive.

James shook his head, dismissing Henry's concern. "I

don't need a doctor. There's only a touch of pain when the weather turns inclement. Don't fuss, Hal. I get quite enough of that from Izzie, and besides, it's unbecoming in a man of your size."

Henry scowled. "Perhaps just one round? It's not very sporting of you to deny me my rightful opportunity to blacken your daylights. Your shoulder should be fine. Outside it's all blue skies and nary a cloud in sight."

James raised a brow. "In England the weather is always inclement."

"Henry Weston, don't you dare think of fighting with James," Isabella warned. "And, just so you know, *I* was the one who did the seducing."

Both Henry and James groaned in unison.

"Hush, love," James told his wife. "I have a reputation to uphold."

"The only reputation you need to be concerned with upholding," Izzie maintained, "is that of the world's most faithful husband and devoted father."

"And if he slips up? Then can I pound him into the ground?" Henry asked hopefully.

"If he slips up, you are welcome to whatever is left once I've finished with him," his sister agreed.

James winced in mock agony. "You have nothing to worry about, my bloodthirsty little wench," he promised her.

"Then neither do you," his wife retorted, a tender smile curving her lips.

"Keep looking at each other like that and I'll drag him to Jackson's, war injury or no."

"When did you turn into such a prude, Hal?"

Henry gaped at his sister.

"It's old age," James explained. "Mellows a man."

"We're the same age!" Henry exploded.

"Why don't you want to fight Olivia's husband?" Isabella asked, obviously trying to distract him.

Henry clenched his hands into fists. His other brother-in-law, the Marquess of Sheldon, was another man he should, by all rights, have been allowed to trounce. Any man who made one of the Weston females miserable was fair game in Henry's eyes, and Sheldon's behavior during his and Olivia's betrothal had left a lot to be desired. That was all in the past, though, and Olivia had seemed disgustingly happy the last time Henry had seen her. "Has Sheldon done something deserving of a beating?"

"Well, no, but Livvy told me"—Izzie dropped her voice to a conspiratorial whisper—"she might be *with child*!"

"I'll kill the bastard," Henry stated grimly. He began to get up, ready to go and do just that, but Isabella waved him down.

"You can't tell anyone. I mean it, Hal. I promised Livvy I wouldn't say anything, but I had to get your mind off this violent obsession with James. Livvy hasn't even told Jason yet. She's certain once he knows, he'll bundle her off back to Wales."

"At least she'll get into less trouble there," Henry muttered.

"Sheldon probably knows already," James said. "Or he will soon. A man tends to notice when certain, ah, activities aren't interrupted each month."

"It doesn't have to be in the ring at Jackson's." Henry looked about thoughtfully. "This room would serve nicely."

Isabella rolled her eyes. "Livvy wants to wait until after Mother's ball next week. Given that it's supposed to be celebrating both our marriages, it would look a bit odd for one of the couples to be in absentia. Not that Livvy's presence or my presence would make that much of a difference, given Mother's *real* reason for the ball." She gave Henry a meaningful glance.

Henry looked at her blankly.

Isabella sighed. "Honestly, Hal, have you learned nothing in all these years of being her son? What is our mother's main purpose in life?"

"To finish her book?" Henry guessed. Their mother had been working on a collection of essays about Shakespeare's heroines for, well, forever.

"Yes, but aside from that." Izzie waved a hand, brushing aside their mother's opus. "What is most important to her?"

"Family," Henry answered easily. "Us."

"Exactly. And what is her most fervent wish for all her children?"

This was easy as well since Henry had heard his mother say it often enough. "To be as happy and fulfilled as she and our father are. Isn't that the whole point of this ball—to celebrate you and Livvy having found happiness and fulfillment and all that namby-pamby claptrap?"

"It's not namby-pamby claptrap," Isabella protested, with a besotted glance at James. "And yes, that's the purported reason for the ball, but Livvy and I have already found what Mama wanted for us. So . . ." She gave him that meaningful look again.

And again he had no clue what the devil she was getting at. "So?"

"Honestly, Hal, I think you're getting more dense with age. *So* Mama's sights are going to turn to her children who have yet to find love."

Henry frowned. "Don't you think the twins are a bit young for her matchmaking efforts? Lia and Genni are only, what, ten? Besides, they're more interested in books than boys."

"The twins are *thirteen*. And as the books they are currently so enthralled with are romantic tales, I doubt they're as immune to boys as you might think. When they were over last week, Lia spent the better part of the visit rhapsodizing over one of the grooms at Weston Manor. Still, I think the twins are safe for now, especially since Mama's current project is well past marriageable age."

Henry tried to think of whom his sister was referring to. His mother had a soft spot for wallflowers and—

"Lord, is she back to Miss Merriwether again? I don't know why she bothers. The girl has been out for at least five Seasons now, and it's not as if she's penniless. The chit simply isn't going to get—"

Isabella set her tea cup down and got to her feet. She came to stand before Henry. "Not Miss Merriwether," she gritted out, leaning over him and punctuating every word by jabbing her finger into his chest. "You!"

"Me?" Henry laughed. "That's preposterous." He looked over at James, expecting to find him equally amused. James's expression was somber. "You're serious," Henry said incredulously.

"I don't know why you're so surprised, especially since Livvy and I deprived her of matchmaking schemes and elaborate weddings," Izzie remarked.

Henry tugged at his cravat, wondering if it was possible that the temperature in the room had risen drastically in the past few minutes.

"Until the twins are out of the schoolroom," Isabella continued, "you are the only child Mama has available to try to marry off."

"But won't this ball satisfy her desire for planning a grand event?" Henry asked, a note of desperation creeping into his voice.

His sister shook her head. "Whet her appetite, more like. No, the real reason for this ball is so Mama can look over this Season's crop of debutantes with an eye to picking her future daughter-in-law."

"Stop tormenting your brother, love, and come see to

your motherly duties. If I'm not mistaken, the princess here is past due for a feeding."

Perfectly on cue, Bride opened her eyes and gazed about. Not seeing the face she associated with food, a distressed whimper escaped her.

Henry knew how she felt. He had a similar urge, only it wasn't from a lack of motherly attention.

Isabella gathered her daughter in her arms and moved toward the door. "No fighting," she reiterated. "Just think how devastated Mama would be if you showed up to the ball with a black eye marring that pretty face."

Henry glared at her back as she swept from the room. If Isabella was right—and he had learned that Weston women were nearly always right—his mother was intending to see him standing at the altar by the end of the Season.

Damnation. It looked like he was going to have to find a new sparring partner.

Also Available

FROM

Sara Lindsey

Promise Me Tonight

Isabella Weston has loved James Sheffield for as
long as she can remember. Her come-out ball
seems the perfect chance to make him see her in
a new light.

James is stunned to find that the impish girl he
once knew has blossomed into a sensual goddess.
And if he remember his lessons correctly,
goddesses always spell trouble for mortal men.

When Izzie kisses James, her artless ardor turns to
a masterful seduction that drives him mad with
desire. But, no stranger to heartbreak, James is
determined never to love, and thus never to lose.
Can Isabella convince him that a life without love
might be the biggest loss of all?

"A real love story...A perfect escape."
—*New York Times* bestselling author Eloisa James

Available wherever books are sold
or at penguin.com

FROM

Emma Wildes

An Indecent Proposition

It's the talk of the town. London's two most notorious rakes have placed a very public wager on which of them is the greatest lover. But what woman of beauty, intelligence, and discernment would consent to judge such a contest? Lady Carolyn Wynn is the last woman anyone would expect to step forward. But if the men keep her identity a secret, she'll decide who has the most finesse between the sheets.

To everyone's surprise, however, what begins as an immoral proposition turns into a shocking lesson in everlasting love…

"A spectacular and skillfully handled story that stands head and shoulders above the average historical romance."
—*Publishers Weekly* (starred review)

Available wherever books are sold
or at penguin.com

From

JO BEVERLEY

The Secret Wedding

At the age of 17, Christian Hill impulsively
defended young Dorcas Froggatt's honor—and
found himself forced into marriage. That didn't stop
him from pursuing his military career abroad,
where he swiftly put his young bride out of his
mind—until the past came back to haunt him...

Not long after her traumatic marriage, Dorcas heard
that her new husband Hill had died in battle. She's
shocked to discover that he's not only still alive,
but searching for her. She's determined not to
sacrifice her independence, not expecting the true
dangers she'll soon face, and even less, the true
love she'll discover with the man who rescued
her all those years ago...

**Available wherever books are sold or at
penguin.com**